T0033359

Someplace Like Home

OTHER TITLES BY BOBI CONN

In the Shadow of the Valley

A Woman in Time

Someplace
Like
Home

A Novel

Bobi Conn

Little
a

Published by Little A, New York

www.apub.com

Amazon, the Amazon logo, and Little A are trademarks of Amazon.com, Inc., or its affiliates.

ISBN-13: 9781662506970 (hardcover)
ISBN-13: 9781662506987 (paperback)
ISBN-13: 9781662506994 (digital)

Cover design by Ploy Siripant
Cover image: © Drop of Light / Shutterstock; © WINDCOLORS / Shutterstock; © Best Selling Images / Alamy Stock Photo

Printed in the United States of America

First edition

To my mother: Thank you for trusting me and sharing everything you did to help bring this book to life. I know this story doesn't represent everything you are or everything you have felt—we knew early on that we wouldn't be able to accomplish exactly that. But what came out of our conversations is a story with meaning, one that can help other people understand some of the difficult experiences and choices so many women face. I am honored to do this with you.

To my children: It would take another book for me to explain how much I love and respect you as individuals. Thank you for being the best part of my story, and I hope you always find the good in yours.

INTRODUCTION

I spent about ten years writing my memoir, *In the Shadow of the Valley*. It was largely a sad story, and a lot of the stories I'm about to tell are sad, too. But when I started grad school at the age of twenty-seven, I began reading books that made me realize some authors can tell a sad story but render it beautiful, so the reader actually wants to stay with the story—unlike how most of us feel about sad experiences in our daily lives. Those authors' writing was so beautiful, their work turned suffering into art. I thought if I could do that, I could find and show the value in *my* life story, which was otherwise full of pain. All the terrible things I had seen and experienced would be redeemed if I could turn them into something that was valuable to the world.

I hadn't yet gotten to the place where I could find meaning in the story of my life—that would come later. In my late twenties, I was still hurting from everything that had happened in my childhood, and I didn't yet have the understanding to put it into words.

What I could put into words was this: It was strange for me to go to grad school, even to have finished college in the first place. Sure, I graduated from college as a single mother with a one-year-old child, but I *did* graduate—and I went on to work, pay my own bills, take care of my child, and then set my sights on more learning. That was not a path that any of my family members had taken. Nobody set me up to achieve anything in life, other than perhaps to get married and have children.

Being a loving, present mother is the most demanding and important achievement I have accomplished and probably ever will. But after I started to understand how transformative the mother-child relationship can be, I realized I had more to do to become my best self, independent of anyone else's experience of me. I had to be the best mother I could be and, at the same time, step into my full and authentic self—for me, but also for everyone around me.

Two days before my memoir was released to the world, I called my mom and told her about it. I had kept it a secret in part because I thought she would hate me for telling *our* secrets. I thought the rest of our family would punish me, call me a traitor for airing our dirty laundry in public—something our class of people knows not to do— and confirm that I never really belonged with them, anyway. I have always felt like the black sheep, and I expected the fallout from the memoir to confirm it.

Instead of criticizing me, my mother asked, "Did I do anything bad to you? I mean, besides the fact that I didn't protect you when I should have?"

I didn't know what to say. It had never occurred to me that she would ask, that she would give me the chance to air my grievances. The idea of expressing my hurt feelings, voicing the resentment and anger that had lurked for decades, unspoken—that possibility had never crossed my mind. I stumbled over my words and reminded her of one event that stood out, a time when she had failed to support me emotionally. It turned out she didn't even remember some of that event happening at all—especially not the part that had caused me the most pain.

We kept talking, and the conversation turned to both of our hopes for my book's success. I shared some of my excitement, but also told her that I understood she might not like everything I had written and asked that, if she ever heard about it or, God forbid, read it herself and was upset, she would try to come to me. We hung up and I thought about her words—words I had never heard before and couldn't have imagined hearing before that night: *I didn't protect you when I should have.*

When my memoir came out, she did read it, to my dismay. I didn't want my mother or my young-adult son to read it. I knew it would hurt them to read about events and emotions I had never shared with them, the kinds of things your parents and children might be better off not knowing once the danger has passed. While strangers and old acquaintances reached out to thank me for my story, or to empathize, something unexpected happened—people reached out to my mother as well. They were sorry they didn't know what she had gone through. They hadn't known her story, just like they hadn't known mine.

In time, I asked my mother for more stories, to go back and forth in the timeline, to show me what had happened. To help me understand the *why*. To let me deepen my compassion, let me know this person who was a sovereign self before I grew inside her and before any man dominated her.

But there is so much she doesn't remember, both in her childhood and during her marriage to my father. Perhaps it is a mercy, not remembering. After she shared everything she could with me, I reached out to other family members to help fill in the gaps even further.

This story is a fictionalized version of my mother's life, and the timeline reaches back even before she was born. These characters have their own emotions and motives, and they let me stitch together a narrative to make sense of my mother's stories and memories, as well as those from other family members. So many of the little details are now gone, but many do remain: the color of her first car, the day of her motorcycle wreck, how many times she dropped the keys the day she finally left my father.

I sought to write this book because I wanted to help my mother find her voice, and I knew I would be changed in the process. Even if Jenny's character ultimately doesn't represent how my mother felt as a child, teen, or young mother, Jenny's story broke my heart open. It helped me find a narrative to explain who my mom might have been, aside from someone in relation to myself. For that, I am grateful.

BOOK ONE

The Caudill Family

1955

Chapter 1

Charles Caudill worked at the Lee Clay tile plant—the one that had the labor strikes—but he made time to work on cars at night. Everybody knew he could drop a transmission or rebuild an engine faster than anyone they'd ever seen, even late at night when a neighbor had to shine a flashlight while Charles worked under the car. He had to be at the plant by five the next morning, before the sun came up, so he tried real hard to get most of the cars finished early in the evening.

His wife, Helen, put all that extra money in an old cigar box. She kept the box inside the ice chest, which kept food cool in the summertime, but they didn't bother buying ice for it in the cooler months. Then, Helen kept food cold by putting it in a little nightstand she set on the six-by-six porch that came standard on all the company houses.

Most technology hadn't made it to their small Eastern Kentucky community of Clearfield. Charles and Helen had both grown up there, just outside the Morehead city limits. They could walk to the company store from their house, as well as Birdie White's general store and the little playground across from the tile plant—in fact, you could see everything worth looking at from their porch. Their oldest girl, Gail, was five years old, so she could walk over to the playground by herself while Helen stayed home with Barbara, the one-year-old. Charles drove them into town every Sunday for groceries. Helen didn't bother learning to drive herself, even though Charles wouldn't have minded.

Morehead was too far west to be a coal town and not close enough to the Licking River to be a river town. There was a railroad, though, and a teachers' college, so Morehead survived after the railroad traffic slowed and then stopped altogether. Eventually, the tracks were taken up and you could hardly tell there was once a railroad that ran through the middle of town and that children had once passed the time counting cars as the trains rumbled through.

Helen saved what she could of Charles's paycheck after the company took out rent and converted half of what was left into scrip that could be spent only at the company store. She was born during the Depression, so she knew how to make clothes for the whole family, how to reuse ham bones until all the flavor was gone, and in a pinch, how much sawdust a person could mix into dough before it ruined the bread.

She saved the last slivers from bars of soap and put them into one of Charles's oldest socks, tying off the open end so the family could use every bit. Charles wasn't even a little surprised when, just five years after they married, his Helen told him they had enough money to buy an acre of land and build a house, complete with a garage for his own business. The last day Charles worked at the plant, mixing clay that had been dug out of the surrounding hills with no regard for anything that lived in them, the factory owner himself came over to say goodbye.

"Charles," he said loud enough so the other workers would hear. Charles looked up but kept mixing as he listened. "You've always been a good worker. I hate to see you go, but we'll have a place here for you whenever you're ready to come back." He smiled, but his eyes glimmered with a meanness he wasn't really trying to conceal.

Charles paused before responding. "I thank you, Mr. Parker, but you won't be seeing me except when you need my help with your vehicles. I ain't moving far away, but I'll be too busy to come to your house and work on them there from now on. We'll find a way to get you to my garage the next time your truck ain't running right, though."

The other workers around them had stopped to listen, but Charles kept on mixing his clay while Mr. Parker stood there, failing to come up with the last word, until he told everybody to get back to work or he'd dock their pay. He didn't come out of his office at the end of the day, until after the last worker had shaken Charles Caudill's hand and wished him well.

Charles walked home, and after hugging Helen a little extra long, he told her to keep a good eye on their money like she'd always done, because he'd starve before he set foot in that factory ever again. Helen nodded, and they both knew the other would keep their word.

About nine months after Charles and Helen moved into their new home, their third daughter, Mary, was born. Two years after that, in 1959, Helen was ready to give birth to the fourth child, and she and Charles hoped for a boy. They had built their house with two bedrooms and a nice front porch for watching the sun go down and the cars drive by. Charles had built his garage right next to the house, decked out with two lifts and filled with all the tools he needed. The garage was always busy, and some of his customers—always men—liked to stand around and shoot the breeze, waiting to crack open a cold beer as soon as it was a decent time. Charles worked from five in the morning until four in the afternoon, hardly stopping to eat, but he always made time to talk to the guys who brought their trucks and cars over to be fixed or to sell for parts.

The baby decided to come on a Friday afternoon, and Charles was in the garage when Dr. Bishop showed up to deliver the baby at the house. There wouldn't be a hospital in Morehead for another four years, so most women went to the doctor's office when they started labor. Helen hadn't done so well when Barbara was born, though, so when she called on the party line to say the contractions had gotten strong, the doctor came to her.

Dr. Bishop was the only female doctor in town and knew more about childbirth and babies than any of the male doctors cared to know, so she was the default midwife on top of being a general physician.

When she arrived to find Helen on all fours on the kitchen floor, the two oldest children trying to calm the youngest, Dr. Bishop went straight back outside to get Charles.

"Help me get her on the table," she told him. "We can't have this baby born on the floor."

They lifted Helen as gently as they could, placing her on her back as she groaned and shuddered. They sent the girls to their room, the littlest one crying. With Helen on the table, Charles joined the men outside, where they could hear Helen every once in a while over the sound of Charles's tools. As she began to push, her screams took on an edge that made everyone nervous, and the men grew quiet and stopped teasing Charles about whether he was ever going to have a boy or just fill the house with girls.

Inside, Dr. Bishop could see the baby's head, but it wasn't coming out as fast as she thought it would, especially for a fourth child. "It's time to get this baby out," she said, and Helen nodded and worked as hard as she could with the contractions. When the head was fully out, Dr. Bishop grasped it and pulled, careful not to put too much pressure on either body, but firmly enough. She laid the baby on Helen's chest, and as the placenta came out, so did a rush of blood that covered the kitchen table.

"Shit," Dr. Bishop whispered before she hollered for Gail. "Grab the baby and stand right there by your mama." Gail lifted the baby off of Helen's chest. Her mother's eyes were closed and her arms had gone limp. As the liquids covering the baby got on her shirt, Gail panicked, wondering if Helen would be mad at her when it came time to wash clothes—these stains might not come out. The doctor was doing something with a serious look on her face, though, so Gail pushed away the thought of punishment and looked at the baby in her arms—another girl.

She stared at her new sister's face, trying to think of a good name. She had heard Charles talk about what they would name a boy but hadn't heard any girls' names. After Gail had stood there long enough that her arms ached from holding the baby, Dr. Bishop got Helen to wake up and sent Gail out to tell Charles the news.

Later on, when Helen was lying down and the men in the garage had gone home for the night, Dr. Bishop sat at the edge of the bed. She looked at Charles as she spoke. "I know y'all have been trying for a boy. This wasn't a good situation today. Give it some time, okay?" Helen and Charles both nodded, and Charles showed Dr. Bishop out with a promise that he would not only pay the bill but also take care of her car anytime she needed it, no cost at all.

Before Helen fell asleep, Gail and the other girls came in to see the baby, and Gail shared the name she had picked: Jenny. Charles nodded and Helen said she liked it just fine, so the baby got her first name, but everyone agreed a middle name could wait until tomorrow.

Chapter 2

Helen was pregnant again soon after Jenny turned one. She and Charles knew it was sooner than Dr. Bishop had wanted, but they also had themselves to think of—this child would be eleven years younger than the oldest one. Dr. Bishop came to the house again once Helen's labor got hard. The day was almost a replay of when Jenny was born, except this time Jenny was the child crying because Helen seemed hurt. Mary was four now, too big to cry. Another difference in this day was that Helen started bleeding before the baby was even born, and Dr. Bishop made Gail help her try to save them both. Gail cried then, too, but she did everything the doctor told her, and to everyone's relief, Helen came back to them in time to push the baby out. And after a smack on the bottom, the baby finally cried.

"That's it," Dr. Bishop told Helen and Charles after everyone was cleaned and settled. "No more babies for you. I don't know that you'll come back next time." She looked at Helen, and then at Charles. "If you do get pregnant again, God help us, you'll have to go to the hospital in Montgomery County to have the baby, and I can't promise you'll get there in time." She paused to make sure that sank in. "It's pretty new, but I'm sure you've heard of the birth control pill. I can put you on it in a few months, which I highly recommend since you all don't seem to have any fertility issues." She gave Charles a look and everybody smiled. She didn't have to worry—Helen and Charles were ready to stop having babies now because the most important difference in this day was that the baby was a boy.

Charles got to name him William, after his favorite uncle, and they called the new baby Billy for short. Helen put his crib outside the girls' bedroom. Jenny slept with Gail in the double bed and the two middle girls were on twin bunk beds. A dresser sat against the wall, giving the girls just enough room to walk between it and the foot of the double bed. There was no closet, so all the girls' clothes had to fit into the six dresser drawers. Gail was the oldest, so she got the top two drawers. Barbara was the next oldest, so she got the middle two drawers. Mary was next, and even though she was two years older than Jenny, she also just got one drawer at the bottom and complained about how hard it was to open with it crammed against the foot of the bed.

During the day, Helen took care of Billy and, while he napped, watched her favorite soap operas on their black-and-white television. The older girls were in school, but Jenny and Billy were still home with their mother. When Helen would lay Billy down in his crib, Jenny would climb onto the couch next to her.

"I'm not sleepy. Can I stay here and watch your stories?"

Helen would always tell her, "Yes, you lay your head down on my lap and be real quiet, and you can watch my stories with me. But remember, you have to stay quiet." Each time, Jenny made a solemn promise to be quiet, and within a few minutes she'd fall asleep on Helen's lap, oblivious to the heartache and deceit unfolding on the small screen.

There were only a handful of quiet times in the house each day. It was quiet when Billy napped. And it was quiet when Charles went to bed, which was sometimes awfully early. The girls knew how important it was not to wake him, so unless the weather was too bad, they spent as much time as possible outside.

Their house was right across from the elementary school, and the kids could walk over to the playground just about anytime they wanted, but they had to come home by dark—it didn't matter if it was summer or winter. That meant, in the summer, they could sometimes be out as late as nine o'clock at night, but in the winter their curfew was closer to five. Jenny didn't mind the early curfew when she was still little. Her sisters would take her over to the playground and push her on the swings and she could go down the slide over and over, as many times as she wanted. It felt good to get back to their yard before dark and see Helen water her flowers in the evening.

Clearfield has always been small. If you were from somewhere else, you might call it a village, but nobody who lived there called it that. To this day, there's never been a traffic light in Clearfield, and there are just a handful of stop signs. Houses, a church, and a school are nestled into the valley. There are hills all around, and they are beautiful, soft, except when it's winter and everything looks so dead it's hard to believe there will once again be a sea of green.

On the weekends, Jenny liked to stay in the bedroom after the older girls got up and spread out around the house, eating breakfast and starting on their chores. That's when she would get out all her dolls—the one Mommy and Daddy gave her for Christmas and the ones Gail and Barbara had grown tired of a long time ago. Mary wasn't ready to give up her doll yet, even though she acted like she was so much bigger than Jenny. In the room alone, Jenny let the dolls talk and say everything they didn't want to say in front of anyone else. Her favorite times were when the Jenny doll and the Mommy doll talked.

"Jenny, you're the prettiest girl. Come here and let me braid your hair."

"Thank you, Mommy. I think *you're* the prettiest."

And then the dolls would smile at each other, and it was like everyone else just disappeared.

As she got bigger, Jenny was able to go outside and explore the jungle of undrivable cars that her daddy kept around. By the time she turned five, the landscape had come into sharper focus: Out the front door she could see the school and the playground. Her mommy's flower planters were in front of the house and on the side where the main driveway was. Out the back door were the gravel driveway and the parking lot where more cars fit—broken cars, cars waiting their turn in the garage, and cars that couldn't fit in the main driveway when lots of family were visiting.

Jenny could sense that the broken vehicles had an order to them. The oldest ones were closest to the garage door, and most of them were painted black. As you walked down the line, the newer ones were green, red, blue, yellow—some pastels, some bright. The shapes changed, the cars and trucks got longer, and there were shiny pieces that reflected the sunlight so it nearly blinded a person, even on a cold day. Every once in a while, someone hauled in a car that was pretty bashed up, maybe even burned, and the men who always seemed to be around would stand there talking in low voices for a little while until Charles had them take it to the back of the garage, where it was harder to see from the road.

Sometimes, Jenny's daddy would pick her up and throw her high into the air, catch her, and swing her around. Then, when she was still laughing and a little dizzy, he would hand her a quarter and tell her to run on and stay out of trouble. He always smiled like he knew she wouldn't get into trouble, and she knew she wouldn't either, but he said it anyway, just so they could know that together, kind of like a secret.

Mostly, Jenny felt like Charles protected her. The only moment with Charles that she didn't like remembering was when he lined up all of the kids and told them that somebody had dropped a plate and it broke, and they needed to confess and take their whipping. Jenny was still so little, she couldn't have gotten a plate by herself. Billy was too little to be accused, so that left the older girls. Charles's last warning was that if the guilty person didn't step forward, all the girls would get whipped, and he knew they wouldn't want to do that to each other. But nobody spoke up.

Jenny was crying after the whipping and Charles kneeled down beside her. "I know it wasn't you," he told her so that nobody else could hear. "I just had to keep my word and do what I said I'd do."

Jenny nodded, confused by what it all meant but happy that he knew she was innocent. She thought back to that moment over and over as she grew up—the injustice of the whipping that had to happen for her daddy to stay true to his word.

But mostly, Charles was kind. A couple times a week, he'd give each kid a dime and let them climb into the back of his truck for the short drive to Birdie's. Jenny needed help getting up the wooden steps when she was little, but eventually she was big enough to grasp the handrail and pull herself up. She still liked it when somebody helped her, so she'd ask her sisters to hold her hand—unless she could get their daddy to carry her, which she liked best.

Jenny would go straight for a Coke and peanuts. She tried to make her Coke last as long as possible on the ride home because her sisters would tease whoever finished theirs first, showing off that they still had more left.

Even when she was as young as four, her sisters picked on Jenny because she was the youngest girl, but nobody picked on Billy that much. When Jenny complained to Mary, who was only two years older, Mary would shrug and say that's just how it was and that Jenny shouldn't act like such a baby. Once, when Mommy was cooking supper and Billy was crying, Jenny had tried to explain to her how unfair it was.

"Don't be so selfish. It's not right to tease a toddler. Why would you even want such a thing?"

Jenny tried to find the words to explain—she wasn't being selfish and didn't want anyone to tease Billy. *She* just didn't want to be teased. But before she could get all the words out, Mommy continued, "Go play with your brother and get him to stop crying. I can't think with all this noise, and y'all are about to make me burn dinner."

At the time, Jenny still liked wearing the clothes her sisters had outgrown, and Helen was busy making all-new boy's clothes for Billy. Jenny could almost always wear the shoes Mary had just grown out of. Helen said it was a blessing that Jenny's feet were big for her age, since she didn't have to stuff newspaper in the toes for any more than a month or so before they'd fit just right. Jenny was proud every time she heard that, proud of her big feet that made life easier and made Helen think of Jenny as a good thing.

When Jenny was in third grade, Billy had just entered first, and Gail—the oldest—was a grown-up, in her senior year and not interested in little-kid stuff anymore.

Gail kept saying she would move out soon, and that made Jenny sad, but she also thought that maybe after Gail was gone, she would get one of the beds to herself. It would probably be one of the bunks, which was smaller than the bed they shared, but it was still exciting. Jenny figured that Billy would have to sleep on the bottom bunk since he was the youngest, and she would get the top. But around then, Charles ended up building a new bedroom for Billy because it turned out that brothers and sisters don't sleep in the same room together.

When Helen was mad at Jenny, or the older girls were hogging the bedroom, Jenny would go outside to her favorite broke-down car—a 1960 Chevrolet Bel Air with teal paint. She'd sit on the ground behind the rear bumper, where the car wasn't mangled. That part was almost perfect.

It was the newest car in Charles's junk collection, and men still stood around it sometimes, talking about how fast it could go and how sharp it was. When they didn't think she was listening, they talked about the boy who eased it out of his father's garage one night—*you know, the lawyer that lives up the hill by the lake*—and how you couldn't even tell who the boy was when they pulled him from the car in the middle of the night. *Had to use dental records. That lawyer ain't so tough now, is he?*

Out there alone, nobody could see her from the house. She liked to daydream about Lassie from the TV and wished she had a dog that would find her, hidden in this jungle surrounded by the foothills of the Appalachian Mountains. A dog like Lassie would be able to find her behind any car, around any corner, probably even if she hid inside a car, like she and Mary did when they were playing hide-and-seek, even though Helen told them not to and they knew there was something dangerous about tucking themselves away like that.

Chapter 3

Over time, Jenny got tired of hand-me-downs and Helen got tired of listening to Jenny whine about them, so she taught her to sew when Jenny was fourteen. Jenny wasn't good enough to make anything from a Simplicity pattern like her mother could, but she could bring in seams or let them out so things would fit her better, or add bows to cover the worn spots and replace straps that had lost their shape. Her sewing skills were enough that Jenny's clothes never looked terribly outdated or old, which other kids would have made fun of even though almost nobody had a lot of money around those parts. The meanest girl in school, Carol Parker, had teased Jenny about her clothes in grade school, and Jenny would have done anything to avoid that again. Even as a kid, she knew that with some people, it was better to be invisible.

Jenny was starting high school, but she still missed most things about grade school. She kept waiting for the day when it would feel good to be older. When she was little, the older kids seemed happier and like they got to do so much, but as Jenny got older, she just got harder chores and more schoolwork. She had a couple of friends, but they didn't laugh together all the time or have inside jokes like she'd imagined they would. Jenny thought it might get better when she could drive, which would only be two more years.

On the morning of her first day of high school, Jenny spent as much time as possible in the bathroom, trying to get her hair just right. It was long and straight, as boring as could be. She wanted to look like

Olivia Newton-John on the cover of her mom's new record: hair parted down the middle but curling out just a little around her cheeks. Smiling and pretty, comfortable in the soft weeds around her. The first time she saw that album cover, Jenny went outside, just past the car jungle, into the only untamed weeds on their property. She checked for snakes first, stomping around a little to scare them off, and then settled into the wild grasses.

The weeds scratched her bare legs and poked through her dress. The chiggers found their way to the elastic line of her panties at her upper thighs, where they bit into her skin and left itchy red bumps for days. She had to be careful not to scratch them in front of anyone because of how unladylike it was. Worst of all, Mary had found her in the weeds and snorted with laughter at how uncomfortable and silly her sister looked, and Jenny worried for days that Mary would tell somebody else and they would all make fun of her.

That had been early in the summer, and Jenny was grateful the chigger bites had healed by the first day of school, but she still didn't have hair that looked like Olivia Newton-John's. Mary banged on the bathroom door so much, Helen got mad and told Jenny to get out and all of them better stop making such a racket in the morning. Jenny started to say how that was unfair because Mary had already been in the bathroom and so had Billy. He had gotten pee on the floor in front of the toilet, but Jenny had cleaned it up without even being told, and now she didn't have enough time to make herself look good for the first day of high school. But her mom had a headache and Jenny thought better of it.

Jenny opened the door for Mary, who sighed loudly as she stepped in front of the mirror. Jenny brushed out her hair and put a bobby pin high on each side. She wasn't a star.

Jenny's stomach flipped and flopped, and she wished she'd eaten something before they left, even just a couple of saltine crackers, but now it was too late. She rolled her window down to get fresh air, and it made her hair fly around. By the time she realized it was getting tangled, her hair was already a wild mess. She tried to comb it back out with her fingers, which shifted the bobby pins around. She adjusted them, trying to look at herself in the sideview mirror because Mary said she needed the rearview mirror to drive.

They dropped Billy off at the middle school and Jenny watched as a group of boys shouted his name and clapped his back, all of them happy in their own skin, never questioning whether they deserved to be liked and to feel so good about themselves.

At the high school student parking lot, Mary's best friends ran up to the car as soon as she parked. Someone had sold Charles a 1970 Chevrolet Chevelle that didn't run, and Charles had rebuilt the engine and given it to Mary for her sixteenth birthday. It was dark blue and had two thick white strips on the hood, which Jenny thought were ugly but everybody else seemed to love.

Mary and her friends stood around the car, babbling about how they would take it to the drive-in sometime, and Jenny got a little satisfaction knowing Mom wasn't going to let Mary drive after dark, even if Mary wouldn't admit it to her friends just then. A couple of boys came over and the girls changed the way they were talking. One of them flirted and made eye contact with all the boys, but Mary acted cool, pulled out a pack of cigarettes, and put one in her mouth. The tallest boy whipped out a lighter and lit it for her. Mary took a long drag while offering the pack to the girl next to her. Jenny hadn't started smoking yet, and she knew she would cough a lot the first time she did, so she didn't ask Mary for a cigarette, even though that made her stick out even more.

Everyone started bragging or complaining about their summers and talking about which teachers they would get. Jenny held her notebooks close to her chest, not sure whether it was worse to stand on the outside of the older kids' circle or walk away, admitting she didn't belong. Mary finally shot her a look. "You'd better get inside, Jenny. You need to figure out where your homeroom is."

Jenny had hoped Mary would show her, but she knew it wasn't worth asking. She nodded and turned away, looking for a friend who could show her where to go, or at least be lost with her.

She wandered around for a few minutes, until she realized she'd made her way to the senior hallway, where seniors leaned against the painted cinder-block walls and taunted lowerclassmen who walked through. A girl wearing a yellow dress and a permanent sneer caught Jenny's eye.

"Now here's a country bumpkin if I've ever seen one!" She didn't laugh, but her friends did, and Jenny turned around to find her way back, pretending she hadn't heard it.

Back toward the entrance to the school, Jenny found a girls' bathroom and ducked in. She wasn't quite ready to cry, but the tears were there, waiting for her to take a breath and let them loose. She wouldn't let that happen in the hallway—not on her first day of high school, in front of everyone. Somehow, nobody else was in that bathroom, and Jenny stood in front of the mirror telling her tears to go away. *You're too old to cry. Act like a baby and they'll treat you like one.*

Her bobby pins were sitting at awkward angles, not at all like they'd looked when she left the house. *Damn it.* She pulled them out and put them back in, but she couldn't get them to line up right.

"Jenny! There you are. I've looked *everywhere* for you!" Peggy Wallace burst into the bathroom. Jenny whirled around, a tear leaking out of each eye, which opened the floodgates.

"Oh, come here. What did you do to your hair? Never mind—we'll fix you right up."

Peggy lived on the hill behind the elementary school, not five minutes from Jenny. Peggy was *Jenny's* best friend, but everybody liked Peggy, so Jenny figured Peggy had a different best friend, or maybe a few of them. All of the popular girls seemed to like Peggy, and anytime Jenny started to feel jealous, she realized that wouldn't be fair. Even though Peggy wasn't rich or even the most beautiful, she smiled all the time and had a great laugh—and she was always laughing because people were always cutting up with her. Peggy was easy to love. Jenny didn't know why Peggy would be looking for her, but her insides relaxed and instead of more tears, she was able to smile.

"There, you look great," Peggy said.

Jenny looked in the mirror and saw how Peggy had pulled her hair back and pinned it. She didn't look like Olivia Newton-John, but it was cute.

"Are you good?" Peggy asked her.

Jenny nodded in response. "Yeah, I'm good."

"Okay, that's great because I have to show you the *coolest* boy I've ever seen. I could just die. He just moved here and all the girls love him already." Peggy grabbed Jenny's hand and pulled her from the bathroom, where, just a moment ago, Jenny had thought she might have to spend the entire day and, who knows, maybe even live there forever if she couldn't pull herself together. The pair went into the hallway and soon wove through a river of bodies that murmured, laughed, and shouted, but they weren't laughing or shouting at Jenny.

Carol Parker was leaning against the lockers, all smiles and giggles, with a little group of girls around her. It was just like grade school and middle school all over again, with Jenny hoping she wouldn't become the center of attention. As Peggy and Jenny walked by their little gaggle, Jenny remembered the first day Carol had talked to her in third grade. It was the first time Jenny remembered anyone looking at her like Carol did that day.

"*What* are you wearing?" Carol had asked with a laugh.

Jenny had felt her cheeks burn, which had also never happened before. "Just my clothes, I guess."

Carol Parker always had her hair in pigtails and her clothes looked like they came from a department store. Everyone knew Carol's dad owned the tile plant and that her family was one of the richest in town.

Jenny had felt so good about her outfit that morning. She had picked her favorite dress, the one Helen had made for Gail and that had been passed down from girl to girl and mended several times along the way. It was still a little big for Jenny, but she hadn't cared. The white fabric had become more of a cream color over the years, and the little dark-pink roses had faded, but it was still the prettiest thing Jenny had ever worn.

Helen had shined the hand-me-down Mary Janes as much as she could the night before. But with Carol staring at her, Jenny noticed that the toes were still scuffed. The straps were also getting tattered, and the little bow on the left shoe was torn. Jenny tried to put her feet where Carol couldn't see.

Carol had tapped the shoulder of the girl in front of her and whispered something into her ear. They both looked at Jenny and giggled until the teacher said it was time for everyone to be quiet and they put on their best good-girl faces, but they went on shooting looks at Jenny all day and whispering when the teacher's back was turned.

All those feelings from third grade flooded back in the high school hallway. Even though Carol hadn't noticed her much since then, Jenny worried that Carol would start making fun of her again. But Peggy waved her hand at the giggling girls and they all waved back. Peggy was in their club.

Jenny had two classes with Peggy and three with her other best friend, Betsy Caudill, who was no relation to Jenny. The new boy Peggy was in love with, Kenny Johnson, was in almost all of Jenny's classes. She knew why Peggy and the other girls liked him and why all the boys clapped him on the back instead of making him earn his place.

He looked just like James Dean, who Jenny and Helen agreed was the handsomest man ever. Kenny wore his hair slicked back but it was a little messy in the front, just enough to show he wasn't some kind of square. When he grinned, which was all the time, one side of his mouth went up a little more than the other. He leaned back into his chair, one leg stuck out straight as if he had been resting before the teachers decided they were going to try to teach geography or algebra.

He was the coolest.

Right away, Jenny didn't want to like him.

She kept her eyes on her notebook whenever he talked in class. He answered the teachers' questions as if he was friends with them. He didn't always get the answer right, but he didn't ever seem embarrassed. He just grinned and the teachers smiled back. Once, Jenny looked up at him in algebra when he gave the wrong answer. She didn't know the answer, either. She didn't mean to look up, but when she did, he looked her way and caught her eye. He smiled and Jenny whipped her head back toward her notebook too fast.

Jenny let herself wonder if she might find him looking at her again sometime, but Kenny was always surrounded by girls and boys who wanted to have him sit at their lunch table, to make him smile at them. And he gave his attention with no kind of attitude, no brooding or dark looks, which made him different from what she liked about James Dean, who had so many deep feelings and hurt pent up behind a handsome face. Jenny decided it was easy not to like Kenny after all.

Chapter 4

Jenny tried to pay attention in class and did well enough, but she always knew she could try a little bit harder. School felt like a place where she was supposed to do good, to prove her worth, but there were distractions.

In the hallways, there were older kids to avoid. She had to remember her locker combination and get there between classes, planning the trip to drop off the morning books and pick up the ones for her next three classes before she was late. There was lunch, where she sat at the same table with the same people every day, but as a freshman, your place wasn't secure—something could always change. Except the food, of course. That was always bland at best, disgusting at its worst. But if she brought lunch, it would only be a baloney sandwich, which was even less interesting.

A month into school, Jenny decided to join the junior varsity volleyball team. All three of her sisters had played, and Peggy was trying out, too. On the gym floor, she didn't feel self-conscious or clumsy. She was able to forget that there were kids and parents in the bleachers. She wasn't afraid of the ball like she was in dodgeball, and she didn't have a hard time hitting a volleyball like she did a baseball. Things were easy. Volleyball was the best part of her freshman year.

The next best thing that year was a boy named Eddie Wilson. He was quiet but really good-looking. Jenny would sneak looks at him during class and think about how, most of the time, when a boy's that handsome, he has a swagger like Kenny. But Eddie didn't. Every now and then, a popular girl would flirt with Eddie and he would act like he didn't know what they were up to. He'd give them the pencil they asked to borrow or he'd accept a piece of gum and thank them, then just chew it and get back to whatever he wrote in his notebook when he wasn't doing classwork.

Sometimes Jenny would get carried away staring at him, and she knew he felt it when he would turn his head just a little in her direction, not quite meeting her eyes. Then Jenny would busy herself with a schoolbook or an imaginary loose thread on her skirt. The only thing that kept her from dying of embarrassment was knowing that there were at least two other girls staring at Eddie at any given moment. He acted like he didn't know a single one of them was there.

In geography class, which was the most boring of all, Jenny made up stories about Eddie: He was writing love poems about her all day, never showing them to anyone out of fear that she would break his heart. Sometimes he was secretly writing a book that was better than anything they read in English class. He was going to be a famous writer and in just a few years, the kids sitting in their classroom would be reading *his* book. Other times, he was the last person alive who knew where to find the lost treasure of Jesse James, and he was writing the directions down in case anything ever happened to him, but they were all in code, buried in some long story like the gold coins themselves.

Jenny tried to figure out who he was like. Not James Dean, but also not Beaver Cleaver or Opie from *The Andy Griffith Show*. He never seemed to laugh, so he couldn't be on *Rowan & Martin's Laugh-In*, which was her favorite show because her mom loved it. When they watched it together, Helen laughed a lot and sometimes looked at Jenny like they shared the jokes. Even though Jenny didn't understand them about half the time, she would laugh and soak in the warmth of those moments.

Maybe Eddie was more like a musician, like someone from the Beatles. It was hard to know what those boys were like, looking at their pictures in the *Hit Parader*.

On Fridays, after Charles was done working, he and Helen would go to Montgomery County to buy wine and beer that would last them a week or two. Helen's favorite wine had a picture of green grapes on the label, and Charles liked his Stroh's beer. And every Friday night, Jenny changed the station on Helen's radio while her parents were gone. Jenny always wanted to hear the new music that she read about, so she would know whether the lyrics she saved really sounded good, or if they just looked good printed in her magazines.

While her parents were gone, Jenny would move the radio to the girls' bedroom and tune it to another station, careful to pay attention to which one Helen had left it on so she could put it back as soon as she heard their truck rumble into the driveway. The university in town had a radio program, and DJ Frankie would play the newest, coolest songs. Jenny couldn't have told you that some of the songs weren't *actually* the newest, though she noticed now and then that she had read about them long before DJ Frankie played them. That didn't matter—she sat by the radio and looked through her latest magazine, trying to connect the words on the page with the sounds spilling into her bedroom, away from whatever Billy was watching on the television and whoever Mary was talking to on the phone mounted to the kitchen wall.

One Friday night, "With a Little Help from My Friends" came pouring out of the speakers, "an oldie but goodie," as DJ Frankie called it. Jenny had heard it before but hadn't paid much attention to the words. Ringo's words made her think about Peggy and smile—she knew exactly what it meant to get by with a little help from her friends.

As the song went on, goose bumps rose on her arms.

She had never thought to ask herself if she needed anybody, and she hadn't thought much about love yet, but that was it—that had to be what was missing in her life. It was as if someone had reached into her and taken all the feelings that had been swirling inside, messy and unnamed, and found a way to make those feelings beautiful, musical.

She cried, sitting on the double bed she now shared with Mary. *Someone gets me*, she thought. *I'm not alone.* She didn't even care if Mary walked in and found her crying—this feeling was so good, nobody could take it away.

When Helen and Charles rolled into the driveway, Jenny almost kept the radio with her, thinking her parents might even share in her newfound joy. But she thought better of it and put the radio back before going outside to see if she needed to help carry anything.

As they unpacked the bottles and a couple of twelve-packs of beer, Jenny got out juice glasses for Helen, Mary, and herself. They poured wine into their glasses, almost to the brim, and Charles cracked open another beer, tossing his empty can from the drive home into the garbage. They all toasted, Jenny more cheerful than anyone had seen in a long time. Before she finished her glass, she knew she wasn't going to cry this time, which usually happened about halfway through her wine. Jenny had found something she hadn't even known she was looking for.

Jenny had to have her *Hit Parader* from then on. She cut out song lyrics that spoke to her and made a scrapbook of albums, lyrics, and musicians. Charles still gave her dimes a couple times a week and even a quarter now and then, only if Helen wasn't looking. Helen didn't like the way Jenny wasted money. Jenny hid the money in a sock in her dresser drawer—not to keep it from Mary or Billy, but so she wouldn't be as tempted to spend it on pop and snacks at Birdie's store.

The magazine came out once a month and Jenny always found a way to get to Birdie White's store on the day it was supposed to come out, even if that meant walking. It wasn't a far walk—you just had to mind the road and watch for cars.

This same year, Jenny started babysitting for a little girl, Mary Beth, who lived behind the elementary school. Her daddy liked to drink, and one night he drove himself headfirst into Dry Creek, which usually did have some water in it, despite the name. But it didn't matter how high the creek was that night. He went through the windshield, and nobody knew it until the school bus drove by the next morning and all the kids saw his body draped across the hood, the car on its side and his fingers reaching into the water. The kids on the bus ended up making fun of the little girl whose daddy was a drunk and killed himself without meaning to, and Mary Beth stopped talking at the age of nine.

Jenny would watch Mary Beth when her mom, JoEllen, went to work at Cowden, the blue jean factory in town. She walked Mary Beth home most days after school and stayed there until JoEllen got home, which had to be before dark. For a time, Jenny tried to talk to the little girl and be nice, play with her and try to cheer her up. If the weather was good, Jenny would ask if she wanted to go to the school playground. Mary Beth wouldn't even look at her, though she did let Jenny push her on the swing sometimes. Other times, she sat at the top of the slide and looked somewhere—Jenny couldn't tell what she was looking at—and wouldn't slide down for the longest time.

So Jenny let her swing or sit while Jenny smoked cigarettes, always careful to make sure Helen couldn't see her if she came out to water the flowers. She wasn't really sure whether her mom would mind her smoking cigarettes, as long as she paid for them herself, but she also didn't feel ready to find out just yet.

Jenny made it through her freshman year of high school without doing anything too embarrassing. She passed everything, and liked math okay, but the meaning of the numbers and most of the stuff in her other textbooks was a little fuzzy, like it was just out of her reach. On the volleyball team, she got to play in some of the games, even though they had a lot of older girls. A couple of times that season, she heard the crowd cheer when she spiked the ball over the net and the other team couldn't get to it in time. *Her*, a freshman, and the crowd loved it.

Little moments marked the highs in her days—a win on the volleyball court, a flicker of emotion in Eddie's eyes, laughing with Peggy between classes. The cars changed in Charles's jungle of broken machines, and she sometimes marveled at what her daddy could make whole again. The sun set next to the parking lot, and she perched on her current favorite car as often as possible, watching the sky light up red and orange and purple. She hummed the best songs and tried to make sense of the lyrics, wondering about things like what the "rock of ages" was and what exactly it meant to have your mama love you that much.

Besides music, the other best thing in life was her dreams. Not daydreams—*real* dreams, the kind you have at night. Jenny didn't know why, but right after she got her monthly for the first time ever, she started having all kinds of dreams. They seemed strange to her at first, so Jenny tried to tell Mary about them, but Mary didn't find them interesting.

Jenny could fly in most of her dreams. She would start out on the ground, maybe in the yard or next to some broken cars, and she would feel something lift her off her feet and take her wherever she wanted. Sometimes, Jenny would look down at the roof of their house or onto the tops of the junk cars. They were a sea of wild color, like a patchwork quilt, beautiful from the sky, not looking broken at all. Helen would be outside watering her flowers sometimes and Jenny would fly over her. She'd try to call out to her mom, but her voice hardly ever worked in dreams and she was afraid to wave her hands around in case that broke the spell. When Jenny was feeling adventurous, she would fly toward town, first over the train tracks and then the buildings, most of them low to the earth. Beyond those buildings, there was nothing, so she didn't go any farther than where she'd been in her waking life.

But Jenny also had bad dreams. She wouldn't call them nightmares, exactly—there were no monsters or bad guys chasing her, like there was when she was little. In one of her bad dreams, Helen was yelling at her and Jenny didn't understand what she had done to make her mom so mad. Helen smacked her in the face, and at first Jenny cried but then got mad and yelled at her. The more Jenny yelled, the smaller Helen got, until she disappeared, and then Jenny had no mother at all, so her own body disappeared, one bit at a time.

In another bad dream, Jenny was little again and Daddy would smile at her and she'd smile back, knowing how much he loved her. But then he made her stand in line with her sisters and Billy. Charles took off his belt and Jenny knew he was about to whip them, and it was going to hurt her body but it was also going to hurt her heart. She didn't want him to hurt her heart because he also made her feel so good when he smiled or gave her dimes, and it took so long to feel good again after he hurt her. Jenny usually woke up right then, before his belt came down, but after she had begun to cry.

Chapter 5

Summer came and dragged slowly across the hot days. Jenny did her chores and tried to find some relief from the heat. She could linger near Helen's fan as long as she ironed laundry or found some other way of looking useful. She liked it for the most part, watching the television with her mom, the fan stirring the thick air almost enough, her hands busy with easy work.

One day, somebody brought an old pontoon boat to the garage and offered it to Charles as payment if he would rebuild a transmission on a 1967 Camaro. The man explained that it had been his wife's favorite car and he couldn't buy her a new one, but she had caught him cheating one too many times and he had to win her back somehow. He swore to everybody who could hear that he wouldn't ever do it again if she would take him back this one last time.

Charles took the job and the boat, and on as many weekend days as possible he'd take the family out to Cave Run Lake, where the kids would jump off the boat and swim to the rocks and the adults would drink as much as they could while still being able to drive the boat safely back to the dock. By most accounts, it was the best summer ever.

In the evenings, Helen had supper ready for Charles as soon as he was done working. It was always hot, and by the time he scrubbed the grease off his hands, she had a plate set for him. After dinner they watched the news, which Jenny didn't care for. She tried to sit through it sometimes—Walter Cronkite on the television, beaming the news of the day—but everything he talked about was so far away, it couldn't be that important. The problems and decisions that blared out had nothing to do with them.

Charles's business grew and Billy started spending his days in the garage. Mary was on the phone every chance she got, and Helen had to shoo her away so people could call and check on whether or not Charles had their cars fixed yet and Helen could tell them how much they owed. Jenny tried to pass the time by sewing clothes for the next school year, guessing as to how much she might grow over the summer, and by filling up her scrapbook with song lyrics and pictures from magazines.

Jenny babysat as much as she could, just to have something different to do. Mary Beth's mama liked to talk to Jenny when she got home from the factory, probably because Mary Beth wouldn't talk and you weren't supposed to talk too much while sewing zippers into blue jeans. One night, JoEllen walked in after her shift and Jenny stood up from the kitchen table where she had been coloring with Mary Beth.

"Thank you, honey. I've got your money in my purse. Come sit on the couch with me a minute while I take these damn shoes off." She kissed the top of Mary Beth's head and plopped onto the couch. They were just a few feet from Mary Beth, but JoEllen didn't seem to think she could hear them.

"I tell you, I cannot wait to get out of that damn factory. It's about to kill me, I swear. On my feet all the time like this, it ain't natural." She eased her shoes off and rubbed her feet, as if to show Jenny how pained they were. "But look here—"

Jenny wasn't sure where to look.

"There's a feller at the factory, Donnie Reynolds, and let me tell you, he is the best-looking man in all of Rowan County, I swear." Jenny thought of Eddie and Kenny, and she wasn't sure JoEllen could be right about this.

"I'm telling you, he's a catch. And get this, he's taking me out to supper Friday night." She opened her fake leather cigarette case and put a cigarette in her mouth. "His wife left him. It don't make any sense—he's so handsome. And no kids." She gave a little nod toward Mary Beth and then reached her cigarette case toward Jenny. "Want one?"

Jenny was surprised at the offer but since JoEllen didn't mind, she figured she might as well take one. JoEllen probably wouldn't tell Helen. JoEllen took a deep drag and blew out the smoke, which she then waved around, as if it had anywhere else to go in that small room.

"This'un's daddy died." She nodded toward Mary Beth again. "I bet you know that already. Everybody knows everything in a little town. Pretty much killed himself—you probably know that too." Jenny nodded, hoping Mary Beth couldn't hear, but pretty sure the poor girl was hearing every word. "He was a good man when he wasn't drinking. Took good care of us there for a while. But then he was drinking all the time and you see where that got him."

In the creek, Jenny thought.

"Most of them are damn fools anyway," JoEllen went on. "Hard to find a man that's got any sense." Jenny felt her eyes widen, but she didn't know how to respond. *My daddy has sense, and he never got so drunk that he would drive into a creek.* She wondered how much JoEllen really knew about men, but however much it was, it was more than Jenny. So she nodded and lit her cigarette, thinking she was about ready to get home. JoEllen's eyes twinkled with amusement.

"Don't worry, I know your daddy's got his head on straight. Everybody loves him. He never gets wild enough to cause trouble." Jenny nodded again and shifted on the couch, taking a long drag.

She thought about last Saturday and how Daddy had passed out on the porch, drunk. Him and Mommy had got into a fight and screamed at each other before he stumbled outside, saying something Jenny didn't hear. You never knew if they were going to end up fighting or dancing in the kitchen when they drank on the weekends, but everything always went back to normal the next day, so Jenny tried to forget how scared she got some nights.

"You haven't coughed a bit. Guess you're used to these."

Jenny didn't know what to say. There didn't seem to be much sense in lying. JoEllen probably figured that Helen didn't know about her smoking, but saying it out loud would make it too real. She coughed a little and JoEllen laughed.

"Don't worry, I ain't telling on you. I know your mama and she wouldn't like it one bit. But I can't have you in trouble and not being able to watch Mary Beth."

Jenny nodded again—that seemed to be the only thing she could do—her eyes stinging from the smoke that hung in the air. She couldn't think of anything to say until JoEllen handed her a few dollars. They both stood up and headed toward the door. "Thank you," Jenny murmured.

"Might get you to come over when me and Donnie go out, okay?"

"Sure," Jenny said, thinking they would have to get home earlier than JoEllen might want, since she had to get home before dark. She slipped outside before JoEllen could say anything else.

As much as Jenny didn't want to go to school, summers got boring. If she stayed inside, she had to be quiet when Helen watched her shows, and be quiet when Helen was on the phone, and don't be such a pest, and don't drink all the damn milk—*save some for your brother and daddy*.

If Jenny spent too much time in the bathroom trying to figure out whether she would ever be pretty, Mary would bang on the door and tell her to stop being a bathroom hog. Mary had no way of knowing that Jenny spent all that time looking at her thighs, where pink and silver stretch marks had appeared out of nowhere. She was definitely bigger than some of the girls on the volleyball team, but not exactly fat. If she kept on growing, the boys in school would oink and snort as she walked down the hallway, like they did to Linda Johnson.

Jenny could go to the garage if she was done with her chores, but something about being in there had changed and it wasn't as fun as it used to be. Now Billy and Daddy talked to each other about carburetors and lug nuts and wrenches like two men who had worked together forever. Charles's folding chair and table were covered in a layer of grime, and she had to check each time she sat down because there was no getting that grease out. Everything *felt* dirty, and she was pretty sure you wouldn't ever smell anything in there again but old motor oil and beer.

Everywhere she went, Jenny didn't fit like she used to. Climbing onto the trunk of an old car should have been easier because she was taller now, but instead, her legs acted like they didn't know what to do. On the playground, her hips were a little too wide for the swings. The metal pieces on each side of the seat pinched into her every time she pushed off from the ground, reminding her that she couldn't fly without paying a price for it. Nothing was all that bad, but nothing was all that good, either. And it started to seem like that was never going to change.

Jenny figured that the best part of summer was that the days were longer, which meant she could stay out later, and she savored every minute. She would sit at the playground or on one of the junk cars and watch the sky, sometimes sneaking a cigarette, her mind wandering over a lyric from a new song or a line from a television show.

On the longest day of the year, she celebrated quietly, knowing it was the day she could spend the most time outside, in the open. There was something sad about that day, though, also knowing that tomorrow's sunset would come a little bit earlier, on and on until it was dark at five thirty. Then she would be stuck inside, trying not to be in the way, waiting for the long days to come back again.

Chapter 6

Despite what Jenny wanted, the days shortened like they always do and her sophomore year started right after Labor Day. Right away, the older girls surprised her by asking if she was trying out for the volleyball team again.

"You have to, Jenny. Look how long your legs got over the summer! We need you up by the net. The other teams won't be able to get a ball past you." She grinned and blushed at the same time, grateful to hear that her long legs were good for something. Peggy told her that she was going to practice after school with some of the varsity girls, and if Jenny practiced with them, she'd be sure to make the team.

It was easier to find her classrooms this year, even easier to get to her locker and make time between classes. She saw the lost looks on so many freshman faces and knew she must have looked like them last year, but now she was a step ahead.

She and Peggy had most of their classes together and played volleyball almost every day after school, even if Coach didn't have a practice or game scheduled. Jenny had to beg Mary to stay late and give her a ride each time, and Mary would grumble but give in. Jenny knew she really didn't mind because Mary stayed at the school and just talked to boys in the parking lot, smoking cigarettes and showing off her car. If they couldn't use the gym, Jenny would go home and do her chores as fast as possible and then meet Peggy at the elementary school playground to hit the ball over an imaginary net.

Jenny still felt awkward most of the time, but Peggy and the other girls on the team didn't notice or didn't mind, and she loved playing volleyball. On the court, she could be something she was nowhere else. She could be strong and graceful, feminine and tough, and best of all, her coach and teammates told her they loved just about everything she did.

They won first place in the regional tournament that year, despite being one of the smallest schools to compete. Most of the younger girls didn't play in that game, but Jenny started in the second set and was playing against a tall girl from two counties over. Jenny blocked and hit as hard as she could each time until she finally made the winning point. Her teammates cheered and hugged her and she almost cried, but she held it in so nobody would see how much this meant to her. Jenny felt like she was on top of the world. That saying had never made sense to her before, but now she finally got it: life could be exciting and fun, and in those moments, a person could forget about what clothes they wore, which boys were out of reach, and even the loneliness that comes with being surrounded by people who don't see you. It was like something out of a show, like rare moments in her mom's soaps when the characters are happy and it seems like everything's going to work out.

Mary started dating Frank Lewis in October. He was one grade behind Mary, and Jenny thought it was weird that Mary wanted to date a younger boy. But Mary acted like he was the best thing since sliced bread. She made Jenny swear not to tell Helen. The girls weren't allowed to date until they turned eighteen.

"I'll try not to let it slip," Jenny teased, knowing she would never say anything in front of their mom that shouldn't be said. She felt bad, though, after seeing the worry on Mary's face. "Don't worry, I won't say nothing. Maybe you could be extra nice to me, though."

Mary turned to look at her. "Yeah, I probably could. You're not too bad for a little sister. Annoying, but not too bad." They smiled, and Jenny realized it had been a long while since she and her sister laughed together. It seemed like they used to laugh as kids all the time, but something had changed.

Jenny missed the days of being in the bedroom with her three sisters, sleeping next to Gail. Now, she and Mary shared a bed and the bunk beds were gone, along with the two older sisters. Mary didn't dote on Jenny like Gail used to do, so Jenny looked forward to the times when Mary treated her like a friend instead of an annoying little sister. There was something sweet about the memory of the four of them all trying to get into the dresser at the same time, even though she had been stuck with one bottom drawer. Now she had three drawers of her own and there was more than enough room for all her clothes.

That night, when Helen poured the girls a glass of wine, Jenny tried to sip hers slowly so she wouldn't end up crying like she usually did. She'd held all those tears in at the game, so it was going to be even harder than usual. Jenny never understood why wine made her cry, but her sisters always thought it was funny. Sometimes they'd offer her a quarter to drink her glass really fast, and then she'd lay on the floor and her sisters would laugh while she blubbered around. Mom would just shake her head and light a cigarette, taking her drink into the living room so she could watch television in peace.

Tonight, Jenny started out drinking her wine as slowly as she could, but after a few sips, it stopped burning the back of her throat and her head began to feel light. Everything she had ever worried about seemed so far away. Mary and Jenny went out to the back porch to sit on the glider. They often took their drinks out there when it was warm out because if Charles was asleep, they weren't allowed to wake him and Mom would be watching a show. The glider was right outside the window, so they had to keep their voices low. But as long as they could hear Mom's laugh and her chatter with Billy, they knew it was safe to talk about their secrets.

That night, Mary wanted to tell Jenny all about Frank. He lived up the holler not far from them—you could see the mouth of the holler from their front porch, where Mill Branch Road disappeared into the hills. They'd never been up there because they didn't have family in that holler, but some of the families on Mill Branch brought their cars for Charles to work on, just like a lot of people in town did.

Jenny had seen Frank hanging around Mary's car sometimes when she got done with volleyball practice. He was good-looking, tall and lean, with sandy-brown hair and strong cheekbones. Like all the other boys, he didn't say much to Jenny, but he also didn't say much to the other boys and they all seemed to avoid him.

As they sat on the glider, rocking it back and forth, Mary told Jenny she was thinking about kissing him soon.

"It's not just that he's cute," Mary told her sister. "There's something about him. He's different from the other guys. They *think* they're cool, but he really *is*."

When the girls had finished their wine, Jenny ducked back inside for the bottle, filling both of their cups to about halfway. She thought back to their volleyball win: *Why not? We have something to celebrate.*

Mary talked about the truck Frank drove on his farm, even though he was too young to drive, and how he grew up in the country—*really in the country, not like one of those drugstore cowboys.* She said he got into trouble a lot but it was only because he wouldn't put up with any disrespect from anybody. Those drugstore cowboys liked to act tough, but everybody knows a man gets strong by growing up rough, and it sounded like Frank liked to fight.

Jenny thought there was something exciting about a dangerous guy, a guy who would protect his family and his home at any cost. A man who knew what he wanted and took it for himself.

Jenny poured a little more wine into each of their cups. They would feel it the next day, but it would be Friday and the girls at school would still be excited about their win, so there would be a lot of chatter in class and the teachers wouldn't mind too much.

Mary kept talking about Frank. Jenny talked, too, but she immediately didn't remember most of what she said. Whatever it was, both girls laughed, and soon it was like they were little again, laughing over things that weren't really funny, and Jenny's head got lighter and lighter, until it almost floated away into the clear sky that glittered with tiny stars. They finally went back inside and Jenny put Mom's bottle in the cabinet, hoping she wouldn't be mad when she saw how much was gone—or maybe she would think she had drank most of it herself.

Jenny and Mary got into bed without changing into their pajamas, their heads swimmy. Mary fell asleep right away, and Jenny lay awake for a few minutes, ready to dream about handsome young men, not knowing that her life was about to change.

BOOK TWO

Jenny

1975

Chapter 7

Frank and his brother showed up at our house on the first Monday after the end of my sophomore year. I was sitting outside on the glider, trying to think of how I could get away from the house. I thought about walking up to JoEllen's to see whether she and Donnie wanted to go out on a date so I could babysit Mary Beth, but since he moved in, they didn't seem to go on dates that much, and their little house seemed even smaller, even darker than before.

Just then, this green Ford pickup pulled into our back driveway. I saw Frank in the passenger side but didn't know who was driving. Whoever it was hit the brakes kind of hard and a little gravel flew up. Mary hurried to Frank's window with a goofy smile on her face. I watched the two of them talk for a minute and figured Momma might come out and wonder what these boys were doing in her driveway. She kept a good eye on people coming and going, especially when they pulled into the back driveway, because that meant the vehicle wasn't heading to the garage.

Frank and the other guy got out of the truck, and I figured they'd all stand around talking to Mary, so I pretended there was something really interesting going on with my fingernails. I felt someone get close and looked up to find this older boy staring me right in the eye. I didn't know what to say so I tried not to look interested, but he grinned and it lit up his face. He had these black horn-rimmed glasses, which is what was in style back then, but he didn't strike me as a big reader or anything.

"What's your name?" I couldn't believe he was asking me. The boys at school didn't usually talk to me. Kenny still smiled sometimes but he smiled at everybody. Eddie acted like he always did, and that had gotten boring.

"Jenny. What's yours?"

"Rob, Rob Lewis. I'm Frank's older brother." He tilted his head toward the truck and just kept looking at me.

"What grade are you in? Or did you graduate already?" I asked, hoping he wouldn't walk away too soon. He didn't look old enough to be done with school, but I couldn't remember ever seeing him before. Rob was lean like Frank, maybe even on the skinny side, and not as tall as his brother. He had a sharp nose and cheekbones, also like Frank, but not quite as handsome.

He laughed and said, "I'm in no grade. I dropped out a couple years ago. School's a bunch of bullshit."

I worried that Momma might have heard him cuss. She was probably sitting in Daddy's chair in the living room, and if she'd noticed the boys standing around, she might have turned the television down so she could listen. We never cussed around her or Daddy.

I think I smiled, not knowing what else to say. I figured he was about to walk away, and I was kicking myself that I didn't know how to talk to boys. Here was this good-looking boy asking me my name, and all I could do was sit there, just like poor little Mary Beth always did when I babysat her. I just about died when Rob sat down in the glider next to me.

He pulled out a pack of Marlboros and lit one up, then offered me a drag. Momma hadn't opened the back door and I didn't see anybody looking at us from the garage, but I still shook my head no. If Momma didn't kill me for sitting next to a strange boy on our porch, she surely would kill me for smoking with him.

"So what do you like to do?"

I looked at him and felt my eyes get big.

"Well, I listen to music." *Of course you listen to music, dummy. Everybody likes music—what kind of answer is that?*

"Yeah, me too. What else?"

"I play volleyball. I mean, I did—at school. We won regionals."

He didn't seem interested in that. Maybe he didn't know what *regionals* meant.

"You seeing anybody?"

I felt my heart race a little. I couldn't tell if he was making fun of me or why he cared. I shook my head again and looked down at my handmade pants. Gail had worn them first, and then Barbara, and then Mary. I wondered if Rob could tell how old they were.

"Good. I'm between girlfriends myself, so this will work out fine." It took me a second to work out his meaning. Was he asking me to date him?

"Momma says I ain't allowed to date boys," I blurted out, but I was embarrassed again because I wasn't really sure he was asking me out. I wished I could go somewhere else and stop being awkward before I had to talk to him again. But Rob just laughed.

"Good thing I ain't a boy," he said. "I'm a grown man. And what your mama doesn't know won't hurt her." He winked, and then took another drag off his cigarette.

"I-I don't know." I stumbled on my words. It felt like we were in a movie. I could hardly believe that, just a few minutes ago, I was thinking about going to babysit, which would have meant missing the most exciting thing that had ever happened to me. Out of nowhere, this boy—this *man*—showed up on my porch and could be the first boyfriend I ever had.

I looked over toward Mary and Frank, but they had walked around the truck and all I could see was the back of their heads. Rob would probably like one of my other sisters better if he spent any time around them. Gail was married, but Mary could drive, and Barbara had moved into town and had a place of her own. I had turned sixteen that past

February but couldn't have a car of my own until Daddy found a cheap one he could fix up or I graduated from high school. Mary said she would teach me to drive, but every time I asked she was too busy. And besides, she didn't want me messing up her car. Momma never learned to drive and Daddy was too busy.

"Hey." He got my attention. "I'll come by and see you again tomorrow." I nodded and he stood up and walked off, flicking his cigarette butt into the gravel.

I couldn't hardly sleep that night. I lay in bed next to Mary, and she talked about Frank and how handsome he was, how everybody was scared of him except her, and how she knew what he was really like on the inside. I thought about telling her what Rob had said to me, but I wasn't sure how she would feel about me dating Frank's brother, so in the end, I was glad I didn't really get the chance to. I didn't listen closely to much more of what she said. She didn't seem to care, and kept going on, so I finally got out of bed and went to the bathroom just so I wouldn't have to hear her talk for a minute.

I sat down on the toilet in case I might be able to pee. There was a window in the bathroom that wasn't far from the glider. You could see it from there if you tilted your head just right. It was dark outside, so I sat there imagining the whole scene over again:

He walks up to her and looks so handsome. He pulls a cigarette from the pack, so cool. He's old enough to drive and dropped out of school because it's a bunch of bullshit.

I cleaned up and went to the sink to wash my hands. I looked in the mirror and imagined my part of the scene in our movie:

She's plain but he doesn't seem to mind. She can't think of anything interesting to say and can't drive. How is she going to keep a guy like him?

I stared at myself a little longer, and all the good feelings of the day faded.

Chapter 8

Rob stopped at our house every day for the next three weeks just to see me. He didn't get out of his truck until I came outside, but I would hear him pull in just a little too fast, and after a few days of that, I knew when he showed up. Sometimes Frank came, too, and him and Mary would stand by themselves and talk, but Rob acted like I was the only reason he was there.

I couldn't believe how lucky I was.

He'd sit with me in the glider or we would stand by his truck if he didn't have Frank with him, and it felt like we were the only two people in the world. He'd tell me stories about going hunting with his dad or about how a cow got loose and he'd used his truck to herd it back inside the fence. I didn't have many stories at all, so I mostly listened and tried to figure out what he saw in me so I could keep showing it to him.

Rob made me laugh so much, and after a while I stopped trying not to laugh like a girl in love. The world got so much bigger all of a sudden. He told me about going to town and hanging out in the pool hall, and how sometimes him and a buddy would hustle some fool in a game. He worked side jobs in town or out in the country, I wasn't sure where. He did what he wanted, and he made everything he did sound exciting. I think that's one of the things I liked most about him—he always knew how to tell a good story.

Just about every time Rob showed up, Billy came over to us and asked if anybody had some change. There was something sweet about

Rob reaching into his pocket and pulling out a handful of shiny coins and a few bills. He'd give Billy a quarter or sometimes a dollar, and Billy would head out to buy a chocolate bar at Birdie's. It felt good to see Rob take care of my brother. Rob could have just told him to buzz off, but he didn't—he was good to Billy.

Mary didn't care about me dating Rob, but she rolled her eyes every time I talked about how great he was. "Yeah, Jenny, he's the best guy ever. A dropout who doesn't have a job."

I never knew how to respond when she said those things. They were true, but that's not all there was to him. And he made me feel good. Those other things didn't seem as important compared to the happiness I got to feel sometimes. I mean, isn't that the point of life—to be happy?

I started daydreaming about what it would be like to run off with Rob, and it seemed like one of those fairy tales where the girl doesn't know she's actually a princess, and all of a sudden Prince Charming shows up and sees her for what she really is: beautiful instead of plain, exciting instead of dull. Momma eventually introduced herself to Rob, and they both smiled so much when they talked, I could tell he was special and she liked him. She might even let me date him and we wouldn't have to just talk outside, standing in our driveway or sitting on the glider. I don't think she liked Frank as much. He didn't try to make small talk when Momma came outside, and he just wasn't as friendly as Rob was. Momma and Daddy both knew Rob's parents, George and Ella. They brought their cars to Daddy to work on sometimes and they went to church just down the road.

One day that summer, I caught a glimpse of Rob's truck driving by as he headed into town. He didn't even slow down, but I told myself he must have something to do and he'd stop on his way back. I watched the front windows for the rest of the day, making sure to stay either in the living room or the bedroom, where I could see the road.

He drove back a couple hours later, and I took a few minutes in front of the bathroom mirror to make sure I looked alright before going outside. I went to the back driveway where he usually parked, but I could see his taillights just disappearing into the mouth of the holler.

I couldn't eat supper when Momma called me to the table a little later. I kept telling myself everything was okay. Maybe his mom was sick and he had to hurry home. Or maybe there was something going on with a cow on their farm and he needed to help. It could have been anything.

I kept an eye on the road in case he came out again that night. For the next couple of days, I cried a little and tried to hide it, but my face was red and my eyes got real puffy. Momma finally got mad. "Get away from the windows and stop worrying about that boy," she told me. "You ain't got no business with him nohow."

I knew she wasn't going to change her mind, so I tried to push Rob out of my mind, at least while everybody was awake.

I drank too much wine that night and threw up in the morning. My head pounded so hard, but Momma told me I couldn't lay around just because I'd done this to myself.

The more the days wore on, the less I felt like I had to see him. On one hand, it was exciting that he liked me and showed me so much attention, but I never could get comfortable when I was sitting next to him. He hadn't tried to touch me, but I was always a little tense, feeling like he might. I had never kissed a boy or even held hands, so I didn't know what it would feel like if he did reach out to hold mine. The thought made me catch my breath and lose track of the stitches I was trying to keep straight, so I had to push that one away too.

After a week of not stopping by the house, Rob came sliding into the driveway one evening while I was sitting on the glider reading the lyrics to "Give a Little Love" in the *Hit Parader*. I figured I understood what they meant now about forsaking love: sometimes things just aren't meant to be.

I knew Momma would get mad if she saw how Rob was flinging gravel around. Nobody came outside, though, so she must not have noticed. I stood up but didn't walk over to his truck. I didn't have any shoes on and wasn't going to make the effort anyway. All the sadness that was left in me turned to anger right then, and I thought I'd tell him to just go back home and don't come here no more.

He got out of the truck and walked right up to the glider and sat down. I stood there for a minute, trying to think of what to say. He pulled out a cigarette and lit it up, and then he patted the empty seat next to him. "You gonna sit down?" he asked. He stared into my eyes like he often did, but now he wasn't smiling.

"You didn't come see me for a week." I looked down at a piece of gravel on the patio and moved it around with my toe.

"Yeah, I was busy."

"Well, I didn't really like that," I told him. I nudged the gravel around a little more. "I didn't know what was going on."

He laughed and I looked up. He stood up and grinned at me, but his eyes still weren't smiling.

"Alright, be like that. Susan doesn't give me a hard time and want to know where I'm at every minute. I'm sure she'll be happy to see me."

My stomach turned and I thought of the pot roast I had eaten for supper, which I might throw up all over the patio. *Who was Susan?* Rob hadn't ever mentioned another girl before. My eyes filled up with tears and I tried to hold them back. But they started spilling out and streaming down my face. I thought that might make Rob feel bad, even if I didn't want to cry. He just walked toward his truck and flicked his cigarette butt onto the ground.

I sat down on the doorstep, put my face down into my hands, and tried not to make any noise. Momma would be so mad if she knew I was upset like this after she told me to stop thinking about him. Everything around me seemed too big all of a sudden: the junk cars that multiplied every week, the fields stretching between our house and the handful of others nearby. Especially the sky, and the stars that we learned in school were already dead—*but how could that be?* Dead things can't shine light on us and bring so much beauty. But that night, the almost-full moon was cold and the stars would be too.

I tried to breathe and calm myself down so I could go back in the house. That's when I realized Rob's truck was still idling in the driveway. I tried to dry my face with the sleeve of my T-shirt. He was sitting in the cab, just looking at me, and I felt my face burn with embarrassment.

I couldn't figure out why he was just sitting there. It was so confusing. Everything was confusing. The too-big world drew in close now, pressing itself onto me.

"Hey, calm down. I didn't think you were gonna break down like that."

Rob was standing in front of me. He had turned his truck back off and somehow I didn't notice him walking back to the patio. He was smiling a real smile.

"Come here," he told me and held out his hand. I let him help me up from the doorstep and a shiver ran through me. I didn't have time to think about how his hand felt because he leaned toward me and pressed his lips against mine. I couldn't believe I was finally having my first kiss. It wasn't like on television, though. He had his hands on my arms and was pulling me toward him just a little too much. I wanted to relax into his arms, melting like a damsel in distress or like the fairy-tale princess, but he held me in place and I couldn't shift to get closer.

I knew Daddy had probably gone to bed, but Momma might look out the window or open the door, and then I'd be in real trouble. It seemed like we stood there for fifteen minutes, our closed mouths pressed against each other's, before he leaned back and let go of my arms.

"Alright, I'll see you tomorrow." I must have looked surprised because he laughed and told me, "I can't stay mad at you for long."

I spent the rest of the night replaying all the scenes in my head: him driving by our house without stopping, the different ways he smiled, how he reached out for my hand, the kiss. It wasn't a perfect romance, but as I repeated all those scenes in my mind, they all grew dimmer until only the kiss was left.

My first kiss—the most special experience I'd had at that point. It would be one of the most important memories for the rest of my life, I knew it. I decided not to think about how he held my arms and how I couldn't sink into the kiss. I wasn't going to nitpick like some girls did. We were falling in love, and I was going to be the best girlfriend ever so he wouldn't even think about any other girls.

From then on, I kept a close eye on the windows, but I was careful not to let Momma catch me. When I saw that familiar green truck hood coming out of the holler, I'd go outside and wait on the patio—I didn't want him to drive past because he didn't see me. Sometimes he'd get out of the truck and sit with me, sneaking kisses and smoking cigarettes on the glider. Other times, he'd keep the truck running and I would walk over to the driver's window and talk to him, the exhaust mixing with Rob's cigarette smoke.

Once or twice, I didn't make it to the patio in time and he drove on past. I was always aggravated that he wouldn't give me a minute in case I was in the bathroom or doing something Momma had told me to do, but he never brought it up, and I figured it was better just to let it go so it wouldn't seem like I was nagging him.

All summer long he came over a few times a week and we'd sit outside, him telling me about his day and all the people he dealt with. We talked on the phone too, but I had to share the phone with Momma and my sisters, and Rob's mom and sister wanted to be on their phone a lot, too. So we just talked when we could.

One night, not long before sunset, he told me how he'd dropped out of school after a couple of boys picked on him and he brought a knife to school to defend himself. As they were getting off the school bus, he pulled it out and told them he would cut them if they ever tried anything again. The school found out and suspended him, but he decided never to go back.

"School don't make you smart anyhow," he said. "Either you've got some fucking common sense or you don't. Nothing else matters."

Without thinking, I smacked his arm. "Don't talk like that! Momma will get mad and make you leave!"

It wasn't like I hurt him, but all the light seemed to go out of his eyes.

"Don't you ever hit me again, Jenny. And I'll say whatever the hell I want."

He didn't wait for me to respond. He stood up from the glider and walked away, taking a long drag off his cigarette before he flicked it behind him, not looking to see where it landed. I was too shocked to cry as he drove off, kicking up gravel. I sat there for a minute and then picked up his cigarette, still burning, and finished it as the sun went all the way down.

Chapter 9

Momma acted different the next day, and I knew something was wrong. She hardly spoke to me as we washed dishes after breakfast, me rinsing and drying everything she washed.

After we finished, she walked over to the kitchen table.

"What else do we have to do today?" I asked, trying to sound unconcerned.

She didn't respond.

"I thought I'd see if you could show me how to mend one of my dresses," I told her, keeping my voice light. "You know, the blue one—it's seen better days." I smiled but she didn't say anything, and I wondered if I'd upset her by criticizing the clothes she had made for my sisters. "I mean, it's a great dress, so I want to take care of it."

She turned around and lit the cigarette she had pulled from the pack, not looking at me just yet.

"Everything alright, Momma?"

She took a drag and blew the smoke out, looking at the floor. When she raised her eyes to look at me, I wished I hadn't tried so hard to get her attention.

"I saw you outside with that boy. I would have come out there but I wanted to see for myself what you would do. And I'm here to tell you right now, if you lay down with dogs, you're going to get fleas."

Her words landed like a slap to the face.

"What do you mean, a dog? He's a man, he ain't a dog."

Momma laughed but not like it was funny. "A man? That's a boy—a reckless boy that ain't as smart as he thinks he is. And he sure ain't as smart as *you* think he is."

My eyes watered and I fought back tears again. "You don't even know him! He's good to me and he's even nice to Billy. He gives him money all the time!"

Momma laughed again. "Oh yeah? And where does Rob get that money from? He doesn't have a job. He ain't in school, and all he does is loaf around up there at the pool hall. All the men that come to the garage tell your daddy about him."

"He works, Momma," I told her, satisfied that I knew more than she did. Soon she would understand just how wrong she was. "He does all kinds of work in town. Those men just don't know." My voice shook a little, and I was mad at those men for talking about things they didn't understand.

Momma looked at me with the first hint of sympathy I had seen from her in a long time. "He's no-count, Jenny. And you better not let him kiss you again. Your daddy will whip you if he finds out. And if I see it again, I'll whip you myself."

My eyes went blurry and my body felt like it would explode—explode all over my mother to show her how much she was hurting me. But there was nothing I could do. It was better to keep quiet. If I said anything, Momma would think I was running my mouth and she might smack me. I didn't hear what she said next, but I nodded and fought back tears until I could walk to the bedroom and squeeze my face against the pillow, screaming but making no sound, the scratchy cotton rubbing against my hot cheeks.

For a while after that, Momma came outside anytime Rob stopped by. She would bring out her broom and sweep the patio even if it wasn't dirty, and sometimes she would send leaves toward us if we were sitting on the glider. I knew when she came outside that Rob wouldn't be able to touch my hand and we couldn't sneak behind his truck for a kiss. Worst of all, Rob would give me a look and get up to leave, and I know he would have stayed longer if Momma wasn't out there being rude to him.

When she did leave us alone, Rob would tell me about his life. His daddy drove a milk truck and used to be a tough guy who'd killed his neighbor's dog for barking too much. After he'd shot the dog, he kicked open the neighbor's door and threw the dog into their living room. This story made me sad, and I wondered what kind of man he was to kill a dog just for barking, but Rob said the neighbors were worthless. They lay around all day and messed with their cars at night but never could get them fixed. The dog sat outside all the time, tied to a fence, barking at nothing, and Rob's dad had to get up long before sunrise to deliver milk all over the county. He wished his dad still stood up to people like a real man.

They moved up to the holler after that, and there were no neighbors or barking dogs to bother them anymore—just little creeks to catch minnows in and plenty of deer and squirrels to hunt. Rob's mama had put her foot down after the move and made his daddy come to church with her every Sunday. After a while of that, his daddy got saved. He went to the altar and asked for forgiveness for his sins and promised to be a better man. But Rob liked him just fine before he got saved, he told me. Now, his daddy did whatever his mama told him to do, and Rob hated it.

He liked to tell the story about taking his knife to school and dropping out after that, and when I reminded him that he had already told me that one, he said it was important—*just listen*. Sometimes that got boring, but I liked being the one he talked to. Every once in a while, I wondered about the girl he had mentioned, Susan, but there was no way he spent as much time talking to her as he did with me.

One day, I realized he was just like James Dean in *Rebel Without a Cause* and I told him so, but he hadn't seen the movie. I still tried to explain. "Nobody understands him, and his dad lets his mom call the shots. He moves to a new town and gets picked on at school—"

"Nobody picks on me," Rob interrupted. His eyes were narrowed and dark like they sometimes got. My stomach sank a little and I wished I could take it back. I knew I had messed up, but my head spun as I tried to figure out what I'd said wrong.

"I told you what happened to those boys—they got what was coming to them." He got up and went to his truck without turning around, even though I tried to explain. Jim was the hero, the good guy, just misunderstood. But Rob drove away, his tires squealing once they hit the pavement, and I sank back onto the glider, wishing I hadn't brought it up in the first place.

Another time, Rob showed up at the house—*slid in*, if I'm being honest. His truck threw up more gravel than ever and he had a big grin on his face when he got out of the truck. I came outside like I always did.

"What's going on, good lookin'?" he asked me. He was trying to walk to the patio but took longer than he should have.

"Not much here," I told him, and I filed away those words to think about later—*good looking*. I don't think anyone had ever said that to me before.

He made his way to the glider and dropped down beside me hard.

"Tell me something interesting."

I searched my mind but couldn't think of anything. Daddy hadn't worked on any good cars that day. Rob didn't really care about anything Momma was fussing over. Before I could stop myself, I blurted out, "I've still got all our old dolls from when me and the girls were kids." Rob raised his eyebrows and I noticed his eyelids weren't all the way open.

"Is that right?"

I laughed a little. "Yeah, I know it's silly. I guess I just like to hang on to things. I used to like to play family with them, pretend like they had that perfect life, like *Leave It to Beaver*."

Rob lit a cigarette, taking a drag as he nodded toward the patio. "No, that ain't silly. I like that. You're a lot like me." He turned and smiled at me before he closed his eyes and leaned back in the glider. Something inside me went wild.

Like me.

Gail and Barbara both came to visit almost every day, Gail with her two little ones and Barbara with her pregnant belly. All of us sisters wanted to have the first girl so we could name her Charlie, after Daddy. I don't know why we didn't want to name a boy Charlie, but for some reason, we all decided that we would give that name to the first granddaughter. I wished I could be the one to have the first girl, but I knew it would be one of my sisters. I couldn't get married for a couple of years, and at this point, it didn't seem like Rob would want to marry me.

School had started back and I was a junior. Mary had graduated from high school and moved out at the end of summer, and she was working at the same factory as JoEllen but wasn't married yet. Things had ended with her and Frank. The last few times they talked on the phone, I could hear Mary whisper-yelling at Frank, trying to keep Momma from overhearing her. Every time I listened in, Mary was telling him he'd better stop whatever he was doing. And then one day I heard him roar out of our driveway in his truck, no longer stuck as a passenger with Rob. Mary stormed in with tears streaming down her face and went into our bedroom. When I checked on her, she wouldn't talk, and Frank never came back to the house again. I didn't ask what happened. Whatever it was, it was between the two of them. I knew she was old enough to take care of herself, so she would let me know if she wanted me in her business.

With the older girls gone, all of the chores were on me. Momma still cooked our meals, but I had to wash the dishes, help with the laundry, and clean the bathroom. I had to clean the floors, and Momma wasn't happy unless they were shiny. Nobody seemed to notice that Billy would track in mud or grease from outside.

I missed Mary more than I thought I would. Even though she ignored me most of the time when she still lived at home, at least we could whisper together as we fell asleep. We could drink wine together and smoke cigarettes on the playground and sometimes we would push each other on the swings, which made me feel like I was a little kid again. Now that she was gone, it was just me and Billy. And instead of me being the older sister who got to boss somebody around, when I wasn't at school, I was at home doing chores or babysitting, while Billy went to the races with Daddy on Saturday nights, and they brought back trophies and talked about the cars and the drivers and the accidents the next day. I wished me and Momma could have something like that, but she had raised five kids and was finally getting to enjoy a little bit of life, so *let me do my crossword in peace, for God's sake.*

Gail and Barbara liked to tease me when they visited, saying things like "You still hung up on that Lewis boy? Don't let him move you into that holler—there's too many copperheads, and you know we ain't coming up there to get bit!"

Momma usually responded with a snorting sound if she was in a decent mood. "Yeah, you won't catch me up the holler, neither. Hope you get some sense and set that boy loose before it's too late." That was annoying enough, but if she was in a bad mood, she'd just give us all a look that said she wasn't going to listen to any foolishness, and to hush up or else. Even after they had grown up, my sisters knew that look and did what Momma said. Or what she didn't say, in some cases.

Mary didn't like to talk about Rob, though. Sometimes she'd chime in and agree with Momma, but most of the time she pretended she didn't hear anything when his name came up. She had told me one time, after her and Frank split up, that Rob was trouble just like his brother and I should end things. I told her she didn't know him—he wasn't Frank. She looked at me for a minute and I thought she was going to say something else, but she changed her mind and walked off.

I knew she meant well, but I wasn't going to listen to anyone talking bad about him if I could help it.

After a while, my sisters stopped asking about him, which was just as well because I didn't know what was going on between us anyway. He came by when he wanted to, but he'd sometimes drive away before I had a chance to come out the door, even if I had been watching for him. Sometimes he did that two days in a row and then on the third day, when I was tired of running outside like a dog looking for a treat, he would show up and wait for me and we would talk for hours. Once every week or two, he brought me my favorite candy bar or a Coke and peanuts, and I knew that meant he was thinking about me not just when he was at my house or driving by, but also when he was at the store.

I compared him to the boys in school, who had all grown older but were never as mature as Rob. I mean, Rob was always going to be older than them, so he was automatically more mature. And he definitely seemed more manly than most guys my age. I imagined bringing Rob to one of our dances. We would walk in, Rob holding my arm, and everybody would stare at us, shocked to see my older boyfriend who was actually too cool for the dance. I knew he would never go, but that was part of what made him better than the guys at school, too. He didn't care about things like dances, never had. He was more of a rebel, not somebody who was going to do what he was told all the time. Of course, sometimes it hurt my feelings, but Rob did things his way, and you have to admire someone who lives according to their own rules.

Each time I thought he was going to end things between us because he didn't come around for a few days or he walked away from me without saying goodbye, he would turn around and do something extra nice. Sometimes it made me mad because it was so confusing, but I knew I was being ugly to think like that, and it felt so good when he was being nice. So I pushed the bad feelings away and hoped that someday, everything would be clear and easy and feel good all the time.

Chapter 10

I graduated in May, a few months after I turned eighteen. Every day of my senior year felt like it was crawling at a snail's pace, but when I walked across the stage to get my diploma, it felt like that whole year had just disappeared. Momma and Daddy bought me a 1964 Mustang, green with a black hardtop, and I loved it. It wasn't running yet—Daddy had to fix the transmission and I had to be patient as he fit that in between his real work. And while I was waiting, Daddy taught me how to drive in a beat-up car he kept around the garage, something he would fix up one day and sell to somebody else.

"Alright, Jenny, two hands on the wheel, two eyes on the road. At all times, understand?"

I nodded but didn't look at him, keeping my eyes focused on the road just beyond our driveway so he would know I was listening.

"Put your right foot on the brake and start it up." I knew what to do from watching Mary drive so much, and I was proud to show Daddy. I wanted this to be easy so he would enjoy our time together, like I knew I was going to. We didn't get much time alone—never had—and now I was pretty much grown. I was going to soak up this time where it could just be me and him.

The engine roared to life and then purred, and I grinned at Daddy without even meaning to. He was grinning back. "It's a fine little car if I say so myself!"

I nodded my head and looked back to the road, ready to follow his instructions. The car sure didn't look good, but Daddy had worked his magic on the engine.

He told me to head left out of the driveway and toward KY 519, just like I hoped he would. "Good girl," he told me as I put on my blinker before he even told me to. He popped open a can of beer and relaxed into the seat, hardly having to tell me anything as I drove us up Clack Mountain, twisting and turning but never jerking the wheel.

When I got to drive my Mustang, I could go anywhere, do anything—I was free.

Me and Peggy went for a few rides down US 60 out toward Farmers, which was the best stretch of straight road you could get on, other than the interstate. I wasn't ready for the interstate yet—better to get a little more practice under my belt.

About a month before I graduated, Momma started telling me I needed to line up a job and start paying rent.

"There ain't no freeloading here. Once you're grown, you pay your own way. And as long as you live under my roof, you still follow my rules, no matter how old you are."

I knew what that meant. I still had to be home by dark, no matter that I was eighteen and an adult. That meant no driving through town or parking in the grocery store lot on Saturday night, my engine idling while I talked with my friends and showed off my car. That also meant no going to the Mount Sterling drive-in and no going to field parties with bonfires and cans of beer. I was going to live like I always had, except I also had to work.

So two days after the graduation ceremony, I got a job at Cowden, the blue jean factory. Mary had gotten a job at a new factory, but I was on the same line as JoEllen, sewing zippers into the blue jeans.

JoEllen looked tired all the time, even after she finished her thermos of coffee and had a Coke before lunch. I babysat Mary Beth a few times before I graduated, but JoEllen said the girl was getting big enough to stay home alone, even if she didn't talk, and Donnie didn't like to spend the money on a babysitter anyhow. Sometimes JoEllen had dark circles under her eyes, and I couldn't tell if it was from not sleeping enough or if maybe she was getting hit at home. We stood outside with most of the other workers during our breaks, smoking a quick cigarette and drinking pop to keep us going. She didn't talk to me like she used to.

When I got home after the first day of work, Momma asked what I'd be doing at my new job.

"I'm sewing zippers, just like JoEllen. Sewing them into the crotch." I couldn't help but grin when I said that last part, and Momma laughed.

It felt good to laugh with her. It was like when I used to lay in her lap to watch her stories and I'd promise to be quiet, and she would smile, knowing I would be asleep in no time.

A few days into my job, the boss came up to where I was working. His name was Mr. Jones and he looked like a mouse or a rat but was mean as a snake.

"What is this?" he asked.

I didn't know what kind of answer he was looking for. "I'm sewing the zippers in."

"Is that what you call it? We can't send this shit out—it looks awful. These are all ruined. How long have you been here?"

My eyes stung. "I've been here three days."

"Three days? And you haven't figured out how to sew a goddamn zipper into some goddamn blue jeans by now?" He shook his head like it was worse than the Vietnam War and Nixon's impeachment put together. "Get it figured out today. If I see this shit tomorrow, I'm reassigning you, and I promise there are worse jobs to have than sewing zippers."

I blinked a few times and hoped nobody could tell I was about to cry. He shook his head again. I looked at JoEllen, but there was nothing in her eyes, no sympathy or sadness or pain. She was just tired. I scanned the room and saw that other workers were looking at me. I knew some of their names. We had smoked together and talked during lunch, but they stared through me like I was a ghost, as if I didn't exist.

Something about it reminded me of my first day of high school, but this was worse. This might be forever.

I went to Mary's after work that day and told her I had to do something, anything besides go home and do chores. She had a new boyfriend named John and he was over all the time, even though she swore they weren't doing anything before marriage. He seemed alright, but I suspected what she liked about him most was that he drove a motorcycle, and that seemed dangerous. Mary was smitten again.

We all hopped into my car, which everybody agreed was the best car they had ever been in, and that made me feel good. We went down US 60 and I popped in my favorite eight-track. I sang along with Donna Fargo's "The Happiest Girl in the Whole USA." It was my favorite song, and I had always thought that one day, it would be true for me to sing it. That didn't seem as likely now as it had at other times. Growing up, there was always something to look forward to that was going to bring me happiness: my first boyfriend, my first kiss. Maybe before or maybe after those things, I would get a car and learn to drive, which would make me free to go wherever I wanted, whenever I wanted. Soon enough, I'd get married and have a house of my own, and babies to show off to my sisters.

It wasn't too late for some of those dreams, but others were already falling apart. Why did I feel confused about Rob instead of giddy with love? Why did my home feel like a trap and the only way to escape it was by running into another trap for eight hours a day?

I was ready for my own adventure.

I stepped on the gas a little, revving the Mustang engine, and John and Mary laughed. "That's right, Jenny!" John hollered, and I smiled for the first time that day. "How fast does this thing go?"

"I haven't found out yet," I told him, and as we turned onto US 60, I hit the gas hard. Mary and John fell back against their seats and laughed even harder, and Mary turned the radio up louder.

We got to the edge of the little town of Farmers—it was so little, there wasn't even a stoplight—and passed the gas station where the cool guys hung out. I knew I would have to slow down soon, but I let my car roar past them, knowing they would notice it. Sure enough, we heard one of them shout, "Holy shit, check it out!" and some of them whistled, clearly impressed.

Mary and John kissed each other and I grinned again, not feeling left out or sad, but knowing I had found a taste of that freedom I had been waiting for.

It was getting harder to predict when Rob would visit me, and it started to feel like he was drifting away for good. Part of me didn't mind. There were a couple of good-looking boys from school who worked at Cowden, and Mary's boyfriend had some friends around sometimes too. And then there were the boys who sat around in their cars at the gas station in Farmers or even closer in Morehead. I knew they would be impressed with my car, if nothing else, and that was starting to be more interesting to me than Rob and how moody he could be.

But then one day in early June, just a few weeks into my job, Rob surprised me. The factory whistle went off to let everybody know it was lunchtime, and I went outside to smoke with JoEllen like I always did. There was Rob, standing with a paper bag in one hand and a Coke in the other. He grinned when I walked over to him.

"Brought you some supper."

I didn't know what to say. "You didn't have to do that. But oh my goodness, it smells amazing!" And it did. Whatever he had in that paper bag was much better than the ham sandwich I had brought.

We sat down on the curb and he ate my sandwich while I ate the cheeseburger he'd brought me from Jerry's, the best restaurant in town.

"This is delicious," I told him. He lit up a smoke and watched me eat. "What made you decide to bring me food?"

He shrugged. "Just wanted to, I reckon." He went on to tell me about how a coyote had gotten into his mama's henhouse last night and he was going to watch for it and try to shoot it tonight, after he went to see his papaw Lewis in Bath County. Rob liked to talk about his papaw a lot. He was a lot calmer now, but when he was younger, Papaw Lewis made moonshine and got into all kinds of trouble with the law. To hear Rob tell it, the old man was in with the mob in Chicago back during Prohibition. He had taught Rob how to make moonshine, too, and he said he would show me his still one day. Papaw Lewis had killed his father-in-law at the dinner table, Rob said, because they were arguing over who made better whiskey. Rob's grandma was still alive and they were still married, which didn't make a lot of sense to me. I can't imagine a man shooting my daddy and me being able to love that man afterward. Maybe she was a real Christian and had forgiven him—I wasn't sure. Rob didn't want to tell that part of the story when I asked.

What I did know was that the cheeseburger made me feel a lot better about Rob and how things had been going with him. This wasn't so bad. A person could work at a regular job and have a good man bring her a bite of supper now and then. Save up some money, get married, have a little family. I could be happy like this.

Chapter 11

Things went on like that for a while. Rob showed up at my house or at the factory a few times a week, and we sat around talking about his days and nights, which were more interesting than mine. Mary and John got married at the courthouse and I got to be there as a witness. I would be the last girl to get married. It's not like that surprised me—I was the youngest—but all my life, it felt like I was left behind as my sisters went on to do more exciting things.

One day in June, Rob came by the factory at lunch and said we should go for a drive in my car after I got off work. That was exciting. He'd never wanted to be in my car. I knew he had to like it—who wouldn't? But he acted like it was nothing special and rolled his eyes when I talked about how fun it was to drive around with Mary and John. I thought he might be jealous because his family couldn't get him a nice car like that. When he asked to go for a ride, I thought it might be a turning point, that he might be more interested in doing something I liked just because I liked it. It was all very romantic.

He pulled into my driveway behind me and I ran inside to get out of my sweaty work clothes. I had a big grin on my face and Momma must have known that meant I was going somewhere with Rob, which she didn't try to stop anymore. Still, she told me to make sure I was home by dark. I said, "I will, Momma," and didn't even roll my eyes when I got to my room.

When I got back outside, Rob was in the passenger seat of my car smoking a cigarette. I hoped he wasn't letting the ashes fall on the seat, but I hopped in and smiled, then revved the engine just a little, trying to make it fun for him but not get myself in trouble with Momma. I pulled onto the road as he fumbled with the radio knobs, looking for a good station.

He seemed a little drunk, which didn't surprise me. I knew he sometimes drank before he came to see me. I could often smell it on his breath and he would slur his words a little, swaying as he stood on the patio and told me about what he had done that day. The ash on his cigarette would get longer and longer, and I would usually get so bored of hearing him talk, I would make a game out of watching that ash, to see how long it could get before it finally fell.

I never knew if his temper would be better or worse when he was drinking, but I learned there were little signs I could watch for. They helped me figure out whether he was in the mood for joking or if he wanted to keep quiet, if he wanted me to ask questions or just let him talk. I hadn't gotten him completely figured out, but I figured we were in love, so it was worth it. He did nice things for me and I accepted him for who he was. That's what couples do, right? They get to know each other and they take the good with the bad. They learn that the other person isn't perfect and love them anyway.

That's what me and Rob were going to have, I was sure of it. Our love was going to take care of all my problems and his, too. It was just a matter of time before we would get married. Then he wouldn't have to live with his mom, who controlled everything at their house, and I wouldn't have to live with mine. We would have a family and jobs and we would decide how to spend our days. There would be cookouts at the lake and trips to the Red River Gorge. We would have bonfires when we wanted to, and watch movies, quiet in our house, if we wanted to. I could see the life we were going to make together.

I headed up KY 519 so we could drive up Clack Mountain. That was one of his favorite places to drive, and I thought it was because when you got to the top of the mountain, you felt like you were floating for a second. The engine had to work hard to get to the top, but once you were up there, it was like you could fly. I knew the Mustang would make that feel even better than his truck.

As we headed toward the base of the mountain, I noticed he wouldn't look me in the eye.

"Everything okay?"

He just looked out the window and didn't say anything. I figured something must be bothering him and once we really got going, he would enjoy himself. You could hear the transmission working as I stepped on the gas and sped us up the hill.

"Go faster."

I smiled and tightened my grip on the steering wheel, pressing down on the gas pedal a little harder. I looked over at him, thinking he would be pleased, but he wasn't smiling.

"I told you to go faster."

I didn't know why he was saying that. I was going 50 miles an hour uphill and would have to let off the gas to get around the curves. It didn't make any sense to go faster.

"I can't, Rob—" The explanation caught in my throat. He had pulled a pistol out of somewhere and was pointing it toward me.

"What are you doing?" I half asked, half demanded. Part of me was terrified and the other part was angry. He was acting crazy, but I didn't know if he would listen to me or not.

"I said go faster." He cocked the gun and lifted it, until it was level with my face. I looked into his eyes, thinking he would see me and snap out of this sick game, whatever it was. I didn't see anything in his eyes, though. They were empty.

I started to cry. "Why are you doing this?"

He pressed the barrel to the side of my head and, more calm than ever, asked me, "Do you not fucking hear me? I said to go faster."

I pushed the gas pedal down farther, tears streaming down my face as I watched the road and glanced down at my speedometer. It climbed from 55 to 60, but he didn't let up. We went to 65, then 70, and the wheels lifted a little as we took the curves much faster than the car could handle—or at least faster than I knew how to drive. We got to the top of the mountain and came over the crest, coming off the road again and landing so my tires had to find their grip on the road.

"Faster," he told me again, and now I was sobbing. The last time I looked at the speedometer, it had said I was going 75. This was the most dangerous road in our county.

Finally, he sat back in his seat and put the pistol on his lap. "That was pretty good, wasn't it?" I looked at him, unable to make sense of his words. He was looking at me and grinning. "I knew we could get this old car going."

I didn't say anything else. He told me when to pull over and turn around. He told me when to drive back to my house. As I parked, my hands shook so much, I could hardly turn off the ignition. He hopped out but I still sat there.

"I'll see you," he called over his shoulder.

I couldn't cry any more, but I had to wait until my face wasn't red before I went inside. Momma didn't look up from her newspaper and the vodka she had poured herself. I went to the bathroom to shower, but first I threw up into the toilet until I was empty, emptier than I had ever been.

I figured it was over between us—I *wanted* it to be over between us. I couldn't tell anyone what had happened. My sisters and Momma would be shocked, outraged. They would tell me what to say and how to feel, and I just didn't know what *I* wanted to say and feel, not yet. Worst of all, they would tell Daddy.

Daddy wasn't known for being mean. When he whipped us kids, it was just enough to teach us a lesson, and he never left bruises like a lot of other kids' dads. He never seemed to enjoy whipping us, like some did. But, when I was about eight, I remember Mary finding me in my hiding place, behind the Bel Air. She whisper-shouted my name and I jumped, knocking my shoulder into the rear bumper.

"Ow, Mary! What are you doing?" I rubbed my shoulder and bet I squinched my eyes like Mary said I did when I was angry.

"Don't be such a baby." That was her favorite thing to say to me. "There's a man in the garage that ain't acting right and I think Daddy's gonna whoop him!"

I could hardly get my footing on the loose gravel. I wondered if this guy was drunk, or if he was trying to run off without paying. Daddy also got stern with men if they cussed around us girls.

They all seemed to listen to Daddy, even though he wasn't the tallest or biggest man out there. He didn't talk in a way that would scare most people, either.

When me and Mary got close to the garage, we saw a man standing just inside the big bay door. He was swaying so much, I wondered how he was still on his feet. Drunk.

"I told that bastard what I'd do if he . . ."

The man seemed to lose his train of thought, and I saw Daddy was watching him close, a tire iron in his hand. I had seen the man at the garage before. He was big, real big. Tall and wide, like you'd want a man to be, but it always made me feel strange when he looked my way, so I went inside whenever he showed up, which thankfully wasn't often. I told Momma about him once and she told me, "Some men you best steer clear of. That's one of them."

On that night, Daddy saw me and Mary and sent us inside. "Get in the house, girls." And we hurried along, knowing he meant it. We peeked out from the back storm door, where we could see Daddy and the man who was running his mouth. I saw a different look on my daddy's face than I had ever seen before.

I'm not sure now whether I saw the tire iron hit the big man's kneecap and him falling onto the driveway. Mary says we heard the men hollering but couldn't see it. I remember seeing it, but no sounds. I remember the sound of Momma's show in the living room, with one of those laugh tracks that was sometimes so empty, so untrue, I couldn't stand it.

That's what Daddy would do to Rob, or worse. And Rob had a gun and a wild brother, so they might do something like that, or worse. And there was his papaw Lewis, who might have taught Rob how to do these things. I imagined them all there, collapsed on the driveway, puddles everywhere, the bay door wide open and the sun setting.

I couldn't tell anyone what Rob had done. Someone would die, and I couldn't have that on my hands. So I kept it to myself. I had kept other secrets before and those stayed buried, like they were supposed to. But this one wouldn't let me forget it. This one did get really quiet. Quiet enough for me to hear other voices on top of it. But it was always there, whispering to me: *He could kill you.*

That's what I heard when he called the next day and Momma handed me the phone. He told me about his day and how he was going to see his papaw and they were going to make some moonshine. He told me there was a stranger that came up their holler and how he went down to the road to make that stranger explain what he was doing there.

I didn't say much of anything, so after a while he asked, "What's got your panties in a wad?"

I felt the barrel against my temple.

"Nothing. I think my stomach's upset from something I ate." I didn't remember ever lying to anyone like that before.

"Oh, well, I'm not stopping by if you're sick. I'll check on you in a couple days."

And then my stomach filled with a dread that was its own sickness. "Sure, sounds good."

He laughed a little. "Alright, Jenny, you be good until I see you again."

What could I say to that? I only ever meant to be good. What did he think I might do?

"I will."

Chapter 12

It was always hot in the factory, but when July rolled around we were miserable. All of us except Mr. Jones. He sat in his office with an air conditioner running, and whenever he opened the door to yell at us, it was like a little winter storm rushed over those of us who were close by. The cold against the hot gave me goose bumps, and I wasn't sure whether it was better to have a little break from the heat or just try to get used to it.

Two days after I told him I didn't feel good, Rob showed up at my work with dinner. And after that, he brought me food every day for weeks. At first, I was too confused and upset by what he'd done to smile and flirt like I used to, but I also had to find a way to pretend everything was okay—I could tell he was watching me more closely than ever. After a while, what had happened in the car seemed like a bad dream. And since I couldn't talk to him about it and couldn't talk to anyone else, I let myself pretend it didn't happen. Soon enough, I didn't think about it all that much.

On the first Friday that month, I went to get my check from Mr. Jones like everybody else. We stood in line outside his office and he would shuffle papers around, knowing good and well that we were all standing out there, hot and miserable, dying to go home, but he took his sweet time. My shirt was sticking to me and pressing into my armpits. Rob hadn't come by that week, and his mom had said he wasn't home each night I called.

I was probably more upset than I should have been because it was the first day of my monthly, and Rob could always tell when it started because he said I got needy and complained an awful lot. It felt like my insides were going to tear me apart all day, but I couldn't tell anyone at work. Standing was the worst, and even though I could have sat to do most of my job, our boss liked to walk around and say things like "Getting awfully comfortable here. I might need to find a harder job for you!" and "Didn't realize I was running a daycare here. Going to have to see if I can get some adults to do some work for me." So we stood as much as possible, even if we didn't need to.

He handed me my check and I rushed out to my car, ready to get home and shower and have a beer next to Momma's fan.

When I walked into the house, Momma was sitting at the kitchen table, like she was waiting for me to get home.

"Did you get your check?" She didn't always ask me as soon as I walked in the door, but Momma always wanted my check the day I got it. As if I was going to do something else with it, besides pay her. By the time she took out rent, there wasn't a whole lot left, but I told myself it was better than nothing.

"Yeah," I told her, and I started to walk past her but she held her arm out to stop me.

"You best hand it over," she told me.

I pulled my check out of my pocket. It was damp from my sweat, which made me feel a little bad, but I thought that was what Momma got for making me hand it to her as soon as I walked in the door, before I could take it out and let it dry. I started to walk to my room to peel off my wet clothes and then hop into a cool shower.

"Wait a minute."

I paused in the doorway to the living room.

"What is this with your check?"

I didn't know what she was talking about. "Nothing, it's my check. It's the same check I get every week."

"I don't think so," she replied. "This ain't what you're supposed to bring home." She handed the check to me and I looked at the number. It was half of what it should have been.

"Why didn't you work like you're supposed to?" she asked. "You been running around instead of going to your job?" She didn't wait for me to answer. "That ain't going to work around here. If you don't pay your own way, you'd better find somewhere else to live."

Right then I would have cried if the tears wouldn't have been hot and unbearable. But I couldn't keep my mouth shut.

"It's not my fault, Momma! I was at work, I swear it! I don't get to do anything and I ain't been anywhere but there and at this house all damn summer. I don't even get to go out after dark!"

Momma looked me in the eye. "That boy's got your mind all twisted up. You best stay right here, where you belong. Learn a little something before you go messing yourself up. Learn how to be responsible and go to work like you need to before you throw your life away on some dumb hillbilly."

Then, I couldn't hold the tears back. They streamed down and I knew how they must look: little clean rivers pouring down my face, making paths through the factory dirt. I turned around and rushed back toward the kitchen door.

"Where do you think you're going?" Momma demanded. "You still owe me for your rent. And you'd better get home on time. You're still under my roof." I went out the door before she could say the rest of it, which I had heard endlessly: "That means you follow my rules."

I drove to Mary's house as fast as I could, but I had to slow down for one sharp turn after another, so I didn't get to speed away like I wanted to. I got out of my car at Mary's with my fists clenched. I wanted to hit something, but the only thing I could think of was my car, and I sure wasn't going to do that. All that was left to do was cry, so that's what I was doing when Mary opened her front door.

"Jesus Christ, Jenny—what's going on?" She looked at me but that just made me cry harder. "Get inside here, before the neighbors think you're hurt or something. Wait—you aren't hurt, are you?"

I shook my head and she took me inside and steered me toward her couch. John was mowing the backyard, and I was glad to have a few minutes alone with my sister. She lit up a cigarette and offered me one, and then lit it for me.

I took a shaky breath. "It's Momma. I can't make her happy. It's like everything I do is wrong, and now she wants to control me even though I'm eighteen!"

Mary rolled her eyes. "Tell me something new. That's how she is, you know. We all had to live with it and you'll have to learn how to unless you find somewhere else to go."

The tears started flowing again. "And Mr. Jones, he shorted me on my check. Momma blamed me when all I do is work at that hot factory and hand over my money to her, and I don't hardly get to see Rob." Mary gave a laugh, but I knew it wasn't because she thought anything I said was funny.

"Why do you think I left Cowden? That guy is a crook. He shorted me all the time. What did he take out of yours?"

"Half."

Mary's eyes widened. "You'd better go back there and tell him you want your money, Jenny. Don't let him do that to you. John will go with you if you want, to make sure he pays you and doesn't push you around."

I nodded my head, relieved that somebody else was going to help me take care of it.

"And Jenny, I thought you and Rob were done," she half asked, half told me.

"No, he's just been busy, I guess."

The look on her face made me doubt what I was saying. The thought of what he had done tried to crawl back into my mind, but I pushed it away. Nobody would understand. *I* didn't understand.

She looked at my messy hair and sweaty clothes. "Why don't you go take a shower. I'll get you some clean clothes. Just don't use up all the hot water because John will be needing a shower himself here soon."

I nodded again and as I let lukewarm water pour over me, I thought everything would be okay now. Mary wasn't going to let me be miserable and John wouldn't let my boss steal my paycheck. Everything was going to work out. *I just need a little help from my friends,* I thought with a smile.

After my shower, Mary and I had a couple of beers while we waited for John, and then we all went for a drive. We headed toward Farmers, which gave me the chance to drive fast like I had been wanting to. We were getting burgers and milkshakes at the Frosty Freeze in a little town called Midland, which was even less of a town than Farmers. Rob said he was related to the people who owned the Frosty Freeze, and his grandparents lived close by, so I could look at their house and wonder what they were like.

We ate and drove all the way to the gas station in Farmers. That's where I saw Rob's truck, which you couldn't miss. My heart beat a little faster, and I was relieved again that my bad day was getting better. I would melt into his arms and he wouldn't mind, no matter how hot it was. He would look into my eyes and I would know everything was going to be alright.

Then I heard Mary gasp beside me. You could see two heads inside the cab of Rob's truck—his and Susan's. Mary had figured out who she was and pointed her out to me one day when we drove through town. Susan had impossibly curly, dark hair that you couldn't miss. They were awfully close together. I swung the Mustang into the parking lot, pulling up next to the passenger's side of Rob's truck.

"Jenny! Oh my god, I can't believe you're doing this!" Mary turned her head and covered her face with her hands. I stared through the window, waiting for them to notice me. John didn't say much of anything.

I imagined what I would do when Susan finally looked at me. I would flip her the bird. I would roll down my window and call her a slut. I would get out of this car and pull her out of his truck and beat her ass right there in the parking lot. I would do something.

What I did—when she finally noticed me and whispered to Rob, and then he leaned over and shook his head like he was just disappointed—was throw my car into reverse, sling it onto the road without looking, and peel out like I was on fire, as Daddy would say. Mary braced herself against the door and dashboard while John muttered something in the back seat. As we made our way down US 60, I finally let off the gas and let my car coast, the hot wind tangling my hair.

I planned to stay at Mary's and drink until I cried, drink until I puked—I didn't care. I was definitely going to drink until I forgot, at least for the night. I would forget my shitty boss and my shitty boyfriend—*was he ever my boyfriend?* It didn't matter. I was going to forget him. Now I had a good reason to get away from him, and he knew it too.

I would forget that my mom was more interested in me paying rent than anything else, that she didn't think I was worth listening to, didn't think I was special. She thought I had my head up my ass and was twisted up over some hillbilly, and goddammit, maybe I was at one point.

I had two more beers at Mary's, and after that I stopped keeping track of how many I drank. She tried to stop me from leaving but I decided I was going to say something to Rob, so I drove up to his house where he still lived with his parents. I wove around the one-lane gravel road all fired up, ready to give him a piece of my mind, but knowing I had to be even more careful than when I was driving to Mary's. His road had a hill on one side and a creek on the other—there weren't many places to go if you messed up behind the wheel. You could barely pass another car on most of this road. Some places, one person would just have to back up until they reached a decent spot to pull over. There was one spot where two trucks could pass, but they'd be close enough so the drivers could reach into each other's windows.

There was Rob. He was standing outside his truck next to Susan. I could have yelled at him, but I couldn't face the two of them together.

The humiliation washed over and through me and I wished I could disappear right there. Instead, I turned around at the end of their long driveway, knowing they saw me. I tore back out of the holler, throwing gravel and driving all reckless, driven by rage. There's a rock wall you have to hug at one point on the road, and I scratched up my car against it. That was the only time I felt anything but anger on my drive home, because I knew I had messed up the paint on my car and Daddy didn't do paint, so it would either be ruined or expensive to fix. And either way, Momma wouldn't be happy about it.

I made it back to Mary's and she came outside, saw my car, and shook her head. But she walked me into her house and helped me get onto the couch with a little blanket. I couldn't tell her how awful the day had been. The whole summer, actually. I couldn't explain how humiliated I was not once, or even twice. How many times had it been? I hadn't told her what he did in my car, how much he scared me. I was still her little sister, still the girl living at home when Mary had moved out and become an adult of her own. She probably didn't care about my troubles.

There was a lot I didn't know that night as I fell asleep on her couch and listened to her and John argue in their bedroom. I didn't know what the ocean looked like or how it tasted or how the sun glimmers at sunrise and sunset over an eternity. I didn't know what it meant to go to Las Vegas and walk beneath the flashing lights, a neon sea lighting up faces and casting shadows all night, all day. I hadn't been on an airplane or a subway in New York City or had a passport stamped. I hadn't been to a concert. I'd never even imagined any of these things. They existed only in songs and movies and, even though I couldn't know it, some of them were in my distant future, less real than a dream.

But I did know that this time, I was done with Rob. I imagined that to be true.

Chapter 13

Mary had called Momma on the party line to tell her where I was sleeping. I didn't know that when I passed out, and I woke up feeling guilty. Then I asked Mary to call her back and tell her I would be gone for the weekend. I didn't know how Momma would take it, but I wasn't ready to go back, not yet.

I did go back on Sunday evening, before sunset. I had a buzz but was okay to drive. Momma didn't say much when I got in, and Daddy was already in bed. It would blow over soon enough and we would pretend nothing happened. That's what families did, after all. We had blowups and crazy times and then we went back to normal, like nothing ever happened.

Momma didn't smile at me as much, though—not that she smiled at me all that much in the first place. But I noticed when I would sit down to watch a show with her, she didn't look my way at all. And if I came through the kitchen while she was cooking, she didn't ask me what I was up to. It was like she stopped caring at all. And even after John helped me get the rest of my check—Mr. Jones acted like it was an honest mistake—and I gave Momma the money that was missing for rent, she didn't apologize or ask me what had happened. She just put the check in her deposit bag, which she and Daddy took to the bank every Saturday morning, and went back to her crossword puzzle.

She did remind me to be home before dark, even when I was just going over to Mary's house. I was afraid if I opened my mouth, all my anger would come pouring out—and there was no telling what it would do. That anger was like a flood inside me, barely contained, and if the dam broke, it would destroy something.

I started thinking about how much money I would have to save before I could move out. It would be a long time before I could get a place of my own, unless I could start picking up extra shifts or babysitting. Mary Beth was too old to babysit, so I would have to find another kid, and it would pretty much have to be on weekends. But if Mary and John would let me move in with them, I could save up money even faster. They wouldn't charge me as much rent as Momma did, just to sleep on their couch. Maybe that could work.

Mary said I could, and I called Momma that night to tell her. She was so quiet on the other end of the line, I thought she couldn't hear me.

"Momma?"

"Come get your things," she told me.

After I moved to Mary's couch, I didn't go back home until Billy's birthday rolled around on July 19. Momma made him a chocolate cake, and Daddy took part of the day off so they could go drive the car he had been fixing for Billy. It was a 1973 Camaro, red and shiny, and I started to feel jealous when I saw how excited everybody was over it—a bunch of guys were still hanging around the garage and acting like it was the best thing they had ever seen. And it was nice, but I liked mine better. I figured I could outrace Billy in my Mustang any day. And besides, red cars were all over the place, but my green car was different, interesting. I tried to be happy for Billy since it was his birthday, even though he didn't have to graduate to get his first car.

After I told Billy happy birthday and ate a piece of cake, Momma said it was okay to take a couple pieces to Mary's house. When I pulled up in her driveway, there was another motorcycle parked next to John's.

I went inside and set the cake on the kitchen table. I was disappointed to discover the other motorcycle driver was David Wilson. He had lost an arm *and* a leg when he was little. Apparently, he was playing on the train tracks and by the time he realized the train was coming, it was too late to move. I always wondered how that could happen. Wouldn't you hear the train coming? I guess little kids don't always know what's going on around them.

His family had money, though, which was good for Dave. Most families couldn't have bought him a prosthetic arm and leg, or taken him to the doctor over and over so he could learn to use them. And here he was, riding his own motorcycle. He had a reputation for being into weed and maybe even pills, but he never got into serious trouble—it's easier not to if your family has money. I figured it couldn't be anything too bad, anyway. He seemed alright to me.

He wasn't the best-looking guy ever, but as we all drank a beer and talked, I started thinking he was cute enough. Him and John said we should hop on their motorcycles and go for a ride. My belly was full of butterflies as I got on behind Dave. He handed me a helmet and put one on himself that had a shield, so he looked extra mysterious. We took off down the road, twisting around turns and following John and Mary. Instead of turning right and heading toward 60, John turned left onto KY 519, which was just about as twisty as Mary's little road, and mostly an uphill drive.

I hadn't been on the back of a motorcycle before. It was even more exciting than being inside my car, where you were protected from the open air. Dave revved the engine and got in front of John as we began climbing up Clack Mountain, and I tightened my arms around him. I hadn't ever put my arms around another guy, nobody but Rob, and this felt strange but good. I didn't know where things could go after this, but I was happy to have something to do besides work, something to feel besides heartache. I hadn't heard from Rob since I saw him and Susan at his house. It hurt me a little every morning when I woke up and remembered again, even though I tried to tell myself I was happy we were over.

A little way up the mountain, Dave pulled off the road onto the grassy shoulder. Soon after, John and Mary pulled up behind us. "What's wrong?" I asked him over the motorcycle engine.

He took his helmet off and rubbed the inside of the shield. "Nothing, just fogging up a little." He put his helmet back on, gave John a thumbs-up, and pulled back onto the road, which was at a steep incline. I looked behind me to see John and Mary back on the road, and a car farther down the hill that was also going from the shoulder to the road.

I settled back into this new freedom and waited for all other thoughts to leave me alone. A few minutes later, though, Dave pulled over again. This time, John got off his motorcycle and came up to us.

"That car pulled over again," he told Dave, who was wiping the fog off his shield once more. Dave glanced behind him.

"That's weird." Then he shrugged and the guys looked at each other in a way that made me think they had an idea they weren't saying out loud. I was ready to get back on the road, though—to climb that mountain and reach the top, where I knew Dave would go top speed, and it would be the best feeling in the world: freedom.

We got to the top of 519 and just when I thought we would tear over the country road, engine roaring and the wind stinging our cheeks, Dave stopped one more time. "Trade helmets with me," he said. "This one keeps fogging up and I can't see a damn thing." I didn't like the idea of trading because that meant maybe I would have a foggy shield and wouldn't be able to see anything. But I figured he was the driver, so I should do what he wanted. John and Mary had pulled onto the shoulder behind us, and the same car was a little farther down the mountain, pulled over once again.

Dave eased the motorcycle back onto the road, and Mary and John pulled in behind us. We got going, and before long, Dave really picked up speed. This was what I had been waiting for. This was what it should be like to be an adult but still young and free, to have your whole life ahead of you. I felt the motorcycle come up off the ground a little and thought Dave was doing a wheelie, so I threw my arms up and shouted, "Yippie!" And that's the last thing I remember.

Chapter 14

The first time I woke up, I couldn't see anything. I tried to talk, but I couldn't move my mouth. I started to panic and reached for my face, but my arms were strapped down. Everything was muffled and dark. I grunted and tried to arch my back and finally, Momma talked to me.

"Keep still. You're okay. You're in the hospital. They're fixing you up, but you've got to stay still." A man's voice started talking to Momma, and I think she was crying. Soon, a wave of exhaustion and bliss washed over me, pulling me back into a dark dream world that started to feel like waking life.

I awoke again to the sound of machines beeping and more low voices, none of them familiar. My heart beat, beat, beat like a bird pounding against its cage and I thought my heart would bloody itself, tear its wings, throw feathers onto the living room floor. It would be free, it would. It would fly in one world or the other, whole or battered. And if it tore itself, was the cage or the bird to blame? Which of them chose violence, the still prison or the beating wings of desire? A machine beeped faster and faster.

"For fuck's sake, Denise, get her blood pressure down. We have *got* to get started." The sounds slowed and slowed and molasses poured into my ears, into my brain, where it was hot and dark and then silent.

They peeled the bandages off my face, pulling at my eyelashes and eyebrows, and I tried to tell them they were hurting me, but I still couldn't talk.

"Oh my God," somebody said. "Is she always going to look like that?"

What the hell are you talking about? I tried to say, but a stabbing pain shot through my jaw and up into my skull and everything went black, blacker than the dark from having my eyes forced shut. Sweat poured out of me all of a sudden and I began to shake. The salt stung my face, as if I had a thousand tiny cuts all over me, and I wanted to cry but my eyes wouldn't make tears and I couldn't open my mouth.

A woman's voice said, "Get back," and it seemed like I was about to have a thought, but then it was more bliss and exhaustion and dark, dreamless sleep.

When I finally opened my eyes, I still couldn't move. My whole body felt like I was sunk into concrete. Out of the corner of my eye, I saw Momma asleep in a chair in the corner. That didn't make any sense. There were some flowers and a balloon on a little table to my right. Above me were bright fluorescent lights and I could hear them buzz and hum. I saw the electricity fly from one end of the fluorescent tube to the other, and back again, and then it filled with flies and those buzzed louder and louder and I shut my eyes against them.

"Jenny?" It was Momma. I opened my eyes and she was there, leaning over me.

"Where am I?" I tried to ask, but my words came out as a moan.

"You all wrecked on that motorcycle," she told me. "You're in the hospital." Her voice shook and I knew she was scared, but there was another feeling there too. She was mad at what I had done, mad that I'd got myself into this mess. This time, tears did come to my eyes, but of course I couldn't wipe them away.

A nurse walked in and leaned over me from the other side. She shined a little flashlight into my eyes and I couldn't turn away or tell her to stop, but I could close them.

"Good," she said.

A doctor came in. I figured he was a doctor because he was a man and also because of how he took charge of the room.

"How's our patient today?" he asked as if I could answer. As if he didn't already know. I just looked at him since we both knew I couldn't do anything else.

"You gave your mom and dad quite a scare, Jenny. All of us actually." He kind of chuckled, like we had gotten to the funny part of a movie, where you find out the bad things aren't going to happen and it was all a big misunderstanding.

Him and the nurse talked about my vitals and what to check next and whether I had gone to the bathroom that day. *Oh my god, how have I been going to the bathroom?*

Then he sat on the edge of my bed and looked at Momma. "Has anybody told her what happened?" I guess Momma shook her head *no* because he looked at me and went right into it.

"Jenny, you were in a motorcycle wreck and you are lucky to be alive. You've gone through surgery and we've got your jaw wired shut. It's probably going to have to stay that way for a while." He inhaled, and for the first time I saw sympathy on his face. "You broke a lot of bones in your face. We're fixing you up as best we can."

My eyes must have shown the fear I felt because he went on: "Now don't you panic. We've got a good team here. And I have plenty of experience. You're in good hands and we will take good care of you."

I tried to lift my arm but could only get my hand off the bed. Still, I pointed at my face.

"You're wondering what you look like, I guess." I tried to say *yes* with my eyes.

The doctor sighed and stood up. "Nurse, you can talk to her mother about whether to show her or not." And he bustled out of the room.

I looked over at Momma, trying to beg her with my eyes.

"She wants to see what she looks like," Momma told the nurse.

"I'm not sure that's the best idea," the nurse told her. "This kind of shock can really be hard on a person."

"Just get her a mirror," Momma told her, and I heard the familiar grit in Momma's voice. The nurse brought a mirror over and held it over my face so I could see myself while I was looking straight up at the ceiling. I didn't see myself, though. I didn't understand what I saw. There was a misshapen lump, covered in bruises and wires. That was my face. A tube was going down into my mouth—and that's when I realized I had a feeding tube in. My eyes peeked out from something that looked like the Vienna sausages Daddy loved to eat. *At least I didn't turn into SPAM.*

Something about that thought made me want to laugh, and I tried to tell Momma how funny it was, but all that came out was *Mmmmh! Mmhhmmhh!!!* And tears were rolling down my face now, lighting it on fire again, but I couldn't explain that they were tears of laughter.

"I knew this would happen," the nurse muttered, as she whisked the mirror away. "Time for her to sleep. You can sit here but she won't be awake for a while." And I tried to tell her to let me stay awake, not to send me back to that sleep that wasn't sleep at all, but my eyes got too heavy and my body went limp.

The next time I opened my eyes after the accident, Mary and John were there, both looking at me as if I was a ghost. Momma was in the corner where I had seen her before. And there was Rob, a vase of flowers in his hand, talking to Momma as if he was her best friend in the world. If I hadn't been doped up on pain medication, I bet I would have vomited, the way my stomach flipped and flopped. Thank God I didn't, since I couldn't have turned my head to the side.

"She's awake," Mary told them, and everybody came close to my bed. It was the first time I could remember everybody in a room looking at me, all care and concern. Like you think it's going to be on your birthday. Rob walked around to put the flowers on my table and he took the old vase off of it.

He laid one of his hands on mine. "You're going to get through this, okay? I'll make sure they take good care of you." Everybody murmured in agreement, like Rob had made a decision and now it would come to be. I couldn't put the words together yet, but the question clanged in my mind: *What is he doing here?* Rob leaned over and kissed the top of my head. I drifted back out of consciousness but heard them all talking as I slipped away, filled with new confusion.

I don't know how many times I woke up and fell back asleep. Sometimes nobody was there, and sometimes it was like a party was going on in my room, there were so many people standing around, chatting as if they did this all the time. Momma was there most of the time. I could smell her cigarette smoke even when I was too tired to open my eyes.

One of the times I woke up, Rob was saying goodbye to Momma and I watched him leave. Momma turned around and saw that my eyes were open.

"He's been here every day," she told me. I knew she meant that was a good thing, but my first thought was that I looked like a monster, and I hated for him to see me like that. My second thought was maybe he was the monster, and now my jaw was wired shut and it was too late to tell anyone what he had done.

Maybe a week later, the nurse took out my feeding tube and explained it was time to start me on a liquid diet. I would have to drink everything through a straw. She fed me my first meal, which dribbled down my lips and onto the bib she had tied around my neck.

"Don't you worry—everybody does that. That's what the bib is for. You'll get the hang of it soon enough."

I ran out of energy before I got full, though, and I started to wonder if I was going to waste away to nothing. With the feeding tube out, I could almost talk, and people tried to understand what I was saying. I learned to use as few words as possible, so there was less for them to decipher.

After Momma started to understand me a little, I asked her, "How long?" She knew what I meant.

"You'll be out of here in a few more days. The doctor says as long as you can eat your liquid diet and get enough calories so your weight doesn't drop any more, you'll be safe to come home."

Come home. I knew what that meant. I wouldn't be going back to Mary's.

It turned out that I wouldn't be going anywhere for a while. When I got back to the house, I didn't have the strength to walk around like I used to, and I was either in pain or on so much pain medication, I didn't want to go anywhere.

Like a miracle, my face went back to looking almost exactly like I did before the wreck, except I couldn't open my mouth. I could feel my teeth, though, and I knew they were out of place. The doctor mentioned that during one of my follow-up visits. "Once we take the wire out, we'll see how those teeth are. With enough time, some of them might get strong enough to stay in. But chances are, some of them will have to come out." I waited until I got back home to cry. Everybody had told me over and over how lucky I was to be alive, how that helmet saved me from the fence post and my sister saved me from the helmet. They weren't sure yet whether Dave would make it or not, and it was his helmet with the foggy shield that had saved me. But I didn't feel very lucky right then.

I didn't realize that my head had been hurting until one day it stopped for a little while. Everything around me got sharp, like the television going from fuzzy to clear when a storm finally passes or you get the antenna situated just right. The doctor told us that was normal after an accident like mine, and my brain was still healing. *My brain, healing.* That didn't make sense to me, but he wasn't worried and neither was Momma, so I figured it wasn't a big deal. Every time I mentioned my headaches after that, the doctor said they would go away someday. I didn't try to tell him about the cloudy, fuzzy feeling.

One day in that late summer, I saw Daddy pull my Mustang around to the driveway in front of the garage. I thought maybe he was going to get the paint fixed, because a man got out of his car and walked up to it. Him and Daddy stood there talking for a while, nodding their heads and smiling. I could tell that man liked my car and I wondered how long it would be before I could drive it again.

"We've got to sell it to pay your hospital bills," Momma told me out of nowhere. She walked into the kitchen to find me staring out the window. "It's a shame, we could have got more out of it but the side is all scratched up." She looked at me, and I knew she was talking about where I had scraped it against the rock on Mill Branch Road. This was the worst moment of the whole accident so far, finding out my car was being sold and I was getting blamed for it not being worth more.

I had been too weak to drive, and with my jaw still being wired, it wouldn't be safe for me for a while yet—any little accident could break my bones as they were healing. I had daydreamed about getting back on US 60 and riding with the music blaring, windows rolled down, but July had disappeared and so had most of August. I would be getting the wire taken out in a couple of weeks, and that gave me something to look forward to during every meal I had to drink through a straw. I was even sick of the milkshakes Rob brought every day. Momma was thrilled by how attentive he was, how much love he showed.

And now, I would have to figure out how I could even go back to work without a car. All the hope I had been holding on to disappeared into a long, dark night that reminded me of the drug-induced sleep at the hospital.

Chapter 15

Mary and John had seen what happened from behind us. They came to Momma's to visit me one night and told me all about it as I drank soup through a straw.

When I thought Dave was doing a wheelie, the front wheel of his motorcycle had come clean off. As the bike flew apart, I flew into the air and straight into a fence post, face-first. Dave had also flown off the motorcycle but missed any fence posts. Instead, he rolled down the hill on the side of the road and was in the same hospital as I was, but for even longer.

Thank God we traded helmets. Thank God for that foggy shield.

When Mary and John got to me, my face was already swelling so bad, they couldn't hardly get the helmet off my head. They finally did, though, and my head quickly grew to the size of a pumpkin—that's how big it was when I first looked in the mirror at the hospital.

Now I was safe at Momma's kitchen table. I looked at Mary sitting next to me as John went on about how crazy the whole thing was. She was trying to light a cigarette, but her hand was shaking too much. I leaned over and took the lighter from Mary and flicked it for her. That's the first time she ever looked so deep into my eyes. All our childhood bickering, all the jabs and resentment—it was gone. She had saved my life. That changed everything between us, forever.

Later that night, I thought to ask why the motorcycle wheel came off. I didn't know much about motorcycles, but I did know that wheels don't just fly off by themselves most of the time. I mumbled my question to Mary and when she finally understood, anger crossed her face.

"Remember that car that kept stopping toward the bottom of the hill?" I nodded. "They think that was somebody trying to mess with Dave. Apparently there was a drug deal that went bad or something." Mary was quiet. "I didn't know how much trouble he was, Sis. I'm sorry." Sometimes I thought I'd like to thank Dave for trading helmets with me, but it seemed like it was his fault the whole thing happened in the first place.

Maybe that conversation should have made my path look different going forward. I had experienced the ultimate freedom you can have on wheels—the open road, an Appalachian mountain, fully unrestrained on the back of a motorcycle with no responsibility for where we went. And look where that got me. I knew what Momma thought of it: *You made your bed. Now lie in it.* That was her answer for every mistake, every bad choice. I wasn't trying to be reckless but the recklessness found me anyway.

I wonder now if I should have taken the wreck as a lesson about danger and dangerous men. Maybe that's what Momma wanted, though she couldn't put it into those words. But Dave was close to my age, barely a man. What was he doing having drug deals, much less ones that could go bad? It was like he was playacting at being grown, and whoever was in that car was playacting at being bad. Or maybe it was Dave who was bad, and the men in the car were getting the revenge they deserved. Maybe they wished I wasn't on the back of the motorcycle and they felt guilty when they saw what happened to me.

Or maybe they were all bad men—playing at being bad, playing at being men—and none of them cared about my broken face and the teeth I could feel moving behind my closed lips. The lips I couldn't open for a month and a half. The words I couldn't say, the songs I couldn't sing, every smile and frown I couldn't show. Maybe none of those men cared about the job I lost and the car I lost and the freedom I had just begun to taste, living at Mary's, and how it felt to have that snatched away from me.

I was an adult, but nothing about my life made me feel like that was true. I knew I had to claim it for myself, take control of my life. I just had to figure out how to do it. It was hard to focus on anything, though. Thoughts came and went, but mostly went. It seemed like I had plenty of feelings but there was only one that never went away, and that was hunger.

Rob came by almost every day when I was recovering through the summer and fall. When they took the wire out and freed my jaw, everybody was able to see what I had known that whole time. Most of my teeth couldn't be saved. They were so crooked and loose in my mouth, I had to be careful when I ate, or I would knock them out myself. We made an appointment to get them removed and to have a bridge made. In the meantime, I spent a couple of weeks with teeth going this way and that. *Looking like that damn pumpkin again.*

A few days before I got my new teeth, the dentist pulled all the ones that couldn't be saved. Ten teeth, gone. Back at the house, I looked in the mirror and grinned, my mouth emptier than I could ever remember seeing it. I was on the pain pills they had given me and didn't have the energy to make a joke in my mind. I watched the girl in the mirror as she cried a little, and I felt sorry for her and how awful she looked.

When I got my bridge—two bridges actually, one for my top teeth and one for the bottom—I stared in the mirror again. My smile was perfect, except for a long time after the accident, I couldn't make my eyes smile with my mouth. A real smile shows up in the eyes. That's how you can tell if someone really means it.

I was so tired from thinking about the wreck and what I could have—should have?—done differently. I was tired from the pain of having my jaw wired shut and not being able to eat or talk. I had no money, no car, no life. It was hard to get excited about returning to normal. Or something close to it.

Rob was so different from what he used to be. He brought me my favorite wine—the one that used to be Momma's favorite, but she mostly drank vodka by that time—and he'd sit with me on the patio, drinking his beer or taking a nip of moonshine as the days deepened into autumn. Sometimes we would sit inside the house with Momma when Daddy was gone to the races and we would talk and laugh until we could hardly stand it.

Things between us were better than ever. He even told me he was done with Susan. When he heard about my wreck and how hurt I was, all he could think of was how much I meant to him and how good I had always been to him. He knew if I made it through, he was going to be a good man to me.

That last part made my belly flip-flop like it did the first time he kissed me. Things were getting so serious between us. I knew that's what I had been wanting, but it was starting to feel real. I wondered if he would ask Daddy for my hand in marriage.

When he wasn't around, Momma would tell me I was too young to get married. "Don't rush into anything," she would tell me. "There's no reason to be in a hurry."

"You got married young," I responded. "And Mamaw was even younger. You all ended up happy, so what's wrong with that?"

Momma would just shake her head. "Some things you can't explain. They just take time to understand. Give yourself time. You don't need him." I wondered why her friendliness toward Rob was starting to wear off. I noticed she hadn't been as talkative with him lately as she was when I first got home from the hospital, and it bothered me.

One day, Momma came outside where me and Rob were sitting on the patio. It was cool but not too cold outside, my favorite time in the fall when the leaves turned red and orange and yellow all around us, like the hills were trying to be just as pretty as the sunsets.

"Jenny, you need to get inside. You've got chores to do."

"But Mom—"

"Now, Jenny. Don't make me say it twice." I stood up and tried not to let her see how mad I was. Rob made light of it, though.

"Oh come on, Helen. I'm sure Jenny'll get her chores done to suit you just fine. You can let her keep me company a little bit longer, can't you?" He smiled like him and Momma were best friends, but she barely looked at him.

"Don't your parents need you to do something? I'm sure they could use some help since you ain't working."

I wished she hadn't said that. I knew Rob would be mad and I'd hear all about it the next time I saw him. He wouldn't say anything back to Momma, though. He just stood up and gave her a smile that I knew meant he didn't like what he had heard, and he walked to his truck.

"See you around, Jenny," he said over his shoulder, and Momma motioned for me to go inside.

Once we were both in the kitchen, I turned around to look at her. "He might break up with me now." I wanted to say, *Because of what you just did*, but I knew better. Momma might be the only person I knew whose temper was worse than Rob's.

She just snorted. "Yeah, don't worry, he'll be back. We ain't lucky enough for him to stay gone."

I wanted to argue back, to tell her how she didn't understand and this was my best chance at love—maybe the only chance I had. I couldn't just let it go. But pain shot through my jaw and into my head, behind my eyes, and I lost the thoughts. I wanted to explain so much to Momma, but those words wouldn't come. Finally, I found some others.

"What do you mean? You saw how he was at the hospital. He was *there* for me, Momma. He loves me," I told her, as if I was making a grand argument.

She just shook her head again. "You're too young. You'll see things different if you give it time."

I didn't want to give it time, though. Life had always moved at a snail's pace and now it felt like I was getting left behind, like all my chances for happiness were going to pass me by.

A few months after my wreck, it was time to go back to work. Daddy had a little junky car and I asked Momma if I could buy it from them. I would have to make payments on it, on top of paying my rent. I couldn't believe how unfair it was. I was back to square one—no money, living with my parents, going into debt for an ugly car so I could work at an ugly factory. But Momma said no, she wasn't a bank and she wasn't handing out loans. I'd have to save up the money to buy it and hope nobody else bought it first. When I told Rob, he said he would drive me to work every day. *He* would take care of me, even if my parents wouldn't.

The days were getting shorter, which meant I had to be home earlier and earlier each day. I got my old job back, and by the time Rob picked me up from the factory, most of the time it was too late for me to go for a ride in his truck or even walk over to the playground. All I could do was sit at my house, and I could tell Rob was getting tired of that.

On Thanksgiving, we had a big dinner and all my sisters came to the house with their husbands. Billy's girlfriend was coming over after she had dinner with her family, and Rob was coming to see me.

Momma made a ham with round slices of canned pineapple on top of it. The taste of ham with pineapple was my favorite and I always tried to get one of the first servings, after Daddy got his, before all the pineapple got snatched up. I made the mashed potatoes and heated up green beans that somebody had canned and given to us—either one of my aunts or one of Momma's friends with a big garden.

Momma and Daddy sat at the kitchen table, of course, but there weren't enough chairs for everybody so we spread out, sitting on the couch with our plates on our laps or standing in the kitchen, leaning back against the counter as we ate. I loved the holidays, loved having everybody in the house smiling and laughing. I thought this is what a home should feel like.

After we ate, the girls sat around the living room, smoking and having drinks, talking about how stuffed we were. The men hung out in the garage, looking at Daddy's latest project or whatever they did out there all the time. Everyone wandered in and out of the kitchen, having seconds if they could make room for more food.

As the sun went down, everybody started going home, until all my sisters were gone. I went onto the patio with Rob to say good night.

"Come on, let's go for a ride," he told me.

I looked at the sky. "You know I can't. It's pretty dark and I'm not allowed."

"What the hell, Jenny? How long is it going to be like this? We can't do anything because of your mom."

"Shhh!" I knew she was in Daddy's chair, right by the window. If the television wasn't too loud, she might be able to hear what Rob was saying.

"Don't tell me to be quiet. I'm tired of tiptoeing around your mom. I won't live like this, having a woman tell me what I can and can't do. This shit is getting old."

I hadn't seen him angry since before my wreck, since that time we went for a ride in my car. Everything was so much better now. I didn't want things to go back to how they were.

He turned around and started to walk to his truck.

"Hey—" I ran toward him and started to reach out but didn't want him to think I was grabbing him or trying to keep him from doing anything he wanted to do. I waited for him to turn around, proud of myself for knowing how to act with him. I knew how to love him the way he wanted to be loved, and there is nothing better than that, is there?

"Just let me talk to her," I told him. "I'll make things better, I promise. I'm an adult now, and she's going to start treating me like one." I held my head high, knowing I had a right to say it. I was ready for a change, and Momma would just have to learn to accept it. My head was swimming, but I tried not to let it show.

Rob nodded as if he was considering what I was saying.

"Alright, Jenny. Let's see it. I'll call you tomorrow." I smiled, letting him see my perfectly white and even teeth. I watched his truck pull away and drive into the holler toward his house. He was waiting for me to show him I could do it, keep my word.

I gathered my courage to talk to Momma. She was in a good mood and probably had a nice buzz by that point in the evening. I would start out with some light talk about the show she was watching. I would compliment dinner, which had been really good, so that would be sincere. And if the timing was right, I would talk to her about how I was getting older. I would be nineteen in February, just a few months away, and we could both agree it was time for me to live my own life while still paying rent and respecting her rules.

I walked into the living room, where she was smoking a cigarette. She looked up from the television.

"I heard what you said to Rob. Don't get any big ideas. This is my house and you'll abide by my rules."

I couldn't find any words. I went to my room and lay on the bed in the dark. A laugh track rang through the house, hollow.

Chapter 16

Just as I feared, Rob stopped coming by the house every day. And for the next two weeks, when I would call his house, his mom said he was out somewhere, she didn't know where. He probably came by three times, but one of those times, he drove off instead of knocking on the door. I had to beg Mary to take me to work each day and pick me up, or sometimes bum a ride from JoEllen. Everything was sliding backward. The third week after Thanksgiving, I didn't see him until Friday night.

He knocked on the door with a bottle of wine and a six-pack of beer in his hands. I tried not to show how relieved I was to see him. We opened the wine and poured me a glass in the kitchen and went to the living room to watch television with Momma. Daddy and Billy were off at the races, as usual. Rob kept talking to me, but Momma didn't want any conversation that night.

"You all go sit in the kitchen," she told us, looking at me. "I can't hear my show."

We did, but I knew she was unhappy about more than us talking. Rob and I smoked a couple of cigarettes—Momma didn't care about me smoking now that I was eighteen and had a job again. Rob told me stories about running the ridges in his truck and having to get it pulled out of creeks, and he made it all sound so funny, I couldn't stop laughing. Of course, I didn't have any tolerance for alcohol after my wreck. It was a long time before I could have a proper drink after it happened, so now I was a cheap date, as they say. I also discovered that if I drank too much, instead of having a regular hangover, I was stuck in bed for the day. Not because I was sick, but because of the pain. It didn't stay in my head, but spread down into my jaw, as if I could feel where the bones had been broken. Momma didn't like me lying in bed during the day, so I had to be careful about that.

"Hush up in there," Momma hollered from the living room. Rob set his beer can down on the table a little harder than he needed to.

"What the hell is her problem?" he asked me, quiet enough that Momma probably didn't hear, although she might have if the television went quiet.

I tried to get him to calm down. "She must be in a bad mood. We can go outside if you want," I offered. It was cold outside, but we could sit in his truck if he didn't mind to turn on the heat.

"I ain't wasting gas," he said, and he stood up without looking at me. He was going to leave, and I couldn't stand the thought of him disappearing on me again.

I stood up, too. "Come on, let's go out there and *talk*," I told him. He knew what that meant—we could go make out in his truck. Hopefully he had parked where Momma couldn't see.

Rob looked at me and seemed to warm up to the idea. He motioned toward the door with his head, telling me to come outside. As soon as I stepped onto the patio, he grabbed me and pressed his lips against mine. He tasted like warm beer and cigarettes. I let him kiss me for a minute and then pulled away to whisper, "Let's go to your truck."

He didn't respond but instead pulled me back toward him and put his hand up my shirt. I knew Momma could see us from the living room or the bathroom, and there's no telling what she would do if she caught us doing that. I tried to push his hand down gently and pulled my face away again.

"Not here. Momma would kill me." I smiled so he would know I still wanted to make out—I just wanted to do it somewhere more private.

He took a step back and dropped his hands. "Alright, Jenny. Have it your way. Guess I'll go home or go out and try to find something else to do."

"No, please. Let's just go to your truck. I'm having a good night with you and don't want it to end. But you know how Momma is."

"Yeah, I'm not interested in living my life to suit your mom forever, Jenny. It's bad enough to have my own mom trying to control everything I do. I guess this just isn't working out."

I started crying. I thought I was going to reason with him, but instead, the floodgates opened and I couldn't hold back anymore. It was too much. There was Momma controlling everything I did and Rob mad at me for something I desperately wanted to change, but couldn't. The wreck had taken away every bit of progress I had made, and on top of that, it left me with false teeth for the rest of my life and having to save up money just so I could buy a junker from my parents. I would probably never have anything as nice as my Mustang again.

The more I tried to stop my tears, the harder I cried.

"Hey, it's okay." Rob put his hands on my shoulders. "I know how you feel."

I didn't understand how he thought he knew that, but this wasn't a time to question him.

"I'll be back in a couple of days. I know how to fix this." Something about his words made me worry, but I pushed that aside. He wouldn't ever hurt Momma. And anyway, Daddy was home all the time unless it was a race night, so Rob wasn't thinking anything crazy. I couldn't let myself think such things.

I nodded, tears still rolling down my face, and I knew I couldn't make myself stop crying, not until the tears were all done. Rob smiled with so much love, there was no mistaking it. He meant what he said. I wasn't sure what had changed or why, but I was relieved and grateful. We would see each other soon. He would help me figure this out and we would stay together, a couple in love.

I wanted him to wrap his arms around me, hold me and make me feel protected and safe. But I told myself this was already a perfect moment, so I let him walk to his truck. Like so many other times, I watched his taillights disappear into the mouth of the holler. I sat on the glider and lit a cigarette, waiting for my tears to stop and for my face to stop looking like I had been crying. The tiny ember somehow kept me warm despite the cold night air.

The weekend took forever. Every time a car door slammed or a truck engine roared past, I thought it was Rob. Every time someone knocked on the kitchen door to pay their garage bill, I thought it was Rob. Monday came and I thought he would show up after I got off work. And if he didn't show up, I thought he would call. He didn't do either of those things. I poured myself a glass of wine that evening and started thinking about all the reasons why he might not have shown up: He had wrecked his truck and was in the hospital. His parents took away the truck and phone, somehow.

But I knew he wasn't in the hospital—his mom would have stopped by and told me. They couldn't take away his truck. He would never stand for that. And even if they kept him off the phone for a little while, he would find a way to use it eventually. He always did. I wasn't ready to think about the options that were left.

He showed up on Tuesday and told me to come outside, which I thought was strange because it was so cold. We sat down on the glider.

"I told you I know how to fix things with your mom."

"Yeah?" My stomach did a flip-flop and something in me panicked a little.

He pulled out his wallet and opened it to show me a row of hundred-dollar bills. "I've got the money to marry you. Let's do it."

And so, we did.

I put on a smile and told myself it was just nerves that were making me feel funny inside. *It makes sense to be nervous! This is life-changing!*

I ran inside to tell Momma that Rob had proposed. She was making cookies in the kitchen when I blurted out, "Rob just asked me to marry him!" She didn't look up but kept mixing the batter. "Did you hear me, Momma?"

"What are you going to tell him?" she asked me. I didn't understand why she would ask such a thing.

"I said yes, of course!" I stood there grinning, waiting for her to smile at me, to celebrate my engagement—something, anything.

She just kept mixing.

"Well, I guess we'll go do the blood test and get ready for the wedding," I went on.

Back then, anybody wanting to get married in Kentucky had to take a blood test just to make sure you weren't related, and the results would be ready in two days. Only then could you apply for a marriage license. We would need to find a preacher. Rob's parents went to church, so maybe that preacher would marry us. And I would need a dress. Maybe we could do the wedding at my house since neither of us went to church. A church wedding seemed better, but lots of people got married at home, so that would be okay, too. I saw everything in my mind, even as the picture changed: me in my white dress, Rob in a suit (*did he own a suit?*), Daddy giving me away. My eyes started to water. This would be the best day of my life.

"Momma?" I realized she still hadn't looked at me.

"What, Jenny?" She sighed. I knew what her different sighs meant. They mostly meant that I had interrupted her—a television show, a crossword puzzle, or in this case, whatever she was thinking about as she spooned cookie dough onto a baking sheet.

"Aren't you going to say something?" I shifted on my feet. "He finally proposed. We're in love." I smiled at her, thinking this time she would understand how important this was.

"We're heading to Jellico here soon."

I turned around, startled. Rob had come in behind me. I hadn't heard the door open or close.

"What do you mean?" I asked him. "Why would we do that?"

"To get married tomorrow. We don't have to do a blood test in Tennessee. There ain't no reason to wait. And there's lots of preachers who will marry us on the spot."

I thought I should be happy to hear him say this. He wanted to marry me right now, not next week or a month from now. And he was right. Everybody knew you could drive just a few minutes over the Tennessee border and get married without so much hassle. I turned back to Momma.

"You'd better get going." She kept her eyes on the stove, the cookie sheet, and then the kitchen window.

"Momma."

Rob took my hand and pulled me toward the door. I watched for Momma to look at me, but I didn't see her eyes that afternoon. There are many times I remember needing to see her look at me, but that's the one that seemed the most important.

The whole drive down to Tennessee, Rob talked about how great things were going to be. "We'll buy you a dress in Jellico," he told me. "I hear there's plenty of shops down that way. And we'll get rings there, too. Lots of people do it this way. And I'll pay for you to have your own motel room tonight."

I know he looked over at me then, but I didn't look back at him. He was saying this was my last night as a virgin. Tomorrow, we would be married and then I would be his, for better or worse, sick or in health, rich or poor. We would make a solemn promise to each other. And not just to each other—to the whole world—and no matter what hardship we faced, we would face it together. For ourselves, for everybody else. Above all else, this was for God, who came up with the idea of marriage and was surely invested in each and every one of them.

I told myself again that the weird feeling in my stomach was nerves. *Every bride is nervous before her wedding night. I'm sure Rob will be gentle.*

Would Rob be gentle? I knew it wasn't his first time. But you can't dwell on the past and start a new future. It was time for a fresh start, and I was going to leave the past where it belonged.

On the way down to Tennessee, I couldn't help but wonder where Rob had gotten the money from. He didn't have a steady job, which was one of the reasons Momma sometimes called him worthless. I always tried to speak up for him when she said those kinds of things. She didn't understand that some people don't live like everybody else, some people are special. Rob was like that. He was wild and different, so he didn't follow some cookie-cutter plan for what to do. Like him dropping out of school. Some people would think that meant he was stupid, but he wasn't. Sometimes I thought Rob was the smartest boy—*man*—I had ever met.

And the way he looked into my eyes. It was like we were the only two people in the world. Even though we had sat on the glider a thousand times, everything around us still disappeared, fell away like it does in the movies, and I would forget anything else existed until Billy came stomping around or Momma hollered that I needed to come inside and do my chores. I tried not to think about when Rob's eyes went black like they did sometimes. That always scared me, but it never lasted for long, and I thought maybe that might be part of what made him special too.

What worried me about the money was I knew he got into arguments with people sometimes and maybe he was selling them moonshine or they had some other deal. He always had a deal going and they ended badly pretty often. It seemed like he almost got into trouble a lot, but his dad knew the judge and the jailer. They weren't exactly friends, but they were all in some kind of group together. Rob wasn't in the group with them, but from his stories, I knew the law didn't come down on him like it would have normally.

Just about a year before we decided to get married, he had a car wreck that could have caused him big problems, but nothing came of it. I felt pretty bad for the woman in the wreck—she was paralyzed and would never walk again. Rob was really lucky. He was driving a truck for the hospital, delivering oxygen, and he had a nitrous oxide tank in there with him. Who knows what would have happened if there had been an explosion. He had convinced the janitor at the hospital to steal the nitrous tank for him, and while he was driving he had put on a mask so he could breathe it in. I only knew a little about nitrous. They call it *laughing gas* at the dentist's office, but I had to be on harder stuff when the dentist pulled all my broken teeth. I didn't understand how a gas could make you laugh, especially with a dentist digging around in your mouth.

Rob didn't mean to hit that woman. It wasn't very responsible of him, but he was just nineteen years old. He worried about what would happen if the Vietnam War kept going and he got drafted. He was always arguing with his parents, mostly his mom, because he wanted to live his life *his* way. He told me his dad had completely stopped standing up for himself when his mom badgered him. Rob really *was* like James Dean, fighting against a world that didn't understand him. But I understood him, and I would love him better than anybody else could.

Thinking about Rob's money made my head hurt and go fuzzy like it often did those days, so I closed my eyes and listened to the eight-track tape playing on his truck radio. George Jones and Tammy Wynette were singing about their golden ring, and I told myself me and Rob wouldn't have an ending like the one in that song, where the woman falls out of love and leaves. No, I'd be like the woman Tammy sang about in "Stand by Your Man." I probably wouldn't always understand Rob's choices and I wouldn't always like them—I was already sure that would happen sometimes. But as long as I could forgive him and accept that men think differently than women do, we would get past any problems. We would make it.

We got to Jellico and found a little chapel where we made our appointment for the next day, and there was a shop with dresses, suits, and rings right next to it. Lots of Kentucky folks crossed the border to get married there, so marriage was big business. The woman who signed our marriage certificate barely looked at us as she recommended the closest motel. I pushed all that aside—it didn't matter if they understood what it meant for me to be here. They didn't have to know how much I had been through for this relationship. I was finally marrying Rob and we would be happy. We would be together and someday have a home and children of our own. I wasn't sure how he was going to provide for us, but I knew he would, eventually. And I would live my life as I wanted from that point on, with nobody telling me what time to get home or how I had to spend my paycheck.

I hardly slept as I lay in the motel bed that night. My stomach hadn't completely settled down and I worried that I was actually getting sick, but I told myself I was going through with this no matter what. *I'll walk to that gas station I saw nearby and get some medicine if I have to.* But I finally fell asleep and had crazy dreams all night. In the morning, I took my overnight bag and new dress to Rob's room and got ready in the tiny bathroom while he returned my room key to the front desk. We would share one room that night.

The whole ceremony took about fifteen minutes and we were sent out as soon as it was over so the next couple could get started. I couldn't help but think about what it would have been like if my family was there, but I pushed that thought away. *What's done is done. I'll get over that.*

Rob drove us straight back to the motel, shooting me looks and grinning. I grinned back to hide my nervousness. Inside the room, he pulled me to the bed right away and I tried to relax. *This is my husband. This is what we're supposed to do.* I knew it would hurt. My sisters always said that's just how it is—the first time or two is painful for the woman and after that, it gets better. We had a couple of bottles of wine in the motel so I was pretty relaxed when the time came. It was kind of like what I expected, but mostly not.

We left with some Polaroid pictures to document our marriage and wedding rings on our fingers. On the drive home, I thought about what my sisters might say. They probably already knew. I wondered if Daddy wished he could have walked me down the aisle like I'd always imagined he would. Maybe Billy wished he could have been a best man or at least could have been there. It was too late now, though. That was okay. Sometimes life happens in the ways you least expect it, but it still works out alright. I knew well enough that the best times were ahead of me.

Chapter 17

After the wedding, we drove back and I packed up my things. We went straight to Rob's parents' home and planned to live with them for the first year, hopefully not much longer. Rob was right—his mom was so hard on his dad. It was like Ella was always mad at George, always criticizing him for every little thing. I wouldn't ever treat Rob like that.

Rob's older sister had already gotten married and had a toddler named Christopher. One time, George set a cup on the coffee table and left it there when he got up to talk to his son-in-law. They walked toward the door but Ella stopped him.

"George, what are you thinking? You can't just leave things lying around like this. The baby could have gotten into your coffee and burned himself."

"Oh, glad he didn't get into it. Can't have my little man getting hurt." George tousled Christopher's hair and none of us would have thought anything more about it, except Ella went on: "None of these kids would be alive if it was up to you. You just can't be bothered to pay attention, can you." It wasn't a question. All of us were quiet except Rob, who kind of laughed and then went out to the front porch to smoke. George stood there for a minute looking sorry, but he didn't say anything. I felt terrible for him. I didn't know why Ella had to be so hard on him. Back then, I couldn't have imagined how anger can spread out over years and spill into places where it doesn't really belong.

Their home was a two-story farmhouse in the woods up Mill Branch Road. Ella raised cows and some chickens and had a good garden. George drove the milk truck for the Spring Grove Dairy, heading out each morning long before the sun came up.

Me and Rob stayed in one of the upstairs bedrooms. There was no door for any privacy. That seemed strange to me until I thought about how I had once shared a bedroom with three sisters and had my baby brother sleeping right outside.

We slept in the bedroom that was farthest from the staircase, and it had a window that faced the head of the holler. I'd lay in bed some mornings, looking at the fields and the creek that cut through them. I couldn't have imagined how I would run through those fields one day, how I would hide in that creek with my children. I didn't know yet that there was something I should run from.

Even if I had known, where would I have run *to*?

It was strange for a while, living with Rob's parents instead of my own. We didn't have a television or listen to the radio, and we weren't allowed to smoke inside. I could listen to my records but I had to keep them quiet because Ella didn't like the noise. I didn't get to hear new music, and it was a long walk to Birdie White's store. I hardly ever got to read through a new *Hit Parader*. It was like we were in a different world.

Sometimes, it was awfully boring. There was nothing but the chickens and cows and creek making any noise. Hardly any cars ever drove by because there was just one more house at the head of the holler. There was no garage, no men hanging around to talk, no laugh track from the television. Looking back, I can see it wasn't the carefree life I wanted for myself. But still, nobody was telling me what to do like Momma had. I helped out because I knew it was the right thing to do, not because somebody said I had to.

Sometimes all that quiet was peaceful. Ella spent the days cooking, cleaning the house, and paying the bills, like Momma. She also took care of the animals and kept the fire going in the woodstove. George drove the milk truck and hunted in the woods during the right seasons. He walked all over their fields, picking blackberries for a fresh cobbler and some for Ella to freeze, and when she made a blackberry cobbler in the middle of winter, the life of summer ran all over your tongue and seemed to light up the dark kitchen, no matter what kind of mood Ella was in. Times like those always made us smile and you could almost forget whatever Ella and George had argued about before sitting down to eat.

Rob drove me to Cowden every morning and sometimes he stopped by to bring me dinner, but soon he got a job at the Rich Oil gas station in Morehead. We were going to have a place of our own and a family, so of course he had to go to work. I didn't work on the weekends, but he did, so there was nothing fun for me to do in my spare time. I still needed to save up a little more before I could buy the junker from Daddy, but I was more motivated than ever before.

That first winter seemed to last forever. By the time spring rolled around, I was stir-crazy and couldn't sit in the house with Ella all day anymore. As soon as it got warm enough, I started walking to Gail's on a lot of the weekend days. It was almost two miles from Rob's house to the mouth of the holler, and from there, it was another mile to Gail's. I had lost so much weight from having my jaw wired shut—I loved how skinny I was now. The curves I had in high school had disappeared and now I was built more like Goldie Hawn. I figured all that walking would keep me thin, especially now that I could eat.

We were saving money to buy a trailer, and Rob's parents would give us a little bit of land to put it on. I couldn't wait to have our own place and real privacy.

In his parents' house, me and Rob could come and go as we pleased and I didn't have to worry about being home by dark anymore, but it was still clear that we were living in somebody else's home, and those *somebody elses* wanted us to live like they did. Go to church not only on Sunday morning, but on Sunday night and Wednesday night too. Get up at four thirty every morning and go to work or start chores. Pray all the time but still be unhappy about life.

We wanted to drink our beer and smoke our cigarettes and listen to music without anybody trying to tell us what to do. And of course, it was weird to be in bed with Rob there, knowing one of his parents might hear us or come up the stairs without us hearing them. I still didn't like working at Cowden, but I knew what I was working for now, and that made it worth it.

One morning in early March, I woke up and got ready to go to work like I always did. Ella always had a little breakfast cooked—she was a good cook and everybody loved that about her. Normally, I could eat up some eggs and potatoes or gravy and biscuits, but on this day, my stomach turned as soon as I drank some coffee. I wasn't sick from drinking or anything, so I figured my stomach was just a little sour and I didn't bother trying to eat. Rob dropped me off at work and right away, I threw up in the bathroom. Whoever was cleaning the bathrooms wasn't doing a very good job, and the smell in there made me even sicker.

After two days of throwing up in the morning, I started to think I might be pregnant. This might be my chance to have the first granddaughter. By then, Gail had two sons, Barbara had a son, and Mary had a son. Somehow, nobody had a daughter so nobody had taken the name "Charlie," after Daddy.

I imagined what it would be like to have a baby in that house with Rob's parents. They were nice, of course, but this wasn't what I had imagined when I thought of starting a family. I wondered how they would like having a baby crying in the house. Rob already argued with his parents a lot, and I knew babies could make everybody more stressed out than they already were.

The best solution was to hurry up and get a place of our own, so I decided I would take on as many extra shifts as I could. I knew that when I told Rob about my plan, he would want to do the same thing.

As soon as I could get him outside alone, I told him I thought I might be pregnant. I didn't know how he would react to the news, and I was so happy when his face broke out into a big grin.

"There you go—I knew it wouldn't take long to get you knocked up! We'll have Rob Jr. running around here in no time."

"I'm not a hundred percent sure," I told him in case I was wrong. "But I think that's what's going on."

"Well, if you aren't already, I'm sure you will be soon. You know how I am."

I smiled and nodded.

"I'm going to tell Mom and Dad," he said, and he walked back into the house before I could tell him I thought we should wait.

It was another week before we could go to the doctor and get a pregnancy test. I went to the only female doctor in town, Dr. Atkins—the daughter of the woman who had delivered me and all my siblings. As I sat there in the exam room waiting for the results, I started imagining what my baby would be like. Hopefully it wouldn't cry as much as Billy had as a baby. It was a lot of work to take care of a baby, but Ella would help me. And the baby would love me like nobody else—I was looking forward to that most of all.

The test was positive, just like I knew it would be. We stopped at Momma's to tell her, and Rob went to the garage to tell Daddy. When I walked in the house, Mary was sitting at the kitchen table with Momma.

"Well, hey there, stranger!" Mary looked happy to see me. Momma looked like she knew I had some news.

I sat down at the table and blurted it out. "I'm pregnant!" Mary's smile froze and faded away. I looked at Momma, and she looked down at the crossword puzzle in front of her.

"Aren't you all happy for me? I'm going to be a *mom*." I couldn't help but show a little anger when I said it. This was the second most important announcement I had ever shared with them, and they should have been as excited as I was.

"Of course, Jenny—we're really excited for you." Mary smiled again and reached out to put her hand on mine.

I looked up at Momma.

"Well, there's no turning back now. How far along are you?" I couldn't make sense of the first thing she said, so I just answered her question.

"About six weeks, we think."

Momma and Mary gave each other a look and I wished right then that I hadn't told either one of them. I wanted to go back in time and tell Rob to drive us to George and Ella's, forget stopping at Momma's.

"I thought you all would be happy. I'm going to have a family." I could hear myself talking and it sounded like I was whining, acting like a baby, but I couldn't help it. I wanted them to show me the same excitement I had always shown for my sisters.

"We're happy for you, Jenny." Mary squeezed my hand a little. "But, uh, how did Rob react?"

"Oh, he's *very* happy," I told them. "He's going to be a great father." I realized the words didn't sound right as they were coming out of my mouth. We all looked around at each other and I tried to think of something else to say, but then I heard Rob honk the horn in his truck. I thought about the junky car I had been saving up for—it was gone now, but Daddy said he'd keep an eye out for another one for me.

"I'd better go," I told Momma and Mary. Mary stood up to hug me and told me to come visit her when I could. I promised her I would and said goodbye to Momma, who was back to working on her crossword puzzle.

From then on, my body quickly changed. My breasts were suddenly bigger and I was nauseous all day long, which meant I was going to have a little girl. I had stopped throwing up, thank goodness, but I had to force myself to eat enough for the baby.

I settled into what it meant to be pregnant when I was around four months along. I loved going to Momma and Daddy's house on the weekends. One of my sisters was usually there to visit with their little boys, and we all talked about the girl I was going to have and how jealous they were. They would talk about the best middle name to go with "Charlie" and I would just smile and rub my belly, happy that one of my dreams was actually coming true. Momma seemed to warm up to the idea of me having a baby, but every time we talked about it, I tried not to mention Rob much.

I wished her or my sisters could come visit me, but I didn't feel right inviting them to come to Ella's house. I still felt like a guest there. And from how they were all starting to act when I talked about Rob around them, I was catching on that they didn't like him very much. His confidence was too much, or they thought he talked down to me, or there was something just a little off about him, they would say. I thought everything would change once the baby came.

Working at Cowden got harder.

Mr. Jones didn't care if a person was pregnant, sick, or dying. He just wanted them to work and make him money, and there wasn't much I could do about that. I was back to sewing zippers, but this time I couldn't find any humor in the thought of working with the crotches of jeans all day.

Me and JoEllen got to sit at tables, a bundle of twenty-five jeans in front of each of us. We worked through each pair, one at a time. We moved the finished jeans to a new stack, and after finishing a bundle, we were supposed to take it to the end of the table so the next person knew they could grab it and do their part to bring the pants one step closer to being finished.

Each pair weighed close to a pound, so a bundle was about twenty-five pounds. I hoped it was making me stronger, all this lifting, but I got tired about halfway through every day and I couldn't work as fast as I was supposed to. I also needed more bathroom breaks than we were allowed to take, and I tried to time those after Mr. Jones had walked by our tables, hoping he wouldn't look our way again for a while. Worst of all, the noise in the factory made my headaches come back, and I had to close my eyes to push them away. Sometimes, JoEllen would do a little bit of my work so I could sneak out of sight and sit down just long enough to get my energy back up.

One day, I went to the bathroom during our regular break. My belly had been hurting and I was afraid I was going to get sick again. But this didn't feel like morning sickness, so maybe I just had a stomach bug. When I turned around to flush the toilet, I couldn't make sense of what I saw. The toilet paper I had used had a streak of bright red on it. I hadn't had my period in at least four months.

Another cramp hit me and I sat back down on the toilet. There was more blood. Someone banged on the door.

"Jenny! Come on, the rest of us have to go, too, you know."

When I opened the door, the redheaded woman who sewed inseams took one look at my face and asked me what was wrong.

"I don't know," I told her. "I'm bleeding."

"Wait right here," she told me, and she walked to the lockers and came back with her purse. She slipped out a sanitary pad and handed it to me.

"I'm not on my period," I told her, knowing she already knew that.

"No kidding, Jenny. Put this on, and you need to get to the doctor."

I glanced toward the office.

"You can't wait," she told me. "It doesn't matter what he says. Call somebody and have them take you now."

Rob came from the gas station and drove me to the doctor's office, speeding the whole way. I wanted to ask him to slow down but I was so upset, I couldn't find the words.

Almost as soon as we got there, the doctor called me into a room and had me lay down. She did her checking and told me, "No more standing on your feet. You're working at a factory?" I nodded my head. "Not if you want to keep this baby."

"What does that mean?" I asked her, and I noticed my voice didn't sound like mine at all, but more like some scared kid's.

"Don't worry too much," she told me, all gentle now. "These things can happen and fix themselves all the time. But you have to take it easy, to be on the safe side."

I looked at Rob. This meant I would have to quit my job again, and who knew when I would be able to go back? Tears came to my eyes. I tried to put everything into perspective, though. We wouldn't be able to buy a trailer anytime soon, but I could still have my baby. And it wasn't bad to be at Rob's parents' house—it just wasn't exactly what I wanted. Things were just going to take a little longer to come together.

When we got into the truck, I sighed and tried to smile. "At least we've got our little family, right?"

Rob laughed. "Well, somebody's got it made. Sounds like you'll be lying around the house while I take care of everybody."

He must have seen how much that hurt me because he said, "That's alright. I'm the man of the family and that's my job." My heart soared to hear him say that. He was going to take good care of me, and I would take good care of him.

He laughed again, but this time it was a real laugh. "Besides, you're the one that's going to be changing all those diapers."

Chapter 18

I tried not to go up and down the stairs too much after that day. And when I did go up to our bedroom or downstairs to eat or use the bathroom, I took it nice and slow. Still, there was a little blood at least a few days a week.

Ella didn't like that at all. She called Dr. Atkins's office and demanded to know what they were going to do to protect this baby. I heard her ask, "Why isn't she on bed rest?" That made me stop and try to hear what the doctor would say. I was already close to being on bed rest—I hardly went anywhere. Even though it was late spring, beautiful and warm outside, most of my days were spent on the couch, watching Ella clean. I hardly got to go to Momma and Daddy's at all now, and I was starting to miss everybody a lot. I thought about asking Ella if somebody could come visit—maybe she wouldn't mind them coming to see me, considering what was going on. I would have to try to find the right time to ask her.

Ella complained to Rob and his dad at supper that night. "Jenny shouldn't be walking around at all," she told them. "She needs to stay off her feet. I told that doctor but she wouldn't listen." Rob and his dad glanced at her and then me but didn't have anything to say. I didn't know what to say. At the time, I didn't understand what it all meant and what was really at stake. Now, it almost seems like I was in a dream for so much of that time.

I made it almost one more month to the day, so I was five months along. Rob had dropped me off at Momma's for a visit while he worked. I went to the bathroom and as soon as I sat down, I felt a gushing and knew something was terribly wrong.

When I looked into the toilet, I couldn't make sense of what I was seeing. I started yelling for Momma and when I showed her what had happened, she hurried away, shutting the bathroom door behind her. My belly tensed and cramped over and over while I sat there, crying, unable to move.

The paramedics got there and helped me off the toilet and onto my back, and they took care of everything while I sobbed, not able to talk. They finally eased me onto my feet and that's when I saw that Ella was standing in our hallway, tears streaming down her face. I had never seen her so upset. It was the only thing that helped me that day and in the days that followed—knowing I wasn't completely alone. Somehow, she understood what I was feeling.

Rob showed up at the hospital and when they finally let me go home, he talked the whole time about how he was going to call my doctor the next day.

"She should have known better. She should have done something instead of letting this happen to my baby. Fucking dumbass doctors think they know everything. Anybody with any sense could have known something was wrong."

My thoughts couldn't keep up with my feelings—they changed over and over, almost as fast as Rob could talk. When I was in the bathroom, I had felt so much, but now it seemed like a bad dream, like it almost wasn't real. And then there were the needles, doctors, the beeping machines and fluorescent lights and nurses who didn't even pretend they cared about what had happened to me. They asked a million questions about what I had done, what I hadn't done, what time I started bleeding, what I did next. I could hardly answer them.

I wanted to be angry like Rob was, to blame the doctor. But Ella had been angry first, and nobody had listened to her, not even me. I couldn't find any anger at the doctors, just at myself. And to tell the truth, I had my doubts that the doctor could have fixed this anyway.

The only thing I *could* feel was some relief that Rob was willing to protect me and his baby. That he would go up against doctors and probably anybody else who could hurt his family. I had always thought he might be protective someday and fight for me, just like he was willing to fight for everything else he wanted. Now it was happening. I felt closer to him than ever.

Other than that, I was just tired. Tired of talking about what happened, tired of crying, tired of remembering what I had seen and how it broke my heart in a new way. I settled into this tired feeling and it wrapped itself around me like a heavy blanket.

That summer was hot like always, but it felt different up in the holler. The sun couldn't peek over the steep hills that shot up on either side of us until later in the morning, and it hid behind them earlier in the evening. Even on the hottest nights, the cool air still settled into the long, narrow strip of flat land where Rob's parents and a handful of other families were trying to raise a few animals or a little bit of hay. That's how it was in all the hollers that snaked through these mountain foothills.

I had grown up going to visit relatives and old women I didn't know who lived in hollers, and they all had a creek or a field or some other wild place to explore. The roads were always narrow and twisty, and going into a holler felt like you were at the mouth of a cave—you couldn't see far ahead, so there was no telling what you would run into along the road. The hills rose up around you like big grandmother arms holding everything together, keeping everything in place.

I always liked it when I got to hunt for crawdads in the creeks and the only sound I could hear was the water flowing over rocks or Mary humming to herself close by, or Billy a little ways down, shouting when he got pinched by a sharp claw. And sometimes we played tag in some-body's cow field, careful not to touch the barbed-wire fences or step in cow patties. Patches of wildflowers sprung up out of the ground in those fields, better than any picture I ever saw.

Now that I was grown, I could see how beautiful it was, but all that quietness sometimes felt like a prison of its own. Just about every day was the same: Rob's parents got up before the sun, before the rooster even had time to crow. George went to work and Ella started doing chores. Rob went to work, sometimes late. I tried to find something to do while I waited for him to get back, hoping he wouldn't go some-where else first like he sometimes did. When he finally did come back, sometimes we would go see a friend or one of my sisters. Sometimes he would take me to get a burger in town instead of eating supper at the house.

Dr. Atkins said I had to wait at least six weeks before I could work again, and that time dragged out. On the weekends, Rob usually visited his buddies. Sometimes he took me with him, but I didn't always like going. If there was another girl to talk to, we could smoke and drink coffee or sometimes beer while the men went outside or into a back room, doing whatever it was they did. If there wasn't somebody for me to talk to, I would listen to the radio or play solitaire while I waited. I learned to bring cards with me anytime we went out.

If we were out in the country, him and the other men would get out their guns and shoot at cans in the backyard. The bangs made me flinch every time, just like it did in the holler when he practiced, the sound bouncing off the hills so a person couldn't tell where it was coming from. By the time we left any friend's house, Rob's eyes were usually bloodshot and either wide open or half-closed. I never knew what he would be like on the way home, but I knew I'd have to drive.

I started looking forward to going back to work.

Finally, in August, I went to Cowden and asked for my job back. Mr. Jones was still there, but he was retiring in a month. He told me I could come back but this was the last time. If I wanted to have a job there, I had to work. Mr. Jones looked at the young guy he was training to replace him—another snake character—like he wanted to make sure he understood the rules, and the young snake nodded, *Yes, last chance for this girl,* and I hated them both but was still happy to go back and be out of the house.

JoEllen looked more tired than ever. She almost never talked to me anymore, never smiled or chatted when we went outside to smoke during break.

"How's Mary Beth?" I asked her one day. I think that was the first time JoEllen looked into my eyes for more than a second since the last time I babysat for her. It was a little uncomfortable, the way she stared. But she didn't answer. She just looked away, as if she hadn't heard me after all. And when she took another drag off her cigarette, I noticed she wasn't wearing her thin gold wedding band. I stopped asking how she was doing after that, even though we still smoked together, and if Rob wasn't there to check on me at dinner, she and I ate our baloney sandwiches together, just in silence.

In early November, I threw up in the morning as soon as I got to work, and I would have cried but I didn't know whether to be worried or excited. The next day, Ella whisked me off to the doctor and she told me I'd better quit my job, *no fooling around this time.* So I was back at the house again, just in time for the cold weather to settle in and for the days to drag on, dark and gloomy, even when it was sunny outside. As bad as Mr. Jones could be, going to the factory had given me something to do, other people to see. I pushed away the thought that maybe I would never get to leave the holler again.

I don't know if I would have made it through another winter like that, cooped up in the house with Ella all day. But one day, out of nowhere, Rob came home from work early and told us that he'd found a good deal on a used trailer. He just needed to borrow a little money and a guy would haul it up tomorrow.

George and Ella glanced at each other over the kitchen table, but I couldn't read the look that passed between them. Were they happy that we were moving out? Not happy about lending us money? Were they going to miss having us there?

"How much?" Ella asked, not looking at Rob.

"Twenty-five hundred," Rob told all of us, clearly proud of himself. I think we all gasped at the same time, and I saw his eyes darken. I know Ella saw that look in his eyes too.

"It comes with everything," he went on. "Delivery, setup, even a woodstove and some appliances. It's a hell of a deal."

Ella's eyes flashed and I knew she wanted to tell him not to cuss in her house. They argued about him cussing all the time and I wished she would just let it go. Nothing she said would make a difference. This time, I got my wish. She looked at her husband before answering, "Alright."

I couldn't believe it. Everybody knew how careful Ella was with money. She made my mom look like a wild spender, Ella was so tight. I didn't know how much a used trailer should cost with or without all the extras Rob had mentioned, but I couldn't wait to move into it. The first thing I imagined was the stereo we would get and all the records I could play. Finally, I would be able to listen to my music anytime I wanted. "I need to go pay him tonight. He'll take a check but wants five hundred in cash."

Ella sat for a moment longer, looking at the kitchen table, and then went to their bedroom. She came back with a check and five one-hundred-dollar bills. She handed it all to Rob.

"I'll pay you back soon," he told her, and she just nodded, though I wondered how we would do such a thing with me not working and a baby on the way. Rob turned to leave. It was a Friday night and I wondered when he would be back, but decided not to try to go with him. I didn't know who he had bought the trailer from, and some part of me thought I'd rather not meet whoever it was.

The next morning, I watched from the upstairs windows as a big truck pulled an old-looking trailer up the gravel road. I thought there was no way they could make it around the curves without the trailer falling into the creek, but they went as slow as molasses and eventually pulled into the cleared area past Ella's cow field. Me, Ella, and George hopped into their truck and drove up to watch the guys start setting it up.

The outside of the trailer was rusted in places and looked tired, like it had been used enough already and needed to be left alone. I kind of knew how it felt.

I looked around and took it all in. The trailer was fairly close to the road, but that meant we had a big backyard, and there was a creek toward the back of the property line. I could see Ella's house from my yard, but not too well—we probably wouldn't really see each other if we were outside.

The men stood there forever, not doing anything, but Rob talked the whole time, pointing his finger this way and that, giving directions like he had done this a hundred times. The bald man who'd driven the trailer up the holler just stood there smoking a cigarette until Rob stopped talking. I couldn't hear what anybody said, but the bald man seemed to be really good at ordering people around—better than Rob was—and when *he* pointed, two skinny guys, who had driven their own trucks and equipment, rushed around to mark where everything needed to go. I was ready for a cigarette too, but couldn't smoke in the truck with Ella and George, and I didn't want to stand out there with the men.

"Could we head back to the house?" I asked. "I better start packing up our stuff." I wondered how long that would take—an hour?

I rolled down the window and told Rob what we were doing.

"Be ready to go," he told me. "We're gonna get this done in no time at all." He grinned, and I was glad to see him happy.

It turned out that everything took some time, after all, and it was a whole week before Rob and his brother carried our mattress and dresser down the stairs and hauled them to the trailer. I waited for them to get everything moved in, and Ella drove me up to my new home. I climbed the makeshift cinder-block steps into the trailer, and it turned out it looked just as tired on the inside. But I didn't care. The trailer was mine, and now nobody could tell me what to do anymore.

Chapter 19

Our trailer turned out to be as rough as it looked. Through the winter, we burned wood in a stove that had a pipe going out the side of the trailer. Sparks shot out of the rusted pipe inside the house, and it's a wonder it didn't burn everything down. Spring had come, and its rain and water dripped through the ceiling and down around the light bulbs that hung in each room. When summer rolled around, the trailer trapped heat all day and would let go of it at night. It wasn't like Ella and George's house, where you could open a window to let the air move around. The air didn't move in the trailer.

But I got used to living there. When Rob went to work, I piddled around the house, drinking my coffee and listening to the radio. We got reception for one country music station that far up the holler, and when I wanted something different, I put on a record and sang as loud as I could with nobody there to hear me. I did housework and picked up any beer cans Rob had left outside. I started cooking dinner every night so it would be ready right when he got home.

I had gotten used to having good well water at Ella and George's, but Rob and one of his buddies dug our well. It always had problems. There was never enough water in it, so sometimes we had to pump water from the creek into it and try to filter it as best we could. I still cooked with that water and used it to wash our clothes, and that's what we took baths in. When it came time to make coffee and Kool-Aid, you couldn't taste the creek at all. We could always fill a jug at Ella's or Momma's if we really had to.

It got pretty lonely at the trailer sometimes, but I wasn't missing Rob all that much. When he was home, it seemed like he always found something for me to do, or that something I had done could have been done better. He didn't like to see me just sitting around. I grew to like it when Ella came up to visit, especially because she usually brought some home-cooked food with her. It would be nice to have the baby for company and I would have somebody to talk to and play with as much as I wanted.

But it was hard to be so excited about the baby this time. I tried to feel what I used to about having a girl and naming her, but that just didn't seem as important as it had. For a while, I dreaded going to the bathroom because every time I was afraid I would look down and see red like I did before. Things got a little better when I was six months pregnant—I knew it wasn't logical, but I felt like if I could make it past the time when I'd had my miscarriage, it might not happen again. I don't think I really relaxed the whole time, though.

When I went into labor, Rob and I were in Flemingsburg, where he was checking out some piglets he wanted to buy. He wanted to start raising hogs and selling them. His parents sold a cow or two every year and he told me, "It's an easy way to make money. And pigs are smart, but they'll eat anything. You never know when it'll come in handy to have a few around."

All I knew was that my contractions were getting more intense. They kind of felt like when I miscarried, but I was a good forty weeks pregnant this time. Still, I couldn't help but worry a little. When Rob was talking to the farmer, I told him I needed to go soon.

"Just a minute," he told me. "We're about done here."

I went to the truck and waited, hoping my water wouldn't break. It seemed like another hour went by before Rob got in the truck and we took off down US 32. When the contractions hit, I couldn't talk.

"Looks like the baby's about here," he said with a grin. I nodded, trying to return his excitement but also trying to remember how to breathe.

"Well, look who it is!" Rob waved at somebody through the window and pulled onto the shoulder. In the sideview mirror, I saw a truck do a U-turn and pull up behind us. Rob's papaw got out of his truck and came to Rob's window. I had been around him a couple of times by then, but he wasn't anything like *my* papaws had been—I can't imagine him bouncing a kid on his knee or teaching them to fish. He seemed worn down, too tired to be mean anymore.

"Where you all off to in such a hurry?" he asked, glancing at me. I tried to smile but another contraction hit, and this time I couldn't help but moan.

"Heading to the hospital. Reckon she's about to pop." Rob motioned his head toward me and his papaw nodded.

"You been out to Flemingsburg?"

"Yeah, checked on those pigs like we talked about. After this is over, I figure I'll go back out there and pick some up. I talked him down on the price."

"Good, glad to hear it. Come out to the house here soon and we'll get going on that new still."

And they went on like that for a whole hour, talking about what they were going to do, who they would work with and who they wouldn't, how much money their plans would make them. I moaned and shifted around in the truck seat with no way to get comfortable. Finally, Rob looked at me again.

"Lord, she's starting to sound like a cow over here. I'd better get her to the hospital before she has the baby right here." Him and his papaw laughed and I thought it would serve him right if I made a mess all over his truck, but I tried to be nice. I'm pretty sure my face wouldn't cooperate to actually make a smile, but I was out of energy to care about anything other than what my body was doing, which was unlike anything I had ever felt before.

It was the summer solstice, the longest day of the year.

At the hospital, they gave me something that calmed me down, and I don't remember anything that happened next. The baby was a girl, seven pounds and seven ounces. I got to name her Charlie, but that didn't bring me the happiness I had always thought it would. I held her little red body in my arms, and while part of me was relieved that she was healthy, the other part of me didn't know what to do with her. Thankfully, the nurses let me sleep for a while longer and when it was time to go home, Ella was there to show me what to do.

In the trailer, the baby seemed to cry and thrash around a lot, and I knew she didn't like to be so hot all the time but there was nothing I could do for her. The diapers made her sweat. Nursing her made her sweat. Holding her made her sweat and so did laying her down. We were hot and miserable together.

Ella liked to come and check on us a lot. I didn't mind, but I quickly found out I would just have to deal with whatever mood she was in. Momma and my sisters had visited right after Charlie was born, but it was clear that none of them were coming up the holler again, so I would have to come see them when I could. So it was nice to have somebody visit who was excited about the baby. The first time she found baby Charlie in her bassinet with nothing but a diaper, Ella got after me.

"Girl, what are you doing? This baby's going to freeze to death!" Ella looked around until she found a baby blanket and wrapped up Charlie, swaddling her like an expert.

"She's been sweating," I tried to explain. "I think she likes to cool off a little."

Ella just looked at me like I had lost my mind. "You've got to keep this baby warm," she told me. "Else the poor thing will freeze to death. She's not ready to fend for herself, you know."

I nodded, sure that no matter what I thought, it was better to keep Ella happy and do what she said. The next time I saw her driving up the gravel road toward us, I hurried and threw some clothes on Charlie and wrapped her in a blanket for good measure.

"Lord, this child is going to burn up!" Ella told me. "You've got her sweating in this hot trailer." She pulled the blanket and clothes off so Charlie could cool down. I figured that was just how things were going to be.

I could tell Rob was proud of himself for being a daddy, but he didn't want to spend much time with Charlie. When he came home, he would usually go see her soon after he settled in and maybe tickle her chin or make a funny face at her. He didn't want to hold her much, and I wished sometimes he would take her so I could get a shower or go outside and just be alone for a minute. I figured he'd get more comfortable when the baby was older, though, and I imagined he would treat Charlie like my father had treated me. She would be *Daddy's little girl*, and she would bring out the sweetest parts of him.

He pointed out the stretch marks on my belly and breasts, and sometimes in bed, he would pat my belly to make it jiggle. "You ever going to lose this?" he would ask. "Don't get fat on me." Things like that made me not want him to touch me at all, but I knew better than to say anything. I just tried to laugh it off, without making him feel like I was laughing *at* him.

I couldn't tell you when Rob hit me the first time. Sometimes I think it must have been before the baby was born, but then again, he never hit my face, and I don't think he would have hit my back or stomach when I was pregnant. And I don't remember if he had been drinking or if he was snorting pills with his buddies that day. Maybe both. Maybe neither. Sometimes he was just mad or I said the wrong thing and then he got mad in a hurry.

After he hit me, he was pretty much always the same. He would either storm out of the trailer and go across the creek to the hog barn or he would get in his truck and roar out of the driveway, his tires spitting gravel behind him. I would clean up anything he had thrown or broken and get Charlie calmed down if he'd scared her. Then I'd try to calm my nerves before Rob came back inside. I learned not to cry too much—he didn't like it when I cried, and it didn't pay to dwell on things anyway.

He didn't like it when Charlie cried either, so I tried to make sure she was fed before he came home. If she was still fighting sleep, I would put a little beer in her bottle and she would drink that and sleep through the night. It wasn't always perfect, but I had a pretty good routine going.

I didn't feel too romantic toward Rob those first couple of months after Charlie was born, but by the time she was three months old, I was pregnant again. I couldn't believe it. The morning sickness wasn't as bad, so I knew I would have a boy this time. But it was still hard on me, taking care of a baby while I was growing another one in my belly. I was tired all the time, but Charlie was still waking up in the middle of the night and she had started taking shorter naps during the day, waking up all of a sudden instead of giving me a couple hours to take a nap myself. Between her and Rob, I couldn't get any peace.

Our little boy was born four days after Charlie's first birthday. We left her with Ella and George while I was at the hospital, and when I got back to the house, it wasn't just twice as hard to keep up with two little kids—it was even harder. Rob didn't change diapers or even want to hold the babies if they were fussy. He would play with them for a little bit and when he decided he was done, he was done. I think he spent more time outside the trailer that summer than ever before. Sometimes I wondered if he was going to change when the kids got a little older, when they weren't so much work. That's when he'd really enjoy having a family, I thought. When the kids were a little older and less work.

We named the new baby George, after Rob's dad and papaw. Rob's parents hadn't named him George because they didn't want that name passed down through the family line any further. It turned out that Rob's papaw had been in and out of prison as a young man, so Rob's grandma had to send George off to live with his grandparents when he was little. Rob still thought his papaw hung the moon. George wouldn't say exactly what he thought of his own father, but I could tell from the way him and Ella acted that they didn't think much of him at all. Ella called Papaw George good-for-nothing, but that's as far as her Christian beliefs would let her go with name-calling. I didn't worry too much about giving his name to my son. Besides, I got to name our daughter after my father. It turns out I had more important things to think about anyway.

It wasn't easy to get into a new routine with two kids, especially with Rob being so impatient with their crying. It seemed like as soon as I got one to sleep or settle down, the other would start up. And Charlie was getting into everything. She started walking as soon as George was born. I would have to keep her away from the woodstove all winter and watch her like a hawk.

It was hard for me to concentrate on what I was supposed to do every day. Rob would be gone to work and one of the babies would start crying while I was fixing the other one a bottle. I would pick the crying baby up and let the bottle get too hot, so the other one would start crying from hunger. At some point every day, I realized I hadn't eaten anything. Some days, I realized I hadn't taken a shower in a while and I'd put the babies in their beds so I could rinse off for a minute. The trailer was so little, I could hear them both crying over the sound of the shower and it seemed like that sound would live forever in my head, bouncing from wall to wall.

Whenever Ella came up, she'd look around the trailer and get that pinched look on her face, like she smelled something but was too polite to talk about it. I stopped caring about that. I was just glad for somebody to hold one of the babies or maybe even both so I could step outside into the quiet. I could smoke a cigarette in peace.

Summer turned into fall and the oaks and maples put on a show, painting the hills bright red and yellow and orange. It was so beautiful out there, a real picture of God's work. But I couldn't enjoy it or anything else because Rob had started staying at work late all the time and I never knew when he was going to come home. I still had supper ready when he was supposed to get back and I would try to keep it warm for him so he could eat as soon as he came in the door. Most of the time, I could hear his truck around the time he passed his parents' house. I would peek outside our bedroom window and rush back to the kitchen to get everything ready. Sometimes, I managed to get his food on a plate and have the babies hushed by the time he came inside. Sometimes, though, I didn't.

Chapter 20

George was about a year old when Rob decided he was going to build a house. It was past time for us to get a bigger place. Charlie didn't always nap at the same time as her little brother, but they had to share a bedroom. Thankfully, Rob decided he was sick of being cooped up in a trailer, so he decided we were going to have a nice house where everybody had their own bedroom.

At first, it was exciting to watch as the builders made progress day after day, week after week. I liked to imagine how much space we were going to have and how I would plant a little flower garden outside our kitchen window. But the builders were there all the time, even when Rob wasn't home, and the house site was just about fifty feet behind our trailer. They kept the kids awake through their naps with all their hammering and hollering, so everybody was tired and grouchy by the time they left.

I couldn't explain that to Rob, just like I couldn't explain why some of the men there looked at me more than they should. *Was it because I was flirting with them all day instead of taking care of my kids, like I was supposed to? Was I out there in the yard showing off, trying to get their attention?* Rob didn't believe my answers. And nobody could tell him any different. The only thing I could do was stay inside so that when he came to check on us or got home from work, he wouldn't catch me near them.

He started having his buddies over to the trailer more often, which was mostly a relief because he would stay outside shooting guns with them and drinking beers and leave me alone. I looked out the window one time and saw they had run an extension cord to a television on the chipboard floor of our new house. The walls were framed but there was no drywall, so it stood like a big empty skeleton. Somebody had brought a VCR so they could watch an X-rated movie, and the girl in it was acting like she was having the time of her life. I just rolled my eyes.

Hopefully Rob would drink and laugh with them until he was ready to pass out. Sometimes, though, he got in a bad mood when the guys left. That's when I tried to stay out of his way, keep the babies quiet, and not let anybody get his attention. As long as I brought him a new beer as soon as he finished the last one and didn't let him lose his cigarettes, things didn't get too bad.

We finally bought a car from my parents around that time, something we could haul the kids around in. It was a yellow Buick, long and bad on gas, but we didn't have to cram everybody onto one seat anymore. And finally, I could leave the holler when Rob wasn't home. Before we got the car, Ella would take me to the grocery store when I needed her to, but she would sigh about loading the kids up and dealing with them the whole time. But with the Buick, I could take them with me to town if I wanted, and most important, I could go see my sisters or Momma and Daddy.

Sometimes, I thought about talking to Ella about how things were going with Rob. I wasn't sure what she would think, though. She called the shots in her house and I was afraid of what she might say to Rob. I didn't need him getting mad at me for another reason. When I told my sisters he was getting mean, they told me they weren't surprised—they always knew he was trouble.

We all tried to tell you, but you just had to marry him. Maybe he'll get better when the babies aren't so much work. Some men can't deal with the babies crying all the time.

I hated to think about that idea, that he might be worse because of the babies. I had hoped he might turn into somebody like my dad, who loved us and carried us on his strong shoulders and even loved Momma, grouchy as she could be. I knew they were right, though. Things hadn't gotten easier. Those times I had seen the best in Rob seemed so far away. I wanted us to go back to those times on Momma's patio when he smiled at me and I was the only person in the world. We could go back to when I was in the hospital and he swore he loved me and was going to be there for me forever. Even back to our wedding, when he made promises to a man we had never met before, and he seemed to mean them.

We still had little moments when that seemed possible. A song would come on the radio that we both liked and we would sing it together, grinning real big. One of the babies would do something funny and he would laugh. Then it was possible he would relax and love having us and even love all the work of having a family. He might see the good we brought to his life, instead of how there was never enough money and somebody was always whining.

I had to be careful, though. I couldn't get too comfortable. When he couldn't hear me, I'd sing "Suspicious Minds" and think how sad it was that Rob didn't understand how much I loved him and how hard I was trying to be a good wife. It was like there was something inside him that couldn't trust my love. Just like the song said, I thought we shouldn't let this good thing die. I was sure that no matter how hard things felt sometimes, the good life we were supposed to have together was waiting for us, right around the corner.

When I was washing the dishes one night, he asked me where his keys were. I hadn't driven his truck all week and he had gotten home from work just about an hour beforehand. I was feeling pretty light-hearted so I didn't think anything of it before I told him, "You tell me and we'll both know."

I shouldn't have said that.

"Goddammit, Jenny, always running your fucking mouth." My insides froze and I stood there holding a plate in the soapy dishwater, a wet rag in my other hand. Before I could decide whether to drop one thing or the other, Rob pulled on my shoulder, spinning me around so I was facing him. His eyes were a night sky on a new moon, when there was nothing to break the darkness, no glimmer on the water.

He pushed me against the kitchen sink so I could feel my lower back pressing into the sharp edge of the counter. Most times, I could pretend I was somewhere else. I would think about what one of the babies needed and it was so clear, I could see it: *There I was, feeding Charlie, changing George's diaper.*

Sometimes I turned my mind back to the dishes: *First, I'll pick up the washrag and swish it around a little to make sure there's no broken glass hanging on to it. Then I'll pick up the plate, careful to feel for a solid edge in case it's broken.*

But this time, I couldn't go anywhere else. Rob's weight was against me. I heard myself telling him, "I'm sorry, I didn't mean it."

That didn't make sense. I was joking, playing. Of course, I didn't mean it. *Who could care about such a joke? Why would anyone have to explain this?*

Rob didn't use many words in times like these, or he used the same words over and over.

"Don't talk like that to me, Jenny. I ain't gonna take it. Not in my own house."

He backed away this time but I still held my breath. Rob pushed things around on the coffee table and then on the kitchen table, and we both knew the keys weren't there but I had better not say it. He finally walked out of the trailer, slamming the door hard enough to wake George and Charlie. I heard his truck roar in the driveway. The keys must have been in the truck.

I visited Momma and Daddy one day and filled up empty bleach jugs at the faucet while the kids lay on the floor and watched cartoons. Momma and Daddy had city water, so we could get some for drinking every once in a while. After I got the jugs filled, I sat with Momma at the kitchen table. There was something strange about being in her kitchen now. I had kids of my own, but I still felt like a kid whenever I was around Momma. Like some part of me wasn't done growing and maybe never would be. She had always been the main grown-up of my life. I didn't think I could ever be like her.

I tried to tell her things weren't going good with Rob, and I tried to tell her without saying too much, in case she got mad. Most of all, I didn't want her to tell Daddy. I hadn't seen him fight many people, but I still remembered how he messed up the drunk man with a tire iron when I was a kid. Everybody knew Daddy loved us girls so much, and we all kept certain things secret so he wouldn't be upset about the bad stuff that sometimes happened. I wasn't sure what he would do to Rob if he found out what was going on, and I didn't want to know. Right away, I think Momma knew more than I let on because tears came to my eyes and I couldn't stop myself from crying just a little.

"He's not being good to me, Momma. He's got pretty rough lately."

Momma took a drag off her cigarette and looked up from the word puzzle in the newspaper. "Well, what did you think you was going to get? Prince Charming?" She laughed a little and that flew right through me. He *had* looked like Prince Charming there for a time. And Momma had believed it too, hadn't she? In the hospital, when he visited me all the time. Even before that, when I was working and he would bring me dinner—who wouldn't love that? But now I was a stupid kid again, the one who should have known better.

And then she said something else, something I wasn't ready to hear. "You made your bed, Jenny. Now lie in it." You could have reached into me and taken anything you wanted from inside me right then, I was so blown open by her words, so torn apart. And I wanted her to know how that hurt me, but she never looked up to see the look on my face.

I wanted to make her look at me, to snatch that newspaper away from her hands and smack the cigarette away. It was like I was a little girl again, full of wants and needs that I didn't have the right words for. *See here*, I would tell her. *I'm right here and I need you and neither of us can change that.*

I couldn't do that, though. I wasn't the kind of person who would smack something out of somebody else's hands. I couldn't tell you what kind of person I was, but there are a few things I knew I *wasn't*.

Momma stood up and walked into her bedroom, probably to get another pack of cigarettes. I heard the kids in the living room. Charlie told George, "Stop it! *My* show!" And she probably tried to push him away from the television screen because he started crying like he so often did. I took a long draw off my cigarette, willing all the noise to go away. I picked up the paper and looked at the crossword puzzle Momma hadn't finished yet, trying to make sense of the empty spaces.

Chapter 21

Rob started staying even later at the gas station, and it was hard to keep his supper warm. But it also meant I could get the kids in bed and take some time alone to sit on our front steps—still cinder blocks, but now they were in front of a house instead of a trailer. I would sit out there and drink a beer, stretching our new phone out through the living room window while I talked with one of my sisters or with Peggy. If none of them were free, I might just watch the smoke from my cigarette as it disappeared into the cool night air. I sat there thinking and not thinking, my mind wandering around however it wanted to.

One night that winter, I was waiting for Rob to come home and couldn't stop scratching myself. It wasn't like a mosquito bite or poison ivy, though—this was in my private area. I didn't know what to do, it was driving me so crazy. When I went to the bathroom, I saw little white spots in my pubic hair and realized what it was. In high school, everybody talked about who had crabs and who had given somebody else an infection.

But I hadn't been with anybody but Rob. My stomach churned, and I knew it wasn't from skipping supper or from the extra beers I had drank. Fear and anger filled my belly, and both of them were about to make me sick. Here I was with my babies, *our babies*, waiting at home for him like I was supposed to. I didn't go anywhere except to see my mom and sisters, or Rob's mom. I was still pretty thin, even if I wasn't as skinny as I was right after my wreck. I didn't know how to do any better. I couldn't figure any way to *be* better than I was.

When he got home that night, I was ready to tell him what he had done to me and make him tell me how it happened. I noticed he smelled like beer when he walked in, and that made me even madder.

"I've got something to ask you," I told him.

He plopped onto a chair at the kitchen table right away, almost like he didn't see or hear me.

"Rob."

"Hmm."

I couldn't tell whether he was responding to me or he just liked the food I had set in front of him.

"There's something I've got to tell you. It looks like I've got crabs," I told him. "And I ain't been with anybody but you in my whole life."

Rob looked up at me and I could see he wasn't mad.

I sat down in the chair catty-corner from him. "Do you know how this could have happened?"

He turned back to his food, shoveling some mashed potatoes into his mouth. After he swallowed them, he finally responded. "I thought something wasn't right. I think it started when I went in that new gas station out by Jerry's Restaurant."

I waited for this to all make sense. He looked straight into my eyes as he started talking, and then looked away as he talked some more.

"Yeah, that's when it started. I used the bathroom at that gas station and I must have caught crabs from that toilet seat. There was some weird-looking guys in there that day. Bet they left them on there."

I couldn't really believe what he was saying, but I wanted to. Ella watched the kids the next day when I went to the doctor's office and got a prescription for the cream.

"You know how this happens, don't you?" the nurse asked me.

My cheeks went hot. I knew she thought I was sleeping around.

"My husband caught them from a gas station toilet."

She just looked at me. As I was saying the words, I knew how ridiculous they were.

"That is *not* how this happens."

I looked down, my eyes blurring with tears. I sounded like an idiot and I would have to go to the pharmacy, where nobody would know it wasn't me who was out cheating, picking up crabs. They would think I was dirty, when I hadn't done anything wrong. All I ever did was be a wife.

I called the gas station a few minutes after they closed.

"Just wondering if you're coming home soon or if you've got to work a while longer. I didn't want your supper to get dried out, and I'm about to cook soon," I lied. The meat loaf I had made was sitting on the stove top and I knew it would be dry by the time he got home, no matter what. The kids had eaten but I didn't have an appetite.

"Yeah, I've got some things to take care of here," he told me. "I'll be there in about an hour." I knew that meant he would be home in more like two hours.

We hung up, and instead of getting the kids in bed, I took them to the car with a blanket to cover them up in case they fell asleep. I let the car coast down the road past Ella and George's with my headlights off so they wouldn't ask where I was going so late at night. After I got around the bend past their house, I flipped the lights on and drove to a parking lot across from the gas station. I parked so my car was mostly hidden, but I could see through the passenger window. Rob's truck was parked toward the end of the building, but I couldn't tell whether there was anything on the other side of it.

The front part of the gas station had big glass windows, so you could see the drink coolers and the counter with the register. I could see the door that led to the back office, where they stored cases of oil, and there was a desk and a chair where Rob sat to count up the money at the end of the day. I couldn't see anybody, so he must be in the back.

"Momma, I'm sleepy." Charlie hadn't fallen asleep yet.

"That's alright," I told her. "Just lay down and close your eyes."

"I want to go home," she told me. I looked at the back seat. Little George was asleep.

"Shhh, you'll wake your brother. We'll be home soon."

Something caught my attention and I turned back to see the office door opening. A woman with long, dark hair came out and Rob followed her, closing the door behind him. My empty stomach churned, and I thought I was going to vomit even though I didn't have food in my belly. I swallowed hard and pushed it back down. I couldn't open the car door and take the chance of him noticing.

The woman adjusted her clothes and smoothed her hair while Rob fixed his belt. She turned around and they talked for a minute, all smiles, and then she left and he locked the main door behind her. I saw him grab a beer off the counter and open it, taking a long swig. He picked up the rest of the six-pack and went back into the office, closing that door. I watched as the woman went to the far side of Rob's truck. A red car backed out and she pulled out of the gas station lot. I wasn't trying to hide at that point, but she didn't see me. She didn't look my way at all.

I started up my car and pulled out, looking back at the office door one more time. It was still closed. I went in the same direction as the red car, even though that wasn't the way home. I had to step on the gas to catch up with her, and when she got to a stoplight, I got as close to her back bumper as I could without hitting her.

I saw her look in the rearview mirror right as the light turned green. She took off a little faster than she should have, squealing her tires as she turned left onto the main road that went through downtown. I couldn't see anything else—not the buildings I had seen a thousand times, not the same Christmas decorations the city put up every year, nothing. But I had seen that woman's eyes and I knew she'd seen mine. We drove past the IGA and I decided I would follow her all the way to her house. I would pull her out of her car and make her tell me who she was. I would tell her how she ruined my life and had no business being with my husband. After that, I didn't know what would happen and I didn't care. Every bit of rage I had ever felt was ready to come out.

"Momma, I see Santa! Are we going to talk to him?" Charlie was still awake and she had noticed one of the fake Santas in a store window. "George, wake up! It's Santa!"

Now they were both awake, pressing their faces against the window. *Shit.*

I drove past the store and they both started crying, wanting to go back. I needed them to be quiet, to go to sleep. I got caught at a red light and the woman got a little farther away, but I could still see her car. I could have caught up. I turned down a side street and made it back to the main road, my heart about to burst it was pounding so fast. The kids kept crying but I couldn't hear them so much over the sound of my heartbeat that got louder and louder until the headache came back. It shot pain through my skull and I couldn't see for a split second. I pulled over on the side of the road and opened my car door, throwing up what looked like water and egg yolk onto the street. The kids were finally quiet, and when we got home, I put them straight to bed.

I poured some whiskey into a glass and added an Ale-8 to it. When Rob got home, he found me at the kitchen table on my second drink.

"Where's my supper?" he asked.

I didn't answer right away like I normally would. "It's on the stove."

He sat at the table and lit a cigarette. "I'll be ready for it in a minute," he told me. "Right after I finish this." He opened the refrigerator behind him, stretching to grab a beer. I didn't stand up to fix his plate. He looked at me as he cracked it open, and I knew he could tell something was wrong.

I was still mad, but it was a good thing that I'd had time to cool off before he got home. I might have flown off the handle right away. In fact, I knew I would have because that's what I *wanted* to do. But I was realizing that might not have gone well. At first, all I cared about was how angry I was and how good it would feel to scream at him, to really let him have it.

He put his cigarette out in the ashtray and looked at me again. I wanted to refuse, but I had seen this look on his face before. He wouldn't mind a fight.

I fixed him a plate and sat it in front of him, hoping it wasn't too dry. I went to the sink and started to wash a couple of dishes. "Sit down here and talk to me," he told me.

Now, I didn't know how to act. He was trying to figure me out, I could tell. And if I let on like I was too mad, he would get mad and blow up. But he had done me wrong and I couldn't pretend everything was okay. Not after he gave me crabs and I caught him cheating.

"I drove up to the gas station tonight," I blurted out. *Dammit. I didn't mean to say that.* I didn't know what I should have said, though— it didn't seem like there was a right way to do this. Rob took another bite of food.

"Oh yeah? What did you do that for?" He acted like it was the least interesting thing he had ever heard.

"I saw a girl come out of the back office with you." I took another drink and noticed my hand was shaking. I hoped Rob didn't notice. I wanted to smoke, but I knew he didn't like for me to do that while he was eating, so I had to wait.

"Oh, Jean Baker. Yeah, she was there tonight," he said. I was shocked. He wasn't even trying to hide it.

"How could you do that to me?" I asked, and tears came to my eyes even though I was more mad than hurt. "That's where you got those crabs from, not some toilet seat!" I waited to see how he was going to react. I had never talked like that to him before.

He laughed and took a drink of beer. "Come on, Jenny. I ain't messing around with that whore." I flinched a little when he said that word. "She's nothing but white trash. She keeps coming around and won't leave me alone, but I told her I'm married." I couldn't believe my ears.

"You sure didn't look like you minded her company," I told him. "You all looked awful happy when you came out of the office."

Rob gave his empty beer can a little shake and I stood up to get another one. He threw his arms around my waist and pulled me toward him instead of letting me get to the refrigerator.

"Come on, Jenny. Don't be jealous." He scooted his chair back and pulled me onto his lap. "We're married. You've got to believe me. You're the most beautiful girl I've ever known and I would never fool around on you."

I wanted to believe him. I wanted to be the most beautiful girl, the most loved girl.

"The nurse said you can't catch crabs from a toilet seat."

Rob's eyes darkened. "What fucking nurse? Was she one of them that made us lose our first baby?" It wasn't, but I knew he wasn't really asking. "Bunch of dumbass, rich motherfuckers think they know everything. I told you it was that toilet. How many times do I have to say it?"

If he kept talking about it, his sweetness was going to completely disappear, so I just said, "It's okay, I believe you." I cried a lot then, and he wrapped his arms around me tightly.

"Don't worry, Jenny. I'm going to be good to you. I'll be a good husband—you'll see. Everybody's going to see."

I didn't know who else he thought was watching, but I decided to let that go. I reached around him to grab two beers from the fridge, and for the rest of the night, we drank, turned on the radio but not too loud, and he told stories about all the crazy people who had come to the gas station that day while I laughed and tried to forget those eyes I had seen in the rearview mirror.

Chapter 22

Now that we had a real house and the kids weren't babies anymore, it was a lot easier to have company over. Rob had a group of guys that would show up on Friday and Saturday nights, and we would let the kids have a little beer so they would stay asleep no matter how much noise we made. Other times, if Ella would let the kids stay at her house, we would go to somebody else's house or trailer to visit. I liked it better when we stayed at the house, because then I didn't have to worry about driving home late at night or even worse, Rob trying to drive us home.

I was still friends with Peggy. Her, my sisters, and a few other girls who had played volleyball in high school all got together to play on Wednesday nights at the elementary school. I could usually take the kids and let them play on the stage in the gym. Peggy was married now, but Rob didn't like her husband and didn't want me going over to their house a whole lot. Peggy didn't come visit me at the house either, but I never asked why. I figured we got to see each other at volleyball and talk on the phone sometimes, and that was better than nothing.

My sisters didn't come up to my house much, but Mary and John had moved into a house close to the mouth of the holler, so I drove past their place any time I went to see Momma or go to town. I stopped there pretty often, and when I asked if she wanted to come up and visit me, Mary would give me a look like we had already talked about this and I needed to let it go. I knew she didn't like Rob all that much, but

I didn't think much of John, either. It was his fault that I ended up on a motorcycle with a druggie like Dave.

I didn't understand why we couldn't just put all that to the side and spend more time together.

The worst part was that Rob could tell when somebody didn't like him, even if I didn't tell him. He would bring it up after he had been drinking, especially if he was drinking whiskey. It always seemed to be my fault, too. He could be talking about anything in the world, and somehow, he would remember that somebody hadn't waved to him when they passed each other on the road that day, and his mood went sour in a hurry.

His temper was worse when he was drinking hard liquor than when he was drinking beer, but the worst was if he had done some pills and the buzz was starting to wear off. That's when everybody had better stay out of his way, especially me and the kids. If they did the least little thing, he might whip them with his belt, and Rob didn't seem to know how to hold back. They were almost three and four years old, big enough to spank, but I still just used my hand. Both the kids were mostly good, though. Even when Rob was being mean, Charlie seemed to think he was a good daddy. And George was such a sweet kid, he never seemed to be upset for long after Rob lost his temper.

There were times when everything went smoothly, though. On those nights, I would put the kids in bed early or even have them spend the night at Ella's. Rob's buddies and their girlfriends or wives would show up and we would drink some beer, smoke a joint, and listen to music while we sat around the kitchen table or in the living room, everybody laughing and having a good time. The guys went outside at some point to hang out in the new barn. I don't know what all they did out there. Maybe watch porn, maybe just snort some pills or whatever else they had. But they usually stayed out there for a while, giving me and the other girls time to really talk. Rob's brother, Frank, would come around sometimes, too, but him and Rob were always quick to get into an argument, so I was glad he didn't visit more often than he did.

Paula and Angie were my friends who came up most often, and they were both fun in their own ways. We were all on the high school volleyball team together, and both of them still lived close by. Paula didn't care who thought what about her—she did and said anything she wanted without giving it a second thought. I was worried about what she would say to Rob sometimes and whether he would think she was running her mouth, but he always grinned even when she was teasing him, and he never got mad at her for some reason.

Angie was quieter and kind of serious, but when it was just me and her, she liked to laugh and joke a lot. If Paula was around, Angie was friendly but let Paula run the show with her stories and opinions. I was always trying to get Angie to relax and enjoy herself, but I also knew there was something special about how she opened up to me and not everybody else. I could tell that Angie didn't like Paula all that much. And even though I thought Paula was a lot of fun, I could understand why another woman would feel that way about her. Paula had all the confidence a person could ever want, and that's not always a good thing in a girl. Every once in a while, being around Paula made me think of the girl in the red car and I would start to imagine how confident *that* girl was, and then I would ask myself what would happen if Rob was alone with Paula. Would they kiss? Would Paula like Rob because they were alike, or would they butt heads because they both said what was on their minds, no matter what? Thinking about that would start to make me feel flustered, so I pushed the thoughts away and told myself that's not what was happening and I needed to quit being stupid.

One time, when Angie came over with her boyfriend, Lou, and Paula wasn't there, she and I started playing gin rummy like we always did while Lou headed out to the barn with Rob. It was more fun with three people, but we still had a good time. Angie was even quieter than usual, though—she didn't smile like she usually did when I tried to cheer her up. I asked her what was wrong.

"Nothing," she said. "Lou's just being an asshole again. He was bitching at me the whole way here." She and Lou had been together since high school, kind of like me and Rob, but I don't think they ever took a break like we had.

"Oh yeah? What's his problem?" I asked, knowing the guys would be loud when they came in—there was no chance of them overhearing us.

Angie shook her head. "I don't know. It's just like he's in a bad mood all the time these days. He's about to lose his job at the sawmill, too. His boss called the house in the middle of the day asking where he was. I thought he was at work, and when I asked him later, he told me that's where he had been all day. I have no idea where he went."

I thought about what Rob told me the last time they had come over, how Lou had got a prescription when he hurt his back at the sawmill six months ago and when the doctor finally cut him off from the pain pills, Rob had told him where he could get them without a prescription. But Lou wasn't keeping it under control like *he* was, Rob told me. Lou couldn't save one for later. He did them too fast and was starting to lose his handle on things.

Rob even had a tape recording from where Lou had called and was asking Rob to help him find more. Rob liked to record conversations as much as possible—I don't know if it was because he thought somebody was going to pull a fast one on him or what. But I learned to be careful about what I said to my friends on the phone.

I wondered if I should tell Angie any of this. Part of me wanted to—she was my friend and I would want to know if I was in her shoes. But Rob had told me not to say anything. It was none of my business and I didn't need to run my mouth about Lou. If it got back to Rob that I'd said anything, there would be hell to pay.

"I'm sure it was just a misunderstanding," I told Angie. "You know how men can be. They don't know how to communicate." She kind of half smiled, as if she wanted to believe it. "I know what will make you forget about him." I went to the bedroom and grabbed a half-smoked joint from one of the ashtrays. We opened the kitchen window a little so the smell wouldn't get too strong. Rob wouldn't want me to do it without him. The pot and cigarette smoke danced slowly around each other beneath the kitchen light bulb until the cool outside air grabbed ahold of it and pulled it through the window.

One of the last things that happened at the gas station before Rob stopped working there had to do with Larry Black. Rob had got mad at Larry for something Larry said—who knows what it was. He told Larry to come up to the station to talk about it one night after the gas station closed. Larry didn't know that Frank was going to be there, too.

Frank's temper was just about as hot as Rob's those days. He was married, and they had a little girl just a couple years older than Charlie and then a boy who was just a year younger than George. The kids all loved playing together, and Ella took them all to church as much as she could. She got Charlie and George there every Sunday because it was so easy for her to come and pick them up—all I had to do was get them dressed and then I could go back to sleep.

I don't know whether it was Frank or Rob that hit Larry over the head with an Ale-8 bottle, but one of them split Larry's head wide open. Frank had a gun, too, so Larry was probably lucky that he didn't get shot that night. Also lucky for Larry, the hospital was almost next to the gas station and somebody got him there in a hurry. Rob called me, drunk as could be, and told me to come pick him up. The whole drive home, Rob went on about how Larry pulled a knife and Rob wasn't going to take that, he wasn't going to be pushed around by anybody. I heard later that when the police searched Larry, all he had on him was a pocketknife. God knows what the whole thing was started over. It could have been anything. It was probably nothing. With Rob, it was all the same.

My headaches seemed to disappear there for a while. I had gotten so used to them after the wreck, I forgot that not everybody has a headache almost every day. Rob almost always had some weed or a pill I could take to make them go away, and if he was out of those things, I could drink a few beers and at least forget the headache for a little while, even if it didn't disappear.

When they went away, it was like the whole world came into focus. I couldn't remember much about the wreck, and now a lot of other things from the past were blurry, too. Living at home with Momma and Daddy seemed like forever ago. Childhood was a flash of memories like on some old film reel where the pictures move and you can see the click-click-clicking between each one. There was Daddy giving me a quarter, Daddy giving me a whipping. Laying my head in Momma's lap, her not looking at me when I told her I was getting married. Volleyball games and school plays and nobody there to see me.

Things with Rob felt like a movie sometimes, too. He would do something, say something, and later, it was hard to believe those things had happened. They were real, but what he meant by them couldn't be real. It was like he was pretending to be someone else for a little while when he did those things, and I was pretending to be the person he did them to. But afterward, when he apologized or was just in a good mood again, the bad things didn't make sense anymore. After each bad thing that happened, it seemed impossible for another to ever happen again.

The kids turned three and four in the summer. I started taking them to daycare so I could work a little bit at the gas station, keeping the books. I got up on one particular morning and we were out of cereal, so I made some pancakes from a mix for the kids. Rob was in a bad mood and I had no idea why. I was trying to avoid him because I could tell nothing I did would make him happy. But he told me to come back to the bedroom and then he started talking about how there was money missing from his wallet and I must have taken it. I would never take money from him. I told him that was crazy, which was a mistake.

"What the fuck does that mean?" He was looking at our dresser mirror, tucking his shirt into his pants.

"Rob, I'm just saying I would never do that. You *know* I wouldn't do that. I'm not stupid."

He had finished with his shirt and turned to look at me. There was the darkness again.

"So *I'm* the stupid one? You think you can steal from me and I'm not going to know what's going on?"

I started crying, thinking he would let it go once he saw how upset I was. But this time I don't think he saw. He came closer until he backed me up against our bedroom door. He started saying all kinds of things—things that didn't make sense. Most of the time when he was mad, he would start yelling. For some reason this time, he was keeping his voice low, but it was like he was about to explode. At least the kids couldn't hear him.

"I'll teach you to get into my stuff." He turned away and walked to the dresser, where his leather belt was lying. I couldn't believe he was going to hit me with it, but something told me to get out of there. I opened the door, walked through the living room, and out the front door.

"Jenny!" I had made it to the yard when he yelled my name. He started coming out the front door—the belt was in his right hand.

"What are you doing, Rob?" I was crying even more. "Why are you acting like this? This is crazy!"

As soon as I said *crazy*, I knew I had made another mistake. He started walking toward me and I turned to run. "Get your ass back here," he told me, but I kept going.

He got a handful of my hair right when I made it to the back of my car. I wasn't trying to get in the car—I was just trying to get away. Where was I going to go? I don't know. I wasn't thinking straight.

I guess Rob had dropped the belt because he started hitting me over and over with his fist. He pulled my head toward the gravel so he could get the back of it—never my face—and hit me in the back, too. For some reason, he kept dragging me toward Ella and George's house, even though they would have said something to make him stop if they had seen it. I guess he knew we wouldn't make it all the way to their house. I probably would have been dead by the time we made it that far.

The kids must have heard the commotion because Rob stopped when we reached the first fence post. He kept my face pointed toward the gravel but turned around to yell at them, "Eat your fucking pancakes!" After that, shooting stars exploded behind my eyes and I dropped to the road, where the gravel bit into my bare arms and legs and the side of my face.

He left me there, and I noticed he went to the barn instead of the house. That meant he wasn't going to say something else to the kids right away, but did he have a gun in the barn? I thought all his guns were in the house. I hoped they were. And then, I was overcome with a wave of exhaustion. I think I laid my head down on the gravel just for a second. *Did I fall asleep?* I don't know for sure. I can't remember walking back to the house.

Later that night, I took off my clothes to shower and stood in front of the mirror. The red marks from the road probably wouldn't turn to bruises. The bruises that were starting all over my back wouldn't be seen by anybody but Rob. A dull headache had settled in and I knew it was going to last for days, maybe longer.

When he came inside later, Rob looked at me and asked, "You okay?" I nodded and he nodded back with a look that seemed friendly.

What he didn't say was: *I'm sorry. Did I hurt you? Is everything going to be alright?* But I thought he meant those things, even if he didn't say them. I thought he felt bad about what happened, even if he didn't know how to apologize. We would smile later, when he remembered what he had spent that missing twenty on. I would push it all away that night, when he climbed into bed next to me.

Chapter 23

Rob was still raising his hogs. He had the corncrib across the creek, and the hogs were supposed to stay over there, but he let them out all the time and I'd find them in the front yard. There was something weird about opening the front door and finding two big hogs there, rooting and messing up the little bit of grass we had growing. I was always a little scared of them, especially after I figured out what Rob meant about how it could come in handy to have some around. Hogs will eat just about anything, including a person.

There was a time when a man came out of the woods behind our house—that was the Daniel Boone National Forest, so people were technically allowed to be there—but the man probably should have known better than to go into a stranger's yard. Rob had his shotgun out before the guy hardly even had time to explain what had happened. I heard him saying he was hiking and had gotten lost, but Rob was sure the stranger was out hunting ginseng. I don't guess we'll ever know the truth of it. The man was still running back up the hill into the woods after Rob fired his twelve-gauge shotgun at him. My point about the man is that he did not get fed to the hogs, but I'm not sure what would have happened if Rob had sunk some buckshot into the ginseng-hunting hiker.

Instead, the hogs had to eat a lot of slop, and we weren't making enough food scraps to feed them from our kitchen leftovers. We hardly had any leftovers, things were so tight. But the elementary school had hundreds of kids who were throwing half their breakfasts and lunches away. So Rob worked it out that we would get those scraps for a pretty small price, and the school just had to make sure the kids didn't throw napkins and milk cartons into the mix.

He wanted me to go pick up the slop every day. I would have to go to the gas station, pick up Rob's truck, and go to the kids' school after lunch. Every day, I had to find the janitor, and he helped me load the giant trash cans into the back of the truck. The thing about the food scraps was that they turn to liquid pretty fast, so as you tried to load the cans, every little bump made the slop slosh around and sometimes it came out, splashing onto my arms or feet or worst of all, onto my face and hair. In front of the janitor, I would try to pretend I wasn't disgusted and humiliated. I pretended I was loved and cared for and this was something I liked to do, something I didn't mind. But half the time I left the school, I was crying before I got very far up the holler. The other half of the time, I was stopping somewhere along the way to throw up out the truck door.

Unloading the cans was even harder because I was alone, but I worked out a way to slide them down a ramp I made out of an old two-by-four. I would feed the pigs and put the cans back on the truck, go wash myself real quick, and then take the cans back to the school so they could be filled up again the next day. Then I'd go to the gas station to take care of the books, adding up all the sales for the day. I left Rob there and took my car to pick up the kids from Momma's—they walked there after school every day—and we would go home while he finished doing whatever he had to take care of.

Rob lifted a case of oil at work one day, trying to move it from the floor and stack it on top of some other boxes. He just about dropped it because something in his back pinched real bad. He took a bunch of ibuprofen at the house and had me make him a hot water bottle, which I had to hold on his back and keep boiling more hot water for because he complained about it getting cold every five minutes.

He seemed fine the next day and went to work like nothing had happened. After we got home that night, he was in the bedroom while I was fixing supper. When I went to tell him it was time to eat, he was lying on the floor under the foot of the bed frame, bench-pressing the end of the bed. I could tell it wasn't easy.

"What are you doing?"

He grunted as he pushed the frame up again. "Hang on."

I stood there while he pushed it up a few more times. "Supper's on the table. It's going to start getting cold." He let the bed frame down and worked his way out from under the bed so he could stand up. He stood there, sweating and grinning.

"I'm about to make us rich," he told me. I was almost afraid to ask what he meant. It seemed like he might have finally lost his mind. He must have seen that I was confused. "You know how I hurt my back at work."

I nodded.

"Worker's comp, Jenny. That was a work injury and I was telling Lou about it and he told me how I can sue the gas station if I want, but a doctor has to look at me and fill out paperwork and some other bullshit. So I've got to do something to make that back injury bad enough to show up on their tests. I'll be able to get a nice little prescription out of this, too." He smiled and I could tell he was really excited about this idea. I hadn't seen him this excited since he decided to raise hogs.

But I didn't understand everything he was getting at. "If you get worker's comp, what happens to your job?"

"That's just it, Jenny. I won't have to work anymore. I'll sue the shit out of the gas station and get rich! Ain't that funny, getting rich off of Rich Oil?"

I didn't think there was anything funny about what he was saying. There was a knot in my stomach. We weren't making a lot of money, but we were getting by. Rob had worked his way up to being a manager at the gas station and now he wanted to throw it away and not work at all? He was going to hurt his back so he could act like his job was the problem, and all he had done was lift a box the wrong way?

I thought about the garbage cans full of food and liquid that I had to wrestle onto and off of the truck every day. I thought about how I carried the babies when they were real little—and when they got bigger too—and sometimes I had to take care of them at the same time, both of them crying and needing different things. I thought about how sore I was after I had them. I thought about the motorcycle wreck and my jaw, the headaches that still came back now and then, and how hungry I was for six weeks with my jaw wired shut. Of course, I could hardly remember the first two weeks. Still, it seemed like a lot for one person to go through. I had never thought about going after more pain medicine than what the doctors gave me. I had taken some with Rob when we first got married, just for fun, but he didn't want to share for very long. That didn't bother me, though—I didn't really want to try them in the first place, but he had pressured me into it. He wanted me to smoke pot with him sometimes, too, but only if he knew he wasn't going to run out of it.

Why would somebody pay Rob to stay home and not work? Nobody ever wanted to pay me for such a thing. Not that I wanted that—it just didn't seem right. I couldn't tell him that, though.

I tried to smile. "Hopefully it all works out. You ready to eat?"

He gave me a look like he wasn't sure what to think about that, but he let it go and we went to the kitchen table. He wolfed his food down like he hadn't eaten in years and I forced the food down my throat so he wouldn't know something was wrong. It seemed like it was hard for me to eat pretty often these days, and sometimes I couldn't help but throw it up later. I had a couple of beers right after I finished eating, hoping that would help me forget how I was feeling, so I could pretend everything was okay and not lose my dinner again.

Things went to hell real quick around this time. Rob kept doing his bench presses until he thought he was hurt enough to go to the doctor.

That's when he started calling off work, telling them he was in too much pain from lifting the boxes that weren't stacked the way they were supposed to be. The doctor did a bunch of scans and saw how Rob's back was messed up by that point. Of course, that was all Rob's doing. Still, he got the prescription he wanted and then some of the papers he needed to file his worker's comp claim, to live on disability forever if he wanted to.

But he took too many pills, all the time. He liked to snort them and get drunk on whiskey. He shared with his buddies sometimes, and I'm sure some of his buddies brought things to share with him, but he got mad at the ones who only wanted to take. I didn't bother trying to tell him none of them were doing good for each other. I knew by then just how careful I had to be. No matter how hard I tried, I could never be careful enough.

Rob would run out of pills before it was time to get his prescription filled. That's when he would make me call the doctor's office and tell them he needed more, he was in so much pain. If that happened on the weekend, he still wanted me to call. He wouldn't listen when I told him the doctor's office was closed. And when nobody answered, he would scream at me that I dialed the wrong number, maybe I even did it on purpose. I was no good, a dumb bitch who couldn't do this one little thing for him. Then the kids would start crying, and that made him even madder, so I tried to send them outside to play before he got started.

All I could do then was keep telling him I was sorry until it was time for me to shut my mouth. I had to hope he wouldn't start hitting me. I hoped he wouldn't go for one of his guns. He kept a loaded rifle by the front door at all times. The kids knew better than to ever touch it—they knew they'd get a whipping if they did. Somehow, I think they knew it would be worse than a regular whipping. Rob was either shooting a gun or talking about shooting somebody so much of the time, it's a wonder he didn't shoot at me.

Frank did, though. I don't know what started it this time, but they were outside one night and all of a sudden, I heard them yelling. They were probably both drunk. I went out there to tell them to quiet down—they were right outside Charlie's bedroom window and both the kids were trying to sleep. Frank started screaming at me and Rob told him he'd better stop, and that's when I saw Frank had a gun. We had moved closer to the car, and when Frank lifted his pistol, I ran and got into the Buick. Bullets hit the side of the car but none got me. When I peeked through the driver's side window, I saw Rob standing there, maybe fifteen feet from Frank, and Rob said, "Go ahead, shoot me."

Frank shot a few times on each side of Rob's feet, like you would see somebody do in a movie when they want to show off but not kill the other person. I don't know which of the Lewis brothers was more dangerous, but that night I decided they were both crazy.

Rob was so mad the next day, he called the police and pressed charges against Frank for attempted murder. But Ella was scared for what might happen to Frank if he got into real trouble and she wanted us to drop the charges. Rob cooled off pretty quick anyway—I think his brother was the one person he knew he could go to if he wanted to fight somebody else. We went to the courthouse and dropped the charges, and I remember how the woman asked twice to make sure, "Drop the charges? For attempted murder?" I let Rob do all the talking and tried to pretend I wasn't even there.

They were like this toward each other. Sometimes, Rob and Frank were on the outs and couldn't be in the same room together. Other times, they paired up and made somebody else's life a nightmare. On their own, they were both a nightmare to everybody they were close to. The only difference between them was probably that Frank liked Valium instead of pain pills and Frank would eventually go to prison for killing someone. So far, Rob hadn't dealt with many consequences for what he'd done.

Rob decided I was flirting with Frank one day and I thought for sure he was going to kill me. Frank was at the house and I don't know what I said or did, but Rob accused me of flirting and I knew I was in trouble then. He didn't yell like he normally did. His voice was calm and steady but so full of hate. I knew he was about to explode. Frank convinced him that they should go to one of the neighbors' houses toward the mouth of the holler—they were growing pot plants with that neighbor. They left, and I only had a few minutes to get out of there.

I couldn't drive the car—Rob would stop me. I didn't even want to think about what he would have done if we had met on the one-lane road, but I know he wouldn't have let me go any farther. I grabbed Charlie and George from the yard and made them run with me to Ella's cow field. They went under the electric fence and I went over it.

"Follow me," I told them. "We have to run and you have to be quiet." They followed me through the field to the creek, which didn't have much water in it right then. We kept walking in the creek for as long as we could, ducking low so nobody could see our heads from the road. We got to the part of the creek where it turned toward the road, so I helped Charlie and George climb up the bank, back into the field. We were running out of time. Rob could come back up the road at any second. Our walk probably took less than ten minutes, but it felt like a lifetime before we made it to Ella's house, crossing another electric fence and carefully going through the strands of barbed wire. The kids knew how to be careful with these fences—that's the kind of lesson you only have to learn once.

I told Ella and George what happened and asked if they'd drive us to my momma's house. I'd have to figure out what to do from there. They looked at each other with that sad look that I saw on their faces so many times. Like they wished there was something else to do, something to make everything better, but we all knew there wasn't. Some things can't be fixed.

We got in the cab of their truck, me and the kids jammed in between George and Ella. The kids got down on the floorboards and I bent over as low as I could. On the way out of the holler, sure enough we met Rob and Frank. George stopped the truck—Rob would have known something was going on if his dad hadn't stopped to speak for a minute.

"Be quiet," I told the kids. "Don't make a sound." They stayed quiet and I held my breath as George rolled down his window.

"Just headed to town to pick up some milk," he told them. And they talked like that for a few minutes. Finally, it was natural for George to move on, and after we got around enough curves, Ella told me I could sit back up. I breathed again but kept looking over my shoulder, sure that Rob had seen us, sure that he knew and was just playing a game and he'd be behind us at any second, ready to kill us all. But that's not what happened.

We made it to Momma and Daddy's, and George parked on the side of the house where Rob couldn't see their truck if he came out of the holler. "Hurry and get out. We'll run to the store and get back to the house."

I took the kids inside and found Momma at the kitchen table, working on a crossword puzzle. Daddy was outside in the garage.

"I need to talk to you," I told her. "I'm going to put something on for them."

She just nodded and looked back at her puzzle.

I set the kids in front of the television and tried to find a cartoon, but finally just handed Charlie the remote. I went back into the kitchen and told Momma what happened, my voice breaking. I kept trying not to cry—I knew I had to stay strong.

Once I was done, Momma looked at me for a minute before saying anything. "What do you want me to do about it?" she asked. "You got yourself into this mess. I can't fix it for you."

I heard what she said, but it wasn't real. None of this was real. So I asked for a cigarette.

Momma nodded yes and when I couldn't light it because my hand was shaking too much, she took the lighter and lit it for me. We sat there in silence. A cartoon voice called from the living room, just nonsense, and Charlie laughed.

Rob had to be home by now. If he had gone into the house, he would know we weren't there and start looking for us.

I didn't have any money. I didn't even have my driver's license with me.

I didn't know what else to do so I called the house phone and Rob answered. He promised he wouldn't hurt anybody. He would be there in a little bit to bring us home.

Chapter 24

I make it sound like life was all bad, but it wasn't. We went camp-
ing sometimes over at Zilpo, the campground at Cave Run Lake
in Bath County. There was a campground in Rowan County—Twin
Knobs—but it wasn't as big. We usually went once a year when Rob's
cousin Bill from Tennessee came to visit with his wife and kids for the
Fourth of July.

One day when they were set to show up—I think the kids were five
and six—Rob got mad for some reason. A lot of that time runs together
now. Maybe he was out of pills and I couldn't get ahold of the doctor's
office on the weekend. Maybe I ran my mouth too much and pissed
him off. Maybe the kids did something. I just know me and the kids
ended up at George and Ella's again. We were upstairs, in me and Rob's
old room, and I saw Bill's car as it drove past us, up to our house. What
would Rob tell them? How would he explain what happened?

I didn't have to wait for long because Bill's wife, Nancy, came to talk to
me. Nancy told me how they had got to our house and Rob was so torn
up about us being gone. He said it was a little argument, no big deal,
but he hurt my feelings and didn't understand what he had done. He
asked her to come down and try to get me to come home. She already
knew us well enough to know there was more to the story, and before
we left there, she knew exactly what I was dealing with. Me and her

both knew I had been right to leave, but we thought that if I went back that night, now that they were at the house, Rob wouldn't be like that. And even if he tried, Bill wouldn't let him.

Nobody had to worry about Rob for that whole week. He was the life of the party, always cutting up and even helping grill the burgers before we left for Zilpo. We let off fireworks on the Fourth and Rob gave the kids beer now and then, but they mostly wanted to catch fireflies and watch the fireworks that Bill and Nancy brought, which were so much better than the ones we could get in Kentucky.

On nights like that, everything seemed like it was going to be okay. Everybody was happy.

But Bill and Nancy had to leave after that week and we were back to our daily life. By that fall, Rob had lost his job but worker's comp wasn't paying because he wouldn't go to his doctor's appointments when he needed to. He wouldn't even let me turn in his paperwork on time. You can guess who he was mad at when each letter rolled in to tell him he was denied.

We still had a big Christmas because of our tax refund. We drove all the way to Mount Sterling to buy the kids a Nintendo and I remember Rob being so proud. When he was proud like that, I almost felt sorry for him. Part of me knew he wasn't doing anything to deserve whatever it was he was proud of. But I also wanted him to be proud—I wanted him to have something to be proud of. I wanted him to be the kind of person who *should* be proud of what they were doing. But this was as close as Rob could get. And he always found a way to mess it up.

He left that Christmas Eve, out to drink the night away and stumble back or maybe not. Sometimes, when he left, I wished he wouldn't make it back. He didn't respond when I asked him to stay that night, told him that he should be home with his kids. I knew better than to say it twice.

"Let us open one present," George begged me after Rob left. I guess it looked like a lot under the tree. I couldn't remember what it was like to be a kid and see all those presents, but for a second, I could feel it. I told the kids they could open just one present, and I tried not to think about how their daddy wasn't there, but he should be. Charlie had something to say about that. She was all the time defending Rob, like he was worth it, like she thought he was good no matter how much he whipped them or yelled at them for no good reason.

"Daddy's working," she told us. "We should wait for him."

I couldn't even pretend. "Your daddy's out drinking. Do you want to open a present or not?"

George opened his present and was happy for it. I couldn't tell what Charlie thought.

I'm pretty sure that's the year I started squirreling money away so I could leave Rob. I couldn't get much at a time—just five dollars here and there. Rob kept a close eye on how much money I spent on groceries and gas, so I had to be really careful. I didn't even dream of taking money out of his wallet. Even if I thought he was too messed up to remember anything else he had done, I knew there would be hell to pay if he ever suspected I took money from him. I had to take our aluminum cans to the recycling center and started crushing the cans in the mud outside the kitchen door so they would pick up a little dirt and weigh more. Every little bit helped. It took months to save up two hundred dollars.

Rob didn't explode every day. He didn't hit me every day or make me have sex with him whether I wanted to or not. Some nights he did, but not every night. There were some things he was doing every day, though. He was snorting pills whenever he possibly could, except when he took too many and ran out before his prescription renewed, which was just about every month. He always knew somebody he could get more from, so every bit of extra money, and some of our regular money, too, was spent on those pills.

When we couldn't pay the electric bill, he fooled around with the meter and turned it upside down so it ran backward. He got away with that a few times, but made it go too far one day and the electric company came out and put a lock on it. He broke the lock and turned it upside down again, but they came back with a better lock.

He always had a scheme for making money. Sometimes he would do a little electric job for somebody, but most of his ideas didn't involve him doing any work. It's not that he wasn't smart, but I think he thought he was smarter than he was. Or else he just took too many pills to keep things straight. Like letting that meter run backward—that would have worked if he had paid attention and put it back in time. Or his worker's comp. He probably would have won that if he had done everything his lawyer said he should do. That was the only thing that kept him from being able to do what he set out to do. He was his own worst enemy.

He also always asked me who all I talked to when I went to volleyball. I would tell him my sisters and a couple of girlfriends who played, but I avoided mentioning the men. One or two of them would play with us sometimes and I avoided them, just to be safe. He was convinced that I was flirting with somebody and was going to cheat on him. Nothing I said could change his mind. It didn't make any sense for him to be jealous because I knew better than to ever flirt with anybody else. Rob would kill me and that guy both. I couldn't take that chance. And second, he was always telling me how stupid I was and how I had gotten fat and he was going to find him a woman who knew how to take care of a man, not like me. It used to hurt my feelings when he said things like that, and I wondered if he was cheating on me and I would get jealous. But by this time, I almost wished he'd find somebody else so he wouldn't want to hold on to me as hard.

At the time, I thought I was fat because I wasn't as skinny as I was after the wreck. But years later, when I looked at old pictures every now and then, I could see that I had been a normal size, healthy. I don't know what made Rob hate me so much, but I wished I could fix it. I tried to.

Sometimes he got so worked up thinking I was cheating on him, I could tell he was going to get violent. I had figured out that crying didn't help when he was fired up like that. He wouldn't stop because I looked scared, and God only knows what he would have done if I tried to stand up for myself. The only thing that calmed him down was if I comforted him.

"Rob, you are the only man I could ever want. You built me a home and gave me a family. I know how lucky I am. There is nobody that could ever make me feel as good as you do."

I would have told him anything, then. Anything to keep him from losing it.

And I told myself I could get through this, but it was wearing me down. I started wondering what the point of living was. I would look in the mirror and see the face of a woman who let a man push her around all the time, who wasn't strong enough to stand up for herself. When I got in the shower, I would see stretch marks on my belly and thighs from the babies and the weight I gained after the wreck. I looked like a hog, just like Rob said. He liked to oink and snort and grab my belly.

Sometimes I'd see bruises on my back and wish I hadn't caught a glimpse of those. They made me think about what I must have looked like when I was trying to get away from him on the floor or on our bed or out in the middle of the yard. The only people who ever saw it happen were the kids. I didn't want to think about what I must look like to them, so I made that thought go away.

I tried to make all my thoughts go away.

That summer, Rob got caught stealing copper off the railroad. With the bank on us for the house payments that we were behind on, he was on to his next scheme. For the longest time, I wished he would just give up on that worker's comp dream, but now, his back was in really bad shape. Every time we went to the doctor, it was something new: a herniated disc, a slipped disc, a disc was deteriorating. Rob had succeeded in doing one thing, which was to destroy his back out of one little injury.

So there he would be in the yard, out past where I hung our clothes to dry, close to where we had a little garden, setting fire to big piles of wire so he could melt the plastic off the copper. Black clouds of smoke went up and I'm sure Ella and George wondered what was going on, but they probably didn't want to know. They always knew he was up to something and it was better not to know the details, most of the time.

Of course, he got caught. I don't even remember how. It might have been his buddy that got caught first. Freddy had gone to Vietnam and come back in one piece, but he liked to smoke a lot of weed and had a taste for the pills, too. Still, he was nice and always friendly as could be. I was pretty sure he never knew what Rob was really like. Over the years, some of his friends had stopped coming up and I think it's because they saw how Rob was treating me. I can't be sure since I never asked.

Rob didn't ever seem to get in trouble for anything, even when he got caught. There was the time he paralyzed that girl, the time he beat up Larry, now this. And plenty of brushes with the law along the way. He just always seemed to be able to get out of every bit of trouble for some reason. Heck, one time the sheriff came up our road and sat in front of the house and honked until Rob came out. He walked out holding a rifle or a shotgun—I'm not sure which, that time—and the sheriff decided pretty fast that it wasn't worth the hassle of questioning Rob about whatever he had done.

The law never came back up to our house after that. It probably would have been better if they did.

I took the kids with me to the IGA to buy groceries one day, but instead of getting right out of the car, I asked them if they wanted to leave their daddy. Rob had gotten drunk the night before and pushed me up against our bedroom wall when I was trying to go to bed. He thought I had rolled my eyes when he said something, but I couldn't even understand because he was slurring his words.

"I'm not gonna take any shit from you, Jenny." The hot smell of whiskey on his breath almost made me gag. "Not from you or anybody else."

"I know, Rob, I'm not trying to do anything. I didn't mean to roll my eyes. I'm just tired." I tried to reason with him, but I knew I had to be careful not to make him think I was telling him he was wrong—that would just piss him off even more.

He just grunted, and right then, the liquor got the best of him. He stumbled backward onto the bed and half fell, then lay down on his back and started snoring. I just stood there for a little while, waiting to see if he would move or wake up, but he didn't. I stepped over his feet—he still had his shoes on—and walked around to lay on the other side of the bed.

I noticed he had set a big hunting knife on our dresser and I stood there for a minute, looking at it. I think it was the kind you would use to gut a deer, but Rob hadn't hunted more than once or twice since we got married. His dad still did all the time, but Rob didn't have that kind of patience. *What was the knife for?*

The way he was lying on the bed, his belly would be easy to get to. So would his neck.

After I went to sleep, *my* belly and neck would be pretty easy to get to. I shook my head and left the bedroom as quietly as I could, turning off the light behind me. I grabbed a beer from the fridge and sat on the couch, smoking cigarettes and drinking while I thought about what I could and couldn't do. Finally, I was too tired to sit up anymore and I got into bed next to him.

So the next day, I took the kids and the two hundred dollars I had saved up to the store with me, thinking I was ready to be done with Rob and all his threats. I told the kids we could go somewhere else, that we didn't have to go home. George said yes right away—I knew he would. He hated the way Rob picked on him, and so did I. Charlie wasn't so sure.

"Where will we go?"

I told her, "I don't know yet. First, we'll go to a motel and I'll figure it out from there."

We went out to the Super 8 by the interstate and checked into a room with two beds and a little color television. The kids were excited at first. We still had a black-and-white television and didn't get much through the antenna. The picture was always fuzzy and the sound didn't always work. Here in the motel, the two local stations were clear as a bell.

I decided I had better call Rob and let him know we weren't coming home. I didn't want him to think we were dead in some ditch. Right away, he started crying and begging me to come back.

"I'll change, I promise. You're my family, you're the most important thing in the world. I can't live without you. Please, please come home. I'll kill myself if you don't."

It figures, I thought. I had heard it all before. Things always went the same way. He had blown up a few times now and I had left, taking the kids with me. He would tell me everything was going to change and talk me into coming back. Maybe there would be roses for me, even though we couldn't afford them and I would have to figure out how to pay for them anyway. He was on good behavior for a little while but never more than two weeks. Usually no more than two days.

He wanted to talk to George. George didn't care about what his daddy had to say. He was partial to me. Rob wanted to toughen him up, but George was a sweet kid and cute as a button. He listened to whatever Rob told him and handed the phone back to me.

"Let me talk to Charlie," Rob told me, sniffing. He probably told her the same things he told me and George, but it got to her. She handed me the phone back, I hung it up, and Charlie started crying.

"He loves us, Momma. He's so sad. He *needs* us."

I knew it was probably an act, but I couldn't tell her that. And I was starting to worry about the same thing I always did when I left Rob or thought about leaving him: *Aren't the kids better off having their father?* When I was sick of Rob, that didn't seem to matter. But after I left, the doubts crept in and I worried that I was making a bad decision. When he promised things would change, I wanted to believe him, even when I knew I shouldn't.

I asked both the kids, "Do you all want to go back?" George shook his head *no* and Charlie nodded *yes*.

"He's really sorry for everything. He promised he would change," Charlie pleaded.

I probably could have convinced her different if he had blown up right before we left this time, but she hadn't seen anything happen before we headed to the store. And who knows what she remembered from all the times before. It didn't seem like a good idea to remind her of all the times he had scared her, whipped her too hard, left bruises on her.

Maybe she didn't remember the night he hit me and pushed me into the coal stove, not far from her door. She might not have heard him tell me to *stop that fucking crying or I will kill your parents, you hear me? If you woke those kids up, I swear to God I'll go kill your mom and dad.* Maybe she didn't actually wake up when he threw her door open, flipped on the light, and stood over her, watching to see if she would open her eyes so he could make good on his promise.

Hopefully she didn't remember. It was better not to ask.

Chapter 25

Getting to see my sisters and playing volleyball were the two things that kept me going. I didn't tell anybody exactly how bad things were at the house. What would they have done? Nobody could have helped. But if somebody ended up telling Daddy, there would be big problems. He knew we argued sometimes, but if he knew how violent Rob was, he would probably want to kill Rob, and I was pretty sure Rob would have liked the chance to get into a fight with my dad. It wouldn't be the kind of fight where somebody walks away the winner and the other person dusts himself off. Rob would have a gun and be itching to use it. I couldn't take that risk.

Besides, I had to wonder if maybe the kids were better off to have a father in their lives. Maybe having one that isn't great is better than not having one at all. And it's not like I had somewhere to go or enough money to support us. What was I going to do, move us to a shelter? I knew other women who were raising kids alone and they could hardly make ends meet. I wouldn't be able to buy us a new house. Hell, I didn't have enough money for a deposit and first month's rent anywhere.

Rob would find us there anyway, after he went looking for me at Momma and Daddy's house. It was safer to try to keep him as happy as possible. Stay out of his way and hope something would get better, or at least not get worse.

Charlie had turned out to be pretty smart, but she was having a hard time with the other kids in her gifted program. I had to talk to the teacher about how much the kids teased her. She was the only kid from her school to go to the weekly classes in Morehead, with kids from all over the county. And to hear her tell it, the kids made fun of her for everything they could come up with—her glasses, her clothes, even her name. After the teacher got onto them, I think the kids acted a little better, but Charlie still came home crying sometimes. It was a mess.

George wasn't the best at school but he did alright. The thing I worried about with him was how Rob still liked to pick on him. Even when Rob acted like he was being lighthearted, everything he said had to have an edge to it. Even if he was laughing, you could tell he was trying to make it hurt a little. I think he wanted George to be tough like him, but I could tell that wouldn't ever happen. George was a normal boy. He wouldn't ever be like his daddy.

I couldn't hardly keep up with Rob's taste for pills anymore. He took out loans against the house, saying he was going to pay them all back when his worker's comp came through. I knew by then that it was never going to come through, but I couldn't tell him that. We started getting letters from the bank and he didn't like that one bit.

"Goddamn bankers think they own everything. They think they can take this house. I'll show them. I'll burn this fucking house to the ground with us in it."

The kids looked scared, but I knew he wouldn't do that—he wouldn't kill all of us like that. And I was pretty sure he wouldn't kill himself like that even though he had threatened to more than once. One time, it was when I had to leave with the kids to get away from Rob. He had started building an addition to the house, one with two stories, that he talked about constantly. It really was going to be beautiful, but I don't know why he thought we had to have a bigger house. Our house wasn't huge, but it had the bedrooms we needed, and I didn't like the idea of taking out money to build more when we didn't have any way to pay it back. Rob just always thought things were going to fix themselves, I guess.

Anyway, something had happened to scare me into leaving again, and when I got the kids into the car, we heard Rob yelling. He was in the addition, which had walls and windows but no drywall or electric or anything like that. Rob was leaning out of what was going to be Charlie's new bedroom, holding one of his rifles out the window, screaming that he was going to kill himself if we left. Charlie cried as we pulled out, but I told her not to worry, he wouldn't actually do it.

How many times did he threaten to kill himself over the years? I couldn't keep track. I didn't want to keep track. I know he didn't talk about killing himself more than he talked about killing someone else. His parents, my parents, a buddy he suspected stole something from him, a stranger that drove by too slowly, a neighbor that drove by too fast. Mostly me. Never the kids, for some reason—that was something I could be grateful for. But he was always mad at somebody and scary enough for me to know he might make good on his word someday, if he hadn't already. I probably would know, though. He always liked to brag when he hurt somebody.

There was a little voice inside me that said, *I wish you would*, when he talked about killing himself. But that wasn't what I really wanted. That would have broke Ella and George's hearts, and they were so good to us. We went to George and Ella's at least a couple times a week and Ella almost always cooked for us. She made everything taste good, even a regular cheeseburger. And she could make all kinds of pies from scratch, the best fried chicken and gravy and biscuits. I don't think anybody ever left their house hungry.

It must have hurt Ella to see how Rob had turned out. She didn't smile hardly at all these days and snapped at George over every little thing. But she took good care of Charlie and little George. I was happy that my kids got to have grandparents like them and that they were so close by. My parents lived nearby, too, of course, but Momma didn't want to take care of them like Ella did—the kids seemed to bring Ella some happiness. She and George still took the kids to church every Sunday but didn't pester me and Rob about going. I would have thought it was a good idea for Rob to go and maybe have a change of heart, but he blamed his mom and the church for turning his dad into a softie, even though he'd been in the military and hunted and worked hard every day. Rob couldn't see his dad that way, though.

Rob found something wrong with everybody, of course. When the kids were still small, one time Rob started in on George while we were eating supper. Poor George just sat there crying while Rob went on and on about something—he was chewing too loud or had a little bit of mashed potatoes on his mouth, something small—until he stopped to see what George had to say for himself. You could have heard a pin drop when George said he just got so sick of Rob sometimes. I couldn't believe my ears. Thank goodness Rob only threw his food across the kitchen and broke some dishes. He didn't hit George or even whip him for saying that. I think he would have gone too far if he had gotten started.

Another time when they were still little, somebody took the battery cover off our tape recorder—the one he liked to use for recording our phone calls—and when Rob saw it wasn't on there, he about lost it. But he calmed himself down and told the kids they could tell him who did it and nobody would get whipped. I don't think either one of the kids could have done it because you had to use a screwdriver to get it off. But Rob was fired up again because he thought the kids were lying to him. He told them he was going to whip them both and send them to bed. Charlie ended up taking the blame. I knew it wasn't right, but what could I do?

That's when I really understood that Rob would never be like my daddy. He didn't whip the kids to show he was true to his word. He whipped them because he liked to.

I spent every day trying not to do something that Rob might kill me for. He didn't care if the kids were around. A whipping wasn't so bad, when you think about what else could have happened.

There was one time that I left and went to Momma and Daddy's with the kids, and I told Rob he had to get some professional help before I would come back. What happened that time? It all starts to run together. Whatever it was, I'm sure I thought he was really going to hurt one of us. I told him he would never see us again, even though I knew Momma was only going to let me stay two nights and then we'd have to go to the shelter, which seemed like a terrible thing to do to the kids.

But Rob took me seriously and checked into the sixth floor at Saint Claire Hospital there in Morehead and stayed for two weeks. He found somebody that would trade him pills and he loved to tell us stories about all the different characters there on the "crazy floor." When he got back home, he hung up the little fruits he had painted in there like they were something to be proud of. He didn't mind looking at them above the kitchen stove every day and being reminded of where he had been, what he had done.

Chapter 26

Once both of the kids had been in school full-time for a few years, I talked Rob into letting me go to vocational school. I think he was starting to realize the bills weren't going to pay themselves, and he sure wasn't going back to work. I always loved numbers, so I started a yearlong program for accounting. I had done the books at the gas station part-time, and between that and the diploma I would get, I should be able to get a decent job.

Rob was on me every day about who I was talking to when I went to my classes. "Don't you fucking lie to me, Jenny. I'll find out if you're messing around with somebody and I'll kill you both, I swear to God."

I would always tell him, "I'm not, I wouldn't ever do that. Please, you've got to believe me. I promise." I figured he must have had a guilty conscience for cheating on me at the gas station and God knows where else.

When I was at my classes, I could pretend none of this was happening. I made good grades and got to make new friends. We could still smoke inside most buildings back then, but we also liked to sit outside at a picnic table for a few minutes before or after class and have a cigarette, shoot the breeze. I could pretend I didn't have bruises on my back and that nobody had shoved me into a dresser or a stove that morning. I could pretend nobody ever talked about killing my parents.

I graduated and found a job at city hall. I loved my job. My boss was great. And our mayor was great, too. He was married to the woman who had been Charlie's kindergarten teacher, which was sweet. Going to work gave me something to do and I got to learn new things. I was good at it, too. That felt good. And with me bringing in a steady paycheck, we weren't always behind on the bills. That was a relief to me and I thought should have been a relief to Rob. But no.

He still wanted to control every penny and he was more convinced than ever that I was going to cheat on him. It just about drove me crazy. City hall was right above the police station, and sometimes I had to call down to them and talk to some of the police. And there were a couple of guys who worked on the same floor as me, but not in the same office. Rob wanted to know all their names, and every day he asked me who I had talked to. He called the office to check on me and make sure I was there. If I was in the bathroom or outside taking a break, I had better call him back real quick or he might call back or even show up.

I wish I could have just been focused on the good things, but when I came home every day, there was hell to pay. Rob used some of my paycheck to buy pills, of course. His doctor had decided to stop seeing him by this point, so he had to find a new one. Most of his pills had to come from regular people who were selling them, and that just seemed like it was getting risky. He kept all that business out in the barn, which was how I liked it. I didn't want any part of it.

All the carefree days were gone. My friends didn't hardly come up anymore. Most of Rob's friends were as bad off as he was, or worse. I didn't want their girlfriends to come to the house and play cards with me. Every holiday was another excuse for Rob to get drunk or be in a foul mood, even if he wasn't drunk.

After just a few weeks at my new job, I started crying at my desk. I don't know what started it. I wasn't thinking about anything sad. I sat in the middle of the office, where everybody could see me. People came to the front window to pay their taxes. The finance manager had an office with glass windows, and she looked at me and smiled during the day. My boss's door was right in front of my desk, so anytime she went anywhere, she saw me first. It wasn't a good place to cry.

I rushed to the bathroom the first time that happened, and I got it all out and put a wet paper towel on my face to make it less red and puffy. I didn't think anybody could tell. Besides, why would anybody care? I was just another dumbass who got herself into a bind and didn't know how to get out of it. I didn't want the people at work to know how awful my life was. They liked to laugh and do their jobs and eat cake when it was somebody's birthday. We could talk about how bad it was supposed to snow or who should get elected or who was booked at the station last week.

And then I would cry. I kept trying to hide it, of course. I kept wiping my face with tissues when nobody seemed to be looking. I went to the bathroom and put wet paper towels on my eyes. I lifted my shirt and looked at my back in the mirror. Nobody could see what was happening. It was always hidden.

I thought so, anyway. One day, one of the women at the office came to my desk right before lunch. She set a book in front of me: *Men Who Hate Women and the Women Who Love Them.*

"What's this?" I asked her. The title was a punch in the gut. I tried to smile and act like I didn't know why she would think I needed something like this. I didn't want her to think that about me.

"Just read it," she said, all quiet and serious.

"Sure, I'll check it out." I kept smiling, but I knew I sounded fake. Me acting like everything was okay was just that—an act. But I wasn't doing a good job of selling it and she sure wasn't buying it. She just gave me a little smile and walked away, and she never mentioned it again.

I called Rob before I left the office and asked him if he wanted me to pick up any groceries on the way home.

"Get me a steak. I want some potatoes and macaroni and cheese too. Stop at Mom's and get an onion."

"Sounds good. I'll be home in a little bit."

"Hurry it up. I'm hungry and don't want you taking forever."

I hid the book in the paper grocery sack under a box of macaroni and cheese and the potatoes, even though they were dirty. I knew Rob wouldn't put any groceries away, but I had to make sure he didn't see the book if he looked into the bag.

When he went to the barn after dinner, I hid it under the clean laundry in the bathroom, but Charlie found it a few days later.

"What's this?" she asked me. She was eleven and liked to read all the time.

"It's a book about men like your dad," I told her.

"Aren't you scared he'll find it here?"

"No," I told her. "He would never go through the laundry." And this was true. I didn't have to worry about Rob finding it as long as I kept it hidden with my chores.

I read it in the bathroom, in little bits. I could sit in the kitchen at night because the bathroom was right there and I could slip it into the laundry real quick if I heard him open the front door. Every word was like a light bulb flashing on in my brain. The bad things Rob did all had a name. So did all the feelings I had been living with, and I wasn't anywhere close to being the only person who had ever felt them. But the book said there was only one way to fix it and that was to get out, before it was too late.

Most of my other memories are gone from around that time. I thought about dying a lot. I wished Rob would die. By that time, I couldn't care about how that would hurt Ella and George. It was hard for me to care about much of anything.

Chapter 27

In the summer of 1991, Charlie turned twelve and George turned eleven. I was thirty-two. It was hard to believe I was so old all of a sudden.

Me and Rob went to town on a Friday afternoon, leaving George at the house by himself. It was hot, like always when the summer really set in. Sometimes you didn't feel like you could catch your breath. Charlie had spent the night with a friend—she was friends with a girl whose parents had money and they would give Charlie her clothes sometimes, after that girl outgrew them. She was Charlie's best friend there for a while.

We went to Rob's doctor first. Even though Rob had started going to a new doctor, it already felt like they'd seen us a thousand times. I had to go to the little window and check Rob in. The girl behind the plastic barrier looked at me and started typing.

"Medicaid?"

"Yes, that's right," I told her. "Work disability." She looked at me like we both knew better.

In the exam room, the doctor had Rob's latest X-rays. "Looks like nothing has changed since last time," he told us, like that was a good thing. "I could recommend surgery but I don't think that's the best course of action at this time."

Rob nodded his head. He didn't want some Yankee doctor cutting on him.

"You've been on Lortab for a while now, though."

And Percocet. And Percodan. Valium. Xanax. Maybe even stuff I don't know about.

"I'm going to step this down a little."

Me and Rob both looked at the doctor, and I know we were both panicking. I didn't want us to leave with bad news, and this was definitely going to be bad news to him.

"Well, I've had a lot of strain in my lower back lately," he told the doctor. I could tell he was putting on his best show. He didn't want to look desperate, but he was. The doctor looked at him with his eyebrows raised.

I spoke up. "It's been awful, really. He can't hardly walk sometimes." I glanced at Rob, glad I thought to say this. *I* wasn't getting a prescription. I figured the doctor would take me seriously even if he didn't think it of Rob.

"Yes, there's evidence coming out that indicates a short-term benefit for this kind of medication, but we need to start weaning you off of it."

Rob's eyes were black as night but the doctor didn't seem to notice.

"I'll write up your new prescription." The doctor walked out, leaving me in the room with Rob. He didn't look at me and I didn't know whether I should look at him or not. We would have to drop off the prescription and come back a little later to pick it up. I already knew Rob wouldn't want to drive home before we got it. I didn't know how much of it he would take in one night—a quarter of the bottle? Maybe half? My paycheck wasn't hardly enough to keep up with what he needed to buy from his buddies anymore.

We went to Holbrook's pharmacy and I took the prescription in. The doctor's handwriting was messy, more like a kid's scribble than anything. Maybe they would just give Rob the same thing they had been giving him.

I drove us to the grocery store and Rob walked beside me, picking out a six-pack of Ale-8 and a pack of honey buns to put in the cart. I already knew what else to get, so he didn't have to tell me. He didn't talk the whole time we were in there, and I knew that meant he was mad. Every once in a while, he would stay calm and everything would blow over. That didn't happen much, though.

We hurried back to Holbrook's. I went inside to pick up the pills while he sat in the car.

"Who's it for?" the pharmacist asked me. He was professional and stuck-up. He knew who I was and what I was there for.

"Rob Lewis. I dropped off his prescription about forty-five minutes ago," I told him.

"Oh, right. Rob Lewis. More pain pills, I assume."

I didn't know what to say. What did he want me to say? I just stood there while he gave me a look and then went to the shelf for the prescription. He came back with the bottle and put it in a little paper sack. "Hope your husband gets to feeling better soon."

He gave me one of those grins to let me know he didn't mean the words. He thought I should be embarrassed about Rob's pills, and I wonder if it would have made him happy to know I was. I knew how they all looked at me when I came in every month. I saw how they looked at each other and rolled their eyes, like I was there because I wanted to be. I couldn't tell them there were worse things than them looking down on me. I couldn't tell them that if I didn't do this, there would be something so much worse than me being humiliated.

"Thanks," I said, and walked out as fast as I could. I stopped right outside the building to wipe my eyes, hurrying even though the car was parked around the corner.

I handed the pills to Rob as soon as I got in—I knew that's what he expected. I started up the car and pulled out to drive home.

"What the fuck is this, Jenny?"

"What do you mean?" I glanced over at him and saw he was reading the bottle.

"Five milligrams? What kind of bullshit is this? You got the wrong stuff!"

I thought about what the doctor had said. "Rob, the doctor must have changed your prescription. He said he was going to wean you—" I didn't get to finish.

"Turn this car around and go fix this." Rob's voice was calm. I knew what that meant. And I knew I couldn't fix it.

"Rob, the doctor did this. They aren't going to give me anything different." He *had* to understand this wasn't something I could change.

"Did you hear me? I said to turn this fucking car around and get your fat ass back in there, and don't come out until you have what I need." His voice was still calm, but it was mean. I turned around in the IGA parking lot and drove back to Holbrook's.

My hand was shaking a little when I turned off the ignition. Rob didn't say anything else. I had no idea what I would say when I got to the pharmacy counter. I hadn't bothered praying in a long time, but I said a little prayer in my head. *Please make them give me what he wants.*

The nicest girl who worked there was at the counter when I walked up. I thought that was good—maybe she would want to help me. "Excuse me, I just picked up my husband's prescription but it wasn't the right one." She looked really concerned right away. "I mean, it wasn't the right strength. He usually gets the ten milligrams." I pulled the bottle out and handed it to her. She read the label, looked at me, and said to wait right there.

I got that feeling in my stomach like I might throw up, but I told myself not to worry. She might just be going to get the right pills. Maybe everything would be okay after all.

When the pharmacist came to the counter holding the bottle, I knew I wasn't leaving there with anything different. But it was too late—he was going to tell me why and tell me how I should have known better. He was going to make me stand there and listen to him talk like I was stupid or a criminal or maybe both. I couldn't keep my eyes from tearing up while he went on about responsible prescription use and doctors knowing best. Worse yet, I couldn't make the people behind the counter understand that I wasn't crying because I wanted those pills. I wanted Rob to have those pills because I wanted the peace they would buy me.

Okay, not peace. But something. It was better than what it could be.

I didn't want to be in Holbrook's with everybody looking at me. And I didn't want to walk outside and have to tell Rob they weren't changing his prescription. But I had to get back to the car because the longer it took, the madder he would be.

"Well?"

"They said they couldn't do anything. They said it was what the doctor wrote on the prescription but I can call him on Monday and see about getting it fixed."

I thought that might make things better—the promise that I would get it fixed on Monday. I didn't know how I was going to make that happen, but at least it could buy me some time. And Rob could just take twice as much as normal over the weekend. Surely, he wouldn't mind that too much. He didn't say anything else. He looked out the window the whole way home, and I relaxed a little, thinking he might be okay with what I said.

He spoke up as we passed my parents' house. "I want you to call the doctor as soon as we get in the house." His voice was still calm. "Get this fixed and get it fixed tonight."

I didn't know what to say. I had already explained and he had to know it was too late to get the doctor to change anything.

"Did you hear me? Answer me when I'm talking to you."

"Yes, I heard you but you know he's gone for the day. I can't get ahold of anybody now."

"You should have took care of this earlier, but you're going to figure it out. I'm hurt and I need my medicine. You've just got your head stuck up the mayor's ass so hard, you don't know what you're doing anymore."

I knew where he was going with that. He would go through a list of people he thought I was kissing up to at work. And then he would say I was brainwashed by them or brainwashed by city hall in general.

It didn't make any sense and never had anything to do with what he was upset about. I had heard it so many times, I was worn out. It used to confuse me and make me wonder if I had said or done something wrong. I used to try to make Rob understand that there was no good reason to accuse me of whatever it was he was saying. But these days, I didn't even try. I just told him whatever I thought would keep him from hitting me or breaking something, and hoped he would let it go.

On this day, he wasn't going to let it go.

"Who are you trying to impress up there? All you think about is those stuck-up pricks and how to make them happy. You don't do anything around the house, don't do nothing for me. You're just stupid and lazy. Just a cow laying around the house and all you do is eat."

I kept my eyes looking straight at the road ahead. When he got like this, I never knew if he would get set off by me talking back to him or if it was better for me to say something. Whatever I did was wrong.

"Don't you ignore me, Jenny. I'm not going to put up with that shit."

We had reached the mouth of the holler. Even though he was telling me to talk, I knew there wasn't anything I could say that he wouldn't get mad about. There wasn't any way for me to win. I tried to remember anything that I had said before, anything that helped. My mind went swimming like it was at Cave Run Lake on a hot summer day when the water was still cool, just right. Me and my sisters were jumping off of rocks into the lake just over our heads. Billy was small and walked around in the shallow water, picking up rocks and throwing them as far as he could. Momma and Daddy sat on another big rock, drinking beer and talking like grown-ups always do. Everything was perfect.

Rob hit my arm like he was trying to get my attention. "Hey! I'm talking to you. You'd better get your head out of your ass and listen to me."

I had heard those words so many times now. What had it been, almost fourteen years? The longest Rob had ever went without being mean was two weeks, and that was after he was real mean, when I had to leave. I knew I should think of an answer—Rob was still waiting—but instead I thought about Birdie White's store and how good those Cokes used to taste. I could see myself, little again, feeling so big when I walked up the wooden steps by myself. The shelves were high up and it was like being somewhere magic because there were a bunch of different colors—gumballs and candies, and even the boring stuff like cans of beans and giant jars of pickles were still interesting, too.

"Goddammit, Jenny, I'm talking to you."

I knew I should say something, but nothing would be good enough. He was hell-bent on being mad. I thought about how good it used to feel when I laid my head on Momma's lap and we both pretended like I was going to watch her soaps, but I fell asleep every time. That's when I got her all to myself. It was just me and her for that minute or two and then for the hours I was asleep. Sometimes she would pet my head and I would forget how it never seemed like I could get enough of her love.

Rob wasn't saying anything anymore. I could feel him looking at me. I knew his eyes were empty and black and he wasn't seeing me. I didn't know what he saw when that happened. I wished I could drive us into the creek and know that we would both die, right then and there. It wasn't a big enough drop, though. More likely, I would be hurt and Rob would come out without a scratch. That's how it always is with people like him. He was too mean to die.

We drove by George and Ella's house. Ella took such good care of the kids. And me and Rob, even though I don't think he ever noticed. Every meal she cooked was the best I ever had. Living next to her might have been the best thing about living in the holler.

I pulled into our driveway and turned off the ignition.

Chapter 28

I didn't have to wait for long to know how Rob was going to act.

"Get your fucking ass in that house and get my prescription fixed."

For just a minute, I was too tired to deal with it. I wanted to tell him to stop talking, stop threatening me. I didn't care if he said he was going to kill me, and right then, I didn't care if he actually did it. I wasn't scared. I was just tired. He walked a few feet behind me to the front door.

"Stupid bitch. I'll kill you and then I'm going to go kill your parents, you hear me?"

When I reached for the keys in my purse, my hands were shaking. I couldn't get ahold of them, and when I finally did, I dropped them on the porch before I could get the key in the lock. I bent over to pick them up and Rob started screaming.

"Get this goddamn door unlocked right now!" Now my hands were shaking so bad, I almost dropped the keys again as soon as I grabbed them. Before I had a chance to stand up straight, he pushed me into the door headfirst.

"Rob, please—" He shut me up by kicking me hard in the side. After that, I'm not sure whether it was his foot or his fist, but he hit me over and over as I screamed for him to stop. He kept pushing me against the door so hard that it finally gave way and swung open, the doorknob still locked.

He kept hitting me—kicking me?—and when I looked up, there was George on the couch, where he had been napping while we were gone. He was sitting up and crying, not trying to be quiet. I covered my head with my arms to try to keep Rob from hitting it.

"Goddamn bitch," I heard Rob say, a little out of breath. He stepped around me and went into the bedroom. I heard him jerk open a drawer—maybe the dresser drawer where he kept his bullets. I pushed myself onto my knees and stood up, grabbing my car keys.

"George," I said as quietly as I could, and I motioned for him to come with me. He had stopped crying but his face was red and wet. I grabbed my keys off the floor and my purse off the porch. "Come on," I told him. "Run."

We ran to the car and I used both hands to put the key in the ignition. I looked back at the front door, still open, and saw Rob step onto the porch. I threw the car into reverse, then into drive, and took off as fast as I could, gravel going everywhere. I looked in the rearview mirror and saw Rob on the porch, looking at me, a rifle in his hand. He wasn't aiming it. Maybe he wouldn't since George was in the car. I drove faster than I ever had on that road before and just hoped we wouldn't meet another car around the corner.

We made it all the way to Momma and Daddy's house without seeing Rob's truck behind us. I pulled George out of the car and we ran into the kitchen, where Momma was sitting.

"You have to help me," I told her. I didn't care if she thought I had made my bed and now had to lie in it. I didn't care if she thought I should have known better than to get mixed up with Rob. If he was going to kill me, it wouldn't be in that holler. I would never go back—that's the one thing I was sure of.

Momma told me we could stay there while I figured out what to do next. But if Rob showed up, she was calling the law. And if he tried to start any trouble, she would tell Daddy what had happened when he got back from his race. He had already left for Flemingsburg and wouldn't be back until real late. I couldn't care anymore. I smoked a cigarette and then another while George watched cartoons in the living room.

"He's going to kill me," I told Momma. "If I go back, he'll kill me next time."

"Well, it's good that you figured that out. You'd better clean yourself up before your daddy comes back."

I went into the bathroom and looked at myself in the mirror. I hadn't even thought about what I looked like until then. My hair was wild and sticking up. When I brushed it, some spots hurt really bad. I touched them and, sure enough, there was blood.

I pulled up my shirt to look at my side and then my back. Bruises were already starting to show—too many to count. Long red scratches—where were those from? Maybe the door threshold. My face was red from crying but there were no bruises or scratches there. None on my arms. I looked normal with all my clothes on. I was always glad nobody could see what he was really doing to me, but I also wished somebody could see. Maybe then it would matter.

I stood there crying, trying to keep it quiet so George and Momma wouldn't hear me. When I was finally done, I came out to find them sitting in the living room. Cartoons were playing on the television.

"Where's Charlie?" Momma asked.

Shit.

"She stayed the night at her friend's house. I'm supposed to pick her up later."

I called her friend's house and talked to the mom.

"Something has come up and I was wondering if Charlie could stay another night with you all?"

The mom sounded surprised but told me, sure, I could just get Charlie on Saturday. They were going to be at the city park for her son's baseball game in the afternoon, if I wanted to come there.

"That's great," I told her. "Thanks so much." I hung up and was suddenly so tired, I couldn't stay awake any longer. I looked at the clock—it was seven. I told Momma and George I was going to lay down for a minute and went into my old bedroom. The bunk beds were gone, but my old bed was still there—the double bed I had shared with Gail so long ago.

I lay down on top of the bedspread, thinking how I needed to change clothes before I got under the covers. *I don't have any clothes to change into.* It seemed like that should make me feel something, but I was empty, blank. I could hear cars go by, birds chirping in the trees, kids laughing on the playground—all the sounds of summer. It was like a scary movie where you think you're watching a normal scene, until you finally spot what's wrong and you understand it was all an illusion.

Even though it was still light outside, everything went dark for me.

The sun was shining when I woke up, but George was next to me, asleep under the covers. I was still on top of them. I got up as quietly as I could and went into the kitchen. Momma was there drinking a cup of coffee and reading the newspaper. I poured myself a cup. The clock on the wall said it was nine o'clock.

I knew Daddy was still asleep—he always slept in after a race. Me and Momma sat there without talking, just smoking our cigarettes and drinking coffee. It almost felt like this could be normal, except all the bruises were hurting, and when I touched my head, it was real tender and there was a little dried blood crusted in my hair. I didn't mention it to Momma.

"What are you going to do today?" she asked me. I couldn't figure out what she meant at first.

"Um, not much, I don't reckon. I need to take a shower."

"You've got to find a place to live. Unless you decide to go back to him."

"I'll never set foot in that holler again," I told her.

"Good. You need to find a place to live."

I started to cry. "I don't have anything. He's been watching every penny I spend and taking anything that was left. I couldn't save any up."

"You need to stay away from him, Jenny. And if you're serious about not going back, I'll help you."

Her words swirled around in my mind but they didn't make sense. Momma didn't believe in lending money or giving family anything for free. Anytime we needed work done on our cars, we had to pay just like everybody else or tell her exactly what day we would pay our bill on. I never expected her to offer me help, especially since I had *made my bed*. I went to the park to talk to Charlie's friend's mom in person. I would take Charlie with me if she wanted, but I was hoping they would let her stay with them for as long as possible. The way she looked at me, I could tell she wasn't surprised to hear about Rob and that I was leaving him. She said Charlie could stay with them the whole week. Charlie was happy to hear she was having a longer sleepover—she always seemed happy to be away from home those days.

I took Monday off from work to find a house for rent and put down a deposit. Funny enough, the one I found was the same house Frank used to live in with his first wife and the kids' cousins. It was in Morehead, not far from Clearfield and the house I had grown up in, but there was a lot more traffic and noise that I wasn't used to. I went back to work on Tuesday, leaving George with Momma. I had to tell my boss—I knew I couldn't pretend like nothing was going on. And there was a reasonable chance that Rob would show up at city hall, ready to shoot whoever he got to first.

I went to her office doorway. "Do you have a minute?"

"Sure, come on in."

I sat in one of the chairs in front of her desk. There didn't seem to be a great way to start, so I just blurted it out.

"I left Rob over the weekend. Me and the kids are staying with my parents for a few days while I get us moved somewhere." She nodded like this was a normal thing for me to be saying. "The thing is, Rob was pretty mad when I left." I took a deep breath. "And I don't know, but he might do something violent. I'm not sure whether he would come up here or not, but it is a possibility."

I waited to hear what she was going to say. I thought she would be mad at me for putting everybody in danger. Maybe she wouldn't even want me there if Rob might come looking for me. I couldn't afford to lose my job. I couldn't even afford to take a couple more days off. I held my breath, waiting to hear what she was going to say.

"I'll go downstairs and talk to the police chief. Rob's still driving that same truck?" I nodded, letting my breath out. She nodded back at me. "Okay, don't worry about it. We'll all keep an eye out for him. And if you need somebody to walk you to your car or anything, just let me know. I'm glad you left that situation. You deserve better."

I realized she wasn't surprised at anything I had told her. Maybe she had known more than I thought the whole time. I tried to keep the tears in again.

She stood up and pretended she didn't notice. "I'm going downstairs to talk to them real quick. I'll be back in a minute. Why don't you take a break in here, until you're ready to go back to your desk."

I nodded as she walked past me, leaving me in her office alone. I let a few tears out, using the tissues from a box on her desk. I cried there for a few minutes, then went back to my desk. When she came back she was smiling.

"We've got everything worked out, okay? You just let me know if you need anything else." I nodded again, knowing I would cry if I tried to talk. "And Jenny, you're doing the right thing. I'm proud of you."

She turned and walked into her office. I went to the bathroom and cried like I had so many times before, but this time, it was different.

It turned out I would have to go back to the holler one last time to get our stuff. A week after leaving Rob, I borrowed Daddy's truck and took the kids with me to load up what we needed. I talked to Ella and she promised me that they would make Rob come to their house and they wouldn't let him leave. I knew this was the one time they would fight against him, if they had to.

I had the kids get their clothes and toys, and I took what we needed from the rest of the house, throwing it into boxes as fast as I could. I could feel Rob staring at the house from Ella's kitchen window, and at one point I thought I could see him in their yard, just outside the house. I hurried to grab forks and spoons, some dishes, a few washrags. We didn't need much. And I didn't want too many things that would remind me of this house and everything that had happened inside it.

Chapter 29

We probably stayed in that house for four months before I moved us to a trailer that the city owned. The house was a lot bigger and we could walk to Dairy Queen and a gas station, but it was so drafty, it would be impossible to keep warm all winter.

So when somebody mentioned that I could live in the trailer and pay less rent as long as I kept an eye on the park, I said yes right away. The city covered utilities too, and that helped me save more money.

We only had two bedrooms—one in the back that I shared with Charlie and a little one just off the hallway, which was George's room. It had central heat and the roof didn't leak, so small or not, it was better than it could have been. And best of all, there was nobody to tell me what to do and put me down all the time. Nobody to threaten me with his belt or gun.

It took a while to get used to this new life. I had nightmares—always about Rob. He would be hitting me, pushing me, hurting me in bed. The stuff I experienced in real life. Charlie had nightmares, too. George never said if he did or not.

The noise of town made me jump all the time after being in the quietness of the holler for so long. For at least the first two months, I flinched whenever a car door slammed or somebody shouted on the park basketball court. I tried to hide it from the kids, but I was always afraid Rob was going to show up to hurt me one more time. One last time.

Rob didn't want to get divorced. He told me he loved me, he would change, he understood this time. And then he told me he would kill himself if I left him. He couldn't go on without me. He couldn't stand the thought of me with another man and if I was already cheating on him, he would find out *by God* and no other man was going to take his kids away, *don't you think for a minute that's going to happen, Jenny.* He said I'd be sorry one day but he wasn't going to fight me in court. *Have it your way. You'll be sorry you did this.*

But every chance she got, Peggy pulled me out on Friday and Saturday nights, usually just to drive up and down Main Street and sit in the parking lot of the new fast-food restaurant or at the other end of town at the gas station. That was about all there was to do in Morehead those days—cruise the little strip and crank up Billy Ray Cyrus on the car radio, windows rolled down. In those moments, it felt like we were teenagers, young and carefree, until it was time to get home to the kids.

Charlie and George had to go see Rob every other weekend for his visits. The divorce was final and I had custody, of course. Neither one of them wanted to go, but Charlie was worse about it. She cried sometimes and begged me not to make her go. I was glad she stopped defending him like she did when she was little. I think Rob showed his true colors to the kids one too many times and both of them saw what he really was now.

I told Charlie every time that I had to make them go to their dad's—it's what the judge said to do. She said she was scared to go up there, so I finally told her that if she was at his house and needed someone to come get her, I would send the police. We made up a code because most of the time when she wanted to leave, Rob was close by and she couldn't say exactly what she wanted. I figured he was still tape-recording phone calls and would probably listen later even if he wasn't in the room when it happened.

One time, Charlie called me and gave the signal—she coughed after she said she was just calling to say hi. I asked her if she was sure and she said yes. I asked again and she wasn't so sure. Finally, she said she was okay. The kids were getting too big to whip, anyway. I figured Rob wouldn't be as bad now that I was gone.

There was one time that he came to the house to pick Charlie up—I think George was already there. Rob got out of his truck that time. He didn't normally do that. He did have to pick the kids up and bring them home. Thank goodness the judge agreed that I didn't ever have to go back up the holler. I wouldn't have felt safe even going to the driveway.

Before I knew it, Rob was at the door. I dialed the police station and left the phone as close as possible so they could hear whatever happened next. Charlie opened the door, and when Rob saw me standing there, he said he wanted to borrow my garden hose. I told him he couldn't, and watched him get mad. I didn't care. I wasn't going to let him push me around ever again. He kept running his mouth and then stepped inside the trailer.

"Stop acting like this, Jenny. Let me borrow the damn hose and I'll bring it back. You don't need to be a bitch about it."

"You can just leave, Rob. I'm not giving you anything."

He took another step toward me. I was shaking on the inside, but I wasn't going to let him have his way, not this time. I didn't care if he hit me or not. The police were listening and they would come. He would finally have to pay for what he'd done.

Charlie stepped in between us.

"Stop it, you all don't need to do this. Please." She looked back and forth at me and her dad. Poor thing, she didn't understand. She didn't know that the police were on the phone and that I wasn't going to back down. Not this time. For some reason, though, Rob decided to.

"I don't need any of your shit," he said as he turned around and walked out the door.

Charlie waited until he was in his truck, then she turned around and hugged me. "I love you."

I told her I loved her too, and I watched as she got in the truck and they drove away. I picked up my phone.

"Jenny? Are you okay?"

"Yeah, I'm okay. He's gone. Thanks for staying on here. I'll let you know if he comes back."

We hung up and I lit a cigarette. I sat at our tiny kitchen table and watched for Rob's truck to come up the road again, but it didn't. That was the last time I ever saw him face to face. From then on, he stayed in his truck when he picked the kids up or dropped them off.

Things went pretty well for the next few months. I kept saving up money. Since we were there next to the park and the city paid for it, Charlie got to go to the pool when it was open and George played basketball as much as he wanted.

There was another family that lived close, a woman and her son who was Charlie's age. They had a lot of money and a nice house. Charlie liked going over there after school—the boy was in some of her gifted classes—but he was mean to George. It was just as well that Charlie stopped hanging around that boy all the time because when they grew up, the boy started funding "pill mills" from Kentucky to Florida and he got into all kinds of trouble over stolen cars. His mom had enough money to get him out of prison, so I still don't know if he ever did any real time. But Charlie was better off to stay away from all that.

I thought I should move on with my life and I went on a couple of dates with different guys, but nothing worked out. One guy was really nice but still in love with his ex-wife. Most men were just after one thing, and I wasn't interested in that. Of course, it could be hard to relax around men after all that happened with Rob.

Me and Peggy still went out on Friday or Saturday nights to drive through downtown, listening to music with the windows down. But that all got old after a while.

And I was lonely.

I found a singles column in the newspaper and decided I would start writing to somebody. Most of the men in the ads were too old.

There weren't many living near me, and I knew most of them that did—and that wasn't a good thing.

Before too long, I was writing letters to single men in other states. What did I have to lose?

Most of the time, me and the guy would exchange one or two letters and then I'd never hear from him again. Sometimes I just got bored because they didn't have anything interesting to say. And then I found Jack.

Jack was from Kentucky, but he'd been living in Nevada for a long time. He was a mechanic for the big machines they used in the gold mines, and that must have been a pretty good living. But he had lost a lot of his eyesight and couldn't work so much anymore. He told me he wasn't the best-looking guy out there and he had to wear thick glasses to see what little he could.

I didn't care about that. I just wanted somebody who was going to treat me good, and Jack was great in his letters. We talked on the phone every once in a while, too, but back then long-distance calls were really expensive. And with the trailer being so small, it wasn't like I could get a lot of privacy.

After a while, Jack wanted to meet me in person. He said we should take a trip that spring. I didn't have a lot of money saved up for something like that, but he said since it was his idea, he was the one that would pay. I couldn't believe it. He wanted me to fly out to Reno—it would be my first time on a plane—and he would pay for the hotel. We would go to the casino and have a great time. It would also be my first time going on a vacation without the kids, which seemed crazy. They were bigger, so it wasn't as much work to take care of them as it used to be, but they were still kids—Charlie was thirteen and George was twelve. I checked with Momma and she said the kids could stay with her and Daddy for a week. I could arrange for the bus to pick them up and drop them off at their house.

All I had to do was save up my vacation time at work.

It was wild to go to a city like that. I loved it. Me and Jack got along good, except one time when I was a little drunk I got mad at him for no reason and told him I was going back to Kentucky. God knows how I thought I was going to manage that. Thankfully, he was patient and didn't get all worked up about it. Jack had been married before but he didn't want to talk about our pasts. If we were going to try to be together, he said we needed to focus on the now, forget about the rest. I would have to stop thinking so much about my ex, and quit bringing him up every time I was the least bit unhappy. I figured he was right. It wasn't fair to take out my past on him.

When I got back to Morehead, I had the kids ride the bus home from school instead of going to Momma's. We hugged and they asked about my trip. I showed them my new ring.

"Your stepdad will be here in two weeks."

BOOK THREE

Charlie

Present Day

Chapter 30

Jack showed up at our house two weeks after Mom got back from Reno. Right away, he let us kids know that as our new stepfather, he was calling the shots and we were going to obey his rules. He gave us a couple of nicknames we could use to address him—he preferred "Pops." We called him Jack.

I can't even remember where George and I slept after Jack moved in. Since I had shared a bedroom with Mom, either I started sleeping in the living room or George did. Before long, George didn't want to deal with Jack anymore. He moved back to our father's house and lived there until he graduated from high school and got married.

Dad wanted his house to be more fun than Mom's—or hell, maybe he didn't think about it and wildness just came naturally to him. He gave us alcohol and weed and eventually pills. Maybe he gave them to George sooner than he gave them to me. And he was always encouraging George to bring girls home. After he remarried, my dad whipped me for sitting on my stepbrother's lap when I was fifteen. Accused me of wanting attention when an old man at the lake told him I was pretty. Called me a whore when I was abused by his brother-in-law.

So I lived at Mom's, still terrified of our father.

But that wasn't the easiest place for a teenage girl to be, either. Jack expected complete obedience at all times. And he had a way of insulting us while making it sound like a joke. If I struggled to open a jar, he'd say, "You've got to be smarter than the jar!" If I asked my mom to change her mind about something, Jack would step in. "No, it's not happening. Now stop asking."

Of course, I didn't love being bossed around by a stranger who suddenly lived in my home. But what I hated most was that he talked to my mom the same way he talked to me.

Despite how angry I was inside, I followed the rules and did what I was told. But it didn't take long before I found ways to follow the rules on the surface while rebelling out of sight. I would follow the letter of the law, but not the spirit.

I remember really arguing with Jack only once. I don't know what it was about, but eventually I told him, "You're not my father." The words didn't even feel right when I spoke them. We both knew he wasn't my father; that didn't need to be said. Jack responded, "I'm more of a father to you than your dad is." He was right, which made me even angrier—part of me wanted to defend my father, but it was useless. And the problem wasn't that Jack was trying to be my father. To me, the problem was that he was a tyrant. But I didn't have words for that. My real father had always treated me much worse than Jack did.

The bar was low. Jack taught me how to drive a stick shift. He introduced me to the Beatles. He didn't beat my mother.

Right after I turned seventeen, my first boyfriend said we should get married, and I went along with it. Not because I wanted to get married, but because I wanted to escape my home. Mom and Jack were about to move us to another county and they told me I would only be allowed to go to school and work—no hanging out afterward to see my boyfriend, who was pretty much my only friend.

My mom told me many times about the curfew her mother imposed on her—*be home before dark, no matter what*. It was a restriction, a terrible one, that my mother had wanted to escape. It was the same curfew she gave me and something *I* wanted to escape. That arbitrary, unyielding rule played a part in driving both of us into our first, too-early marriages. Mom's had worse consequences, but it also brought me into being, so I can't wish it away.

When I was a teenager and angry at her rules, I thought my mother was unreasonable and uncaring. When I learned it was the same curfew she was given, I thought my mother was repeating the past without understanding the consequences. (We do that, don't we?) Now, I wonder what it was my grandmother feared about the dark, and where this fear began.

Home is supposed to be a place of safety, refuge. My mom and I both found our childhood homes to be a sort of prison, rather than a haven. We didn't feel protected, so we ran the first chance we got. We were both short-sighted, but something had to have been missing for a long time before that. Something children can't provide for themselves.

So, I said *yes* to my boyfriend and became a wife before I became an adult. I left home so I could be free, and I discovered all manner of danger awaited me.

Growing up in Eastern Kentucky was complicated. Not because of the poverty and drug abuse everyone already knows about, but because Appalachia is also full of life and beauty—it's a place that resists simple explanation. Running around with George in our holler, I absorbed lessons from nature without knowing it. Most importantly, life flourished all around us year after year, regardless of what my father said or did to us.

No matter how scared or confused I was, I knew the blackberries would grow wild in the fields and ditches, and I could indulge in their sweetness if I was mindful of the thorns. I knew where the crawdads would be hiding in our creek, and if I was gentle with them, they would be gentle with me. I looked forward to picking up enormous sycamore leaves, watching silver maples wave from the edge of a field, the fireworks show of sugar maples and red oaks in the fall. I didn't know it at the time, but all that consistent, persistent beauty gave me hope.

In the holler, I often carried a book with me into the woods, especially when I could still hear my father shouting even after I went outside. If I was stuck inside the house with his rage, I learned how to force my mind into a story. There on the page, kids were going through adventures and navigating friendship, loneliness—normal things. I knew most of the stories I read weren't real, but I could *feel* what the characters felt, and that was often much better than what I was going to feel when I put the book down.

In some ways, my father helped inspire my love of reading, both with his violence that I was trying to escape and with all the stories he told me. He told wild stories that were never age-appropriate or related to my interests. I don't know why he found me to be such a good audience, but I was. I soaked up his stories like cold spring water on a hot summer's day. Who Great-Grandpa Lewis had killed and why. Who had wronged my father and how he had gotten revenge. Large and small dramas among our family and people I didn't even know. He showed me his knife collection over and over, explained who made which handle out of a buck's antler, which brands were good to collect, which blades would stay sharp. He showed me newspaper clippings of my great-grandfather with Al Capone in prison, and other clippings that told of deaths and tragedies in our county.

Why did he tell me all these things? Maybe because I was listening.

Now, my own kids love to hear the stories I tell from my childhood. My moonshining great-grandfather and his exploits are fascinating, but even the most ordinary experiences feel meaningful if you look at them right. Like how around the age of ten, I was trying to show off as a wild hillbilly to my cousins from west Tennessee. I lifted a little aluminum boat in the yard to show them Kentucky's trademark venomous snake, the copperhead. I didn't bother looking under the boat as I crouched beside it and lifted it up. For some reason, I didn't really expect a snake to be under there, even though I knew they loved the shade. I turned to my cousins and smiled as I watched fear come to their faces, not realizing there really was a snake waiting.

I can't say for sure that it was a copperhead—when I turned around and saw what they were scared of, I dropped the boat and ran as fast as I could. Any snake will bite, and I'd invaded its cool resting place. But maybe it could sense I wasn't there to hurt it. Maybe it somehow knew that there was no need to hurt *me*. That just because it could be dangerous doesn't mean it had to be.

Chapter 31

A few days ago, I drove my teenage daughter, Rose, to Lexington, the closest city to the little town where we live. We were meeting up with her brother, Orion, who's fresh out of college. This was technically our Mother's Day celebration, even though we were already far into June. All of us had been sick with a cold on Mother's Day, so there we were, making up for lost time.

As soon as we got on the interstate, Rose took over the car radio. A couple of her rap songs have grown on me, but for the most part I just tolerate them for as long as possible. I tried to focus on the road and let my mind wander instead of paying attention to the lyrics. Soon though, Rose quizzed me on some of the artists she thinks I should recognize by now.

"Come on, Mom—think about how his voice sounds."

"Um, is it Kendrick?"

She sighed in mock exasperation. "No, the last song was Kendrick, remember? He sounds totally different."

I knew I had heard the voice before but I couldn't place it. "I give up."

"It's Drake."

"Oh yeah, that's what I was going to guess next." I smiled and gave her a quick glance and she grinned.

"Sure, Momma, sure you were."

A few minutes later she turned on a Waylon Jennings song— one I've had memorized since I was younger than her. We sang along together, deepening our voices for the low notes and adjusting to the rhythm when Willie Nelson joined in. I figured as long as she has a favorite old country song, who am I to complain about the new music she likes? We spent the rest of the drive listening to my "Hillbilly" playlist, which is mostly made up of songs I grew up listening to. I imagined myself at eight years old next to our radio with a record and cassette player. This was the soundtrack to my life, and now it's part of the soundtrack to my daughter's, though the scenery is much different.

At the restaurant, we all got different sushi rolls, swapping pieces and talking about little details from our days. Orion has been to New York and San Francisco and wants to move to a city someday. Rose wants to move to France either during college or right after. They've both already traveled and seen more in their young lives than most of my family has, but they claim my history as part of their own. Maybe not always with pride, but with love.

Later, we stopped to take pictures of ourselves in front of the theater where the movie we were going to see was playing. They grinned and hugged me, then took silly pictures together that I knew would lead to more laughter in the future. I used to hate pictures of myself, but I've gotten better about that. It's not so hard to smile anymore.

I spent years trying to understand my father, and it finally occurred to me that I still didn't understand my mother all that well. She always seemed passive, like she was a supporting character in my childhood—there, but not influencing our lives. When I think back, I see her folding the laundry, cooking our meals, even mowing the yard. But when it came to our family interactions, she didn't *do* so much as she was *done to*. She was a victim at my father's hands, just as my brother and I were, just as his future wives, girlfriends, and youngest children would become.

I've always wanted to understand my mother, though. I met up with her for lunch recently—cheap Mexican food, something we both love—and I asked her if she would be willing to tell me about some of the most significant moments of her life. I expected she'd respond like she often has in the past: "I've tried to forget all that. There ain't much to tell anyhow."

But this time, she surprised me. As we ate greasy tortilla chips and watery salsa, waiting for our orders to come out, she told me a few stories I wasn't part of. They were mostly hard times, even before I was born, going all the way back to her childhood. She told me what her life was like when she was pregnant with her first child, and then with me.

The more she told me, the more questions I had. It was like starting to put a puzzle together but finding that it keeps getting bigger, expanding so the picture reveals itself as more complex, more detailed.

When I felt like she was comfortable enough, when this question wouldn't hurt her, I asked, "When did Dad start getting mean?"

"Oh, let me see. Hmm, that's hard to put my finger on."

"Was it when I was little? Or after George was born, maybe?" I imagined any patience he had for one young child would have disappeared when there were two.

"Yeah, it was probably sometime after that. Seems like things were pretty good there for a while." That surprised me.

"What about your family—did they like Dad? I know you didn't tell them everything he did, but did they know what he was like?"

"I can't really remember. My mom liked him pretty good there, for a while. He made her laugh a lot when he'd stop by the house to see me, back when we were courting."

But she couldn't give me the details I needed to stitch the whole story together. I wanted to understand more, so I called up Aunt Mary last weekend.

I started out by asking her to tell me about when she dated my uncle Frank, back when they were teenagers. Mary surprised me with how much she remembered and was willing to share.

I took my phone to my front porch and sat on one of the white rocking chairs out there, watching a few cars go by as Mary talked.

The bushes in front of my house are a little overgrown and need to be shaped up. The Bradford pears ought to be trimmed soon, before limbs start breaking. We're surrounded by brick houses on one-acre lots and there's no traffic going anywhere except to their homes. It's safe, quiet, friendly. I miss the forest.

"I had the biggest crush on Frank," Mary said. "But one time at the house, we were out there on the patio and he drew back his fist like he was going to hit me. Daddy came around the corner and saw what he was doing and told him to get out of our driveway and don't come back. And I was done with him—I wasn't going to put up with that."

That was Uncle Frank, always handsome, always violent. He was so tall, he had to duck when he walked into Granny Ella's dining room, which had wide, arched openings instead of walls separating it from the kitchen and living room. He wore a mustache, no beard, and I always thought he was the only man who could pull off that look. This was in the eighties and nineties when a lot of men were trying to.

Uncle Frank told me a story one day at Granny's house when I was eight or nine. We were eating hamburgers after church—I had gone to church with Granny, not Frank. I don't remember ever seeing Frank there. Granny always made us food after church, and somehow, even her burgers were the best I ever had. How did she always do that? I think it was the love she poured into her food.

Anyway, Frank asked me a question.

"You know how coal miners always take their food in a lunch pail down in the mines with them?"

I nodded. I didn't know, but it made sense.

"When they eat their sandwiches, they hold them with a finger on one side and their thumb on the other, like this." His thumb and forefinger were on his burger bun, opposite one another. "Their hands are filthy with coal dust and this way they can eat all around their dirty fingers without getting the rest of the sandwich dirty."

I nodded again—this seemed smart to me.

"They eat all that sandwich until the only part that's left is the little bit between their fingers." He had taken bites all around, demonstrating how the miners would eat. "You know what they do with that last bite?"

"No, what?"

And without another word, Frank threw the last little bit of his hamburger into his mouth and ate it.

That story has stuck with me for more than thirty years. My reaction is still vivid in my mind, and when I revisit that scene, I think about how perfect Frank's storytelling was: the suspense, how easy it was to visualize, the surprise ending that was also the only sensible ending, because who ever heard of a coal miner who would throw away a bite of food? And me, now so picky about cleanliness—it gives me a horrified thrill each time to imagine carefully eating around the one dirty spot on a sandwich, just to pop it into my mouth after all that effort. But that always made sense to me too. We had times when there wasn't much to eat. A person learns not to waste.

That is the one good story I have about Uncle Frank. I don't think he ever hugged me. I don't remember him smiling much. Maybe he smiled for a brief moment at the beginning or end of some event along the way.

I have other stories about him, though—like the day my dad thought Mom was flirting with Uncle Frank, and for some reason, the men drove off together and Mom took me and George running through Granny's field, dodging cow manure and hiding for our lives. Certainly hiding for hers.

There was the night I woke up because of yelling and gunshots. I could see Uncle Frank from my bedroom window. I remember wondering if someone was going to shoot toward him and hit me. Or would he catch me looking at him and turn his gun to me in anger? I don't remember whether I cried myself to sleep. I remember a woman in an office asking my dad a few days later, "Drop the charges? For *attempted murder*?" And though I was little—maybe six?—I understood what she was saying: *This is crazy.*

And then there are stories like the one my cousin told me about what Frank did to her mom, his first wife. He drove her head through the fish tank. That probably happened in the drafty house on Main Street where me, George, and Mom lived for a little while. Maybe that's why it felt so cold and uninviting. Maybe the walls remembered the broken glass, the broken skin.

Mary didn't tell any of those stories on the phone, though. She was lucky enough to leave Frank early—to avoid getting stuck in that violence. But Mary did divorce her first husband when I was pretty little, and I always thought he must have been abusive. As we talked, I asked her if that was the case. It felt so intrusive to ask, and I was afraid she would shut me out. But she told me no, it wasn't like that at all. He drank too much, but he was never violent. She divorced him and it took a while, but he cleaned himself up like people sometimes do after they lose their family.

Before that conversation, I had thought three out of the four sisters, including my mother, had married abusive men. That didn't make sense when I thought about how gentle Papaw Caudill—their *daddy*—always seemed to be, but I wasn't sure what he was like when he was younger. Some men calm down as they get older, like my own father did. They're not as eager to fight and hurt as they once were, or maybe their bodies just can't see it through.

Either way, a parent's legacy is established pretty early in their children's lives. We make our deepest marks on them when they're young, and they tend to remember. I have a few pictures of me and Papaw from when I was little. I'm always sitting on his lap, grinning. I don't need a picture to remind me that I always felt safe, loved.

As I sat on the porch talking to Mary, the neighbor across from us waved at me before they pulled into their driveway. I waved back and smiled. They don't drive past our house too fast. I asked Mary what she thought of my dad when Mom first met him, when Mary was still in high school and dating Frank.

"He was always trouble." She told me about Grandma's metal box, where she kept all the money from Papaw's work in the garage. This old money box had a four-digit combination lock and you had to roll the wheels for each number, lining them all up perfectly before it would open. Maybe my father saw Grandma carry it to and from the garage, or perhaps when he was allowed inside the house, he watched her lock money away after counting it at the kitchen table. According to Mary, he wanted to try to figure out the combination just about every time he was at their house, and for some reason Grandma let him try.

I can see him sitting on the patio glider, not paying attention to my teenage mother, with her impressive cheekbones that make me think Grandma really might have been one-eighth Cherokee. My mother, who was beautiful like so many girls are when they don't know it. Unassuming, unaware. In pictures of her from before I was born, she is the quintessential girl of the seventies. I wish I could talk to that girl.

What would I tell her, though? Don't fall for the first boy that gives you attention? There's somebody better out there?

Maybe: *So much depends on what you choose next.*

Chapter 32

Mary told me a story about Grandma Helen, too.

She'd had a younger sister, Laura, who she was really close to. Laura had a stroke when she was sixteen. The doctors found that she had a brain tumor and said they could operate, but there was a 95 percent chance she would die during surgery. Or they could let her go on, and she would probably die from the tumor, though they couldn't say how soon.

They didn't do the surgery, and Laura ended up paralyzed on her left side, so she couldn't get around very well and stayed in bed most of the time. That tumor gave her awful headaches every day. She would beg Helen to go get her some aspirin to ease the pain. Helen felt so bad for her, she would go to Birdie White's store and get the aspirin, but then their mother would get mad because they already had medicine for Laura—probably something the doctor prescribed. Still, Helen would get the aspirin because that's what Laura wanted, even if it got her in trouble. Laura died six years after they discovered the tumor. She was in bed, and when they found her, she had gotten her shirt off and was flopping around. It was awful. Mary said she didn't think her mom ever recovered from that.

I think I understand. I can imagine a heartache that follows you for a lifetime.

I walked inside the house to listen to the rest of Mary's story. I didn't want to smile and wave if someone else drove by. I just wanted to listen.

Mary went on to talk about how my grandma started taking "Black Beauties," the very legal, very addictive pill also known as Biphetamine 20. Similar amphetamines were given to soldiers in Vietnam to keep them alert and battle-ready even after many sleepless, brutal nights. Black Beauties were also good for helping a woman keep her figure, or get it back after having a baby or three. Maybe that's why Grandma started taking them, or maybe it was that heartache from Laura. Who can say? It was the 1950s—women were prescribed all kinds of drugs to cope with their lives. But Mary remembers the day that her mother said, "I'm sick of taking these pills!" That's when Mary thinks she started drinking.

I felt a pang of sadness for my grandmother when Mary told me that. She must have been trying to numb, then drown, something that wouldn't leave her alone. And that struggle would have had an impact on the whole family.

Mary always has to sleep with her bedroom door open, just a little. "If Dwayne gets up and goes to the bathroom and shuts our bedroom door behind him, or if he comes to bed after I go to sleep and he shuts it, I'm awake. I can't sleep unless that door is open."

"Wow, do you have any idea why?" I asked.

"I know exactly why," she responded.

When Mary was little, she remembers Grandma going into their single bathroom at night. And then, she would hear the sound of Grandma vomiting. That's when Mary would open their bedroom door—just a little—and listen for her mother to stop throwing up and go to her bedroom, where she must have passed out for the night.

One night, Grandma threw up until she wasn't making any more sounds, but she didn't leave the bathroom. Mary found her in there, collapsed into the sink, her face a mess. Mary went and got her daddy and watched as he wiped off her mom's face and then carried her to bed. He wasn't very gentle, though. These were acts of necessity, not tender concern.

"I always thought that was so cold of him," Mary told me. That's the only time I have heard Papaw described as *cold* and the only time I could imagine him being that way. But we all know how things can be inside a marriage, when you're dealing with another person's pain. He was probably tired, and so was she.

Was Grandma Helen drinking to forget anything else, besides the death of her beloved sister? There's probably a lot I don't know about my grandmother's young life. Maybe something else happened, or more than one thing, that nobody else will ever know again because she took those memories with her when she passed away. But her pain is part of my aunt Mary's story now, just as her pain is woven into my mother's story, but in a different way. And eventually it became part of mine. But it won't be passed to my daughter.

My mother remembers Papaw whipping her over a broken plate, but Mary swears he never did, that he never whipped any of the kids. Grandma, though, would hit them with whatever she happened to have in her hand—a hairbrush, a wooden spoon—you name it and she probably swatted one of the kids with it.

Swatted. That's better than *hit*, isn't it? It sounds better, anyway. It might not feel better.

When I asked Mary if I could call her again sometime, she told me, "Sure—anytime. I love you kids, you know." It's funny how the kids of the previous generation always remain "kids," even when they have children of their own. When she said that, I realized how lucky I am to have this family, even far away, who'll take the time to talk to me. For so many of us, stories are a love language.

I didn't wait long to call again. This time, I sat on my couch, looking out the window to watch hummingbirds hover and flit as they sipped sugar water. Grandma Helen always had a hummingbird feeder.

I couldn't understand the appeal when I was little. Now, these simple pleasures make sense.

Mary remembers a warm, beautiful day when my mom showed up at Grandma's house after all of them were grown and had moved out. The adult kids visited often, so it wasn't unusual for them to run into each other there. But on this day, Mary was sitting on the patio—the site of so many conversations, many of them lost now. Mary was talking to Grandma and all of a sudden, my mom came around the side of the house. Her arms were bloodied and her legs were bloodied from the knees down.

"Jenny, what on earth happened to you?"

"Oh, I just fell." And that's all she would say of it. She acted like nothing was wrong.

Mary said she always thought it was strange that she hadn't heard a car before my mom appeared. There was no crunching of gravel, no car door slamming. Just my mom, bloody, out of nowhere.

"I always wondered if your dad dragged her down the road."

And that's when it hit me: what had probably happened next after I saw my dad drag her down the road by her hair, beating her along the way. He probably left her in the road when he got tired. How do two people go back to their normal lives after such a thing? We had a lot more days in the holler after that one. I imagine she lay there, crying, shaking, but knowing it was best to stay limp, now that he had let go.

No fight, no flight. Just play dead, or something close to it.

Where would my dad have gone after that? Maybe to the barn. Maybe he came inside the house and us kids pretended we didn't know that anything was wrong. Maybe we hid in our bedrooms. Or maybe that was one of the many times we ran into the woods, scrambling up the steep foothills of the Daniel Boone National Forest. In there, we followed deer paths and found little spots where they bedded down. We got to know the land with its poison ivy and snakes, which you had to learn not to bother, and they usually wouldn't bother you, either. Oaks and maples towered over us, but they didn't loom; they didn't threaten.

And there were wildflowers, squirrels, creatures in flight—so much life that our father couldn't control or destroy.

So yes, there's my dad in the barn. Me and George on a hillside somewhere. Mom pushes herself up when she can, all out of tears. She walks the two miles to her mother's house, brushing gravel out of her cuts, trying to smooth out her hair. And before she reaches the mouth of the holler, where other people will drive by and her family will soon see her, she does the most important thing. She puts on a smile. But if anyone is going to believe the smile or believe she fell, she has to do something else—she has to push everything inside her into a dark room. The sorrow, the fear, every tender part of herself that has been brutalized—pretend none of that exists. Close the door and try to forget. If she tried hard enough, maybe she would.

Not long ago, I was listening to Mavis Staples sing "You Are Not Alone." Her words washed comfort through me until she sang that every tear tastes the same. I started to cry when it hit me: That's not quite true. Most of us weep in salt water. My mother's tears would have tasted like gravel and copper that day.

Chapter 33

When we visited Grandma and Papaw Caudill as kids, George and I got to run around the same junkyard that my mother grew up with. And don't get me wrong—this wasn't a really big junkyard. I didn't even see it as a junkyard when I was a kid. Back then, it looked like old cars that probably had some usefulness, even if they didn't run. We would search for unexpected treasures—a coin that somebody had dropped and forgot or a set of keys that made me think each time that maybe we could start the car after all. Where did I think we would go? Maybe just somewhere else. But we never did.

It was so different at Grandma Helen's than it was at Granny Ella's. I thought of Grandma's house as pretty much being "in town" even though it was still a couple of miles from the city limits. But there, we could watch cartoons if she would let us and endure soap operas if we had to. Either way, the picture on the TV was always clear and you didn't have to go outside to fool with a giant antenna like we did at home.

Granny Ella had a well and I think it still worked when I was real little. Eventually, somebody sent city water all the way up the holler to Granny's house, but they didn't go the extra quarter mile or so to reach ours. We could drink the water at Granny's but we took Clorox jugs to Grandma's and filled them up so we could have clean water to drink at home. The taste and smell of bleach was enough to make a kid avoid drinking water for a long time. Maybe that's part of why I'm always after good water to drink now.

I got a call one day from one of Granny's nieces, Elaine. She'd read my first book and wanted to talk. I was thrilled—she told me how Granny made the best peanut butter pies and would always have one ready when she knew Elaine was going to visit. "She was the best cook I ever knew," Elaine told me. "But she sure went through some hard times."

I wanted to hear more and I sat on my front porch again, listening as she wove stories of Granny's younger life into my understanding.

She told me about Granny's father, a man I had never heard much about. I've seen one picture of Granny's mother holding me when I was real little and I think I remember her, though I can't be sure. This relative told me how Granny's dad ran off and left my great-grand-mother and their children—all twelve of them—and started a new family. Eventually, my great-grandmother found out, and my granny found out. I started wondering if that was why she always looked so sad in pictures from her childhood. Or was it something else? I wish I had known to ask while she was still alive. I doubt she would have told me, though. So many times, we think we're doing the people we love a favor by hiding the truth.

Granny Ella always made me my favorite birthday cake every year—usually a strawberry cake with white frosting and rainbow sprin-kles. And she'd make chicken and dumplings for my birthday, too. She may have even killed one of her own chickens for me once or twice. I don't think there were more than a handful of times when I walked into her house that she didn't ask me if I was hungry and offer to fix me something to eat.

She took me to church because she believed it was good for my soul. When I was a teenager and later, a young adult, she gave me money because she wanted to make my life better, even if I wasn't great at doing that for myself. She wasn't perfect, of course, but she was so good.

There was that time my father told me to walk to her house and tell her she was a whore.

I was four or five years old and was used to walking to Granny Ella's alone by then. Our holler was so isolated, almost nobody drove past our house other than the neighbors who lived another mile up the holler. They knew to watch out for us kids—my dad made sure of it one time when he poured motor oil and screws on the gravel road in front of our house, so the family's teenager would get the message to slow down.

As I walked down to Granny's house, I knew it was wrong to call her that word, even though I wasn't sure what it meant. I walked in through the back door without knocking, straight into the kitchen like always. Granny was at her table and I stood just inside, afraid of what I was about to do.

"What's wrong?" she asked me.

I started sobbing. I cried because I hated the words I had to say and I feared what my father would do to me if I didn't say them. I cried because Granny knew something was wrong just by looking at me and even though I got really good at hiding my feelings soon after that day, it was important that someone cared then. She could see me.

"Dad said to come down here and call you a whore."

She pulled me onto her lap and let me cry.

"Now, it's okay. Shhh, it's okay." I was surprised by how she responded. I think I expected her to be angry, indignant. But in that moment, all she showed me was that she cared more about how *I* felt. As an adult, I know I would respond the same way if I was in her shoes. But as a child, I had already learned that my feelings didn't get factored into much of anything.

Granny comforted me until I stopped crying and drove me home. That surprised me too—I had expected to have to walk home. It was a mercy I didn't know I needed.

Dad came out of the house when we got out of Granny's truck.

She told him, "Don't you do that to my little girl again. Don't you treat her like that." Her voice shook but I knew it was from anger, not fear.

I was surprised again that she defended me, not herself. And my father didn't try to retaliate, though I was afraid for her because I knew what he would have done to my mother.

That day is my earliest vivid memory.

My dad didn't listen to my granny and stop hurting me after that, but it mattered that she said it. It mattered more than I can say.

Chapter 34

As a child, I told myself that my father was hurting inside. I told myself he felt vulnerable and weak, and he took that out on us, his family, because he didn't know how to feel powerful unless he was hurting someone else. I could forgive him for that, understand it, and love him. In reality, I was the one who felt powerless. *Was* powerless.

I can see the tragedy in my childish desire to believe the best about my father. Like on that Christmas Eve when I told Mom and George we shouldn't open a present without Dad because he was working to support our family. I thought they were being selfish, and even at six or seven years old, I felt like a fool when Mom told me he was out getting drunk, not working.

I kept on wanting to see my dad turn into the good man I believed he could be. One time in my thirties, he told me he was sending me a birthday card with some money. I thought about it countless times after that when I checked the mail, wondering each time if that was the day it was going to appear.

It never would have been too late, not even years later. I would have felt loved in that moment.

That stubborn desire to see the good in him—that fundamental *need* I had to see the good in him—set me up for some early failures.

I gave the men I dated the same grace, believing more in their goodness than they did. I was so often convinced that they would transform into their best selves with the love and support I could give them. It's an illusion I finally saw through, but it caused a lot of heartache first.

Now, after years of trying to understand our family, I'm finally not angry or hurt. I know how much love I tried to give and where that love came from.

For my birthday this year, my daughter bought me a green mug from an antique shop. "I thought you'd like it because it reminded me of *The Lord of the Rings*. But I was worried you already have too many mugs. Do you like it? It's okay if you don't."

"I love it," I told her. "And it *is* like something a hobbit would drink from. This is really special."

She grinned and gave me a hug.

Orion brought me two miniature orchids, one full of white blooms and the other with deep pink. "Happy birthday, Momma. I hope you like them."

"They're perfect."

The three of us ate some of my birthday tiramisu and settled onto the couch to watch one of our favorite shows and laugh together, Orion's arms around me and his sister. It was perfect.

I remember going to the gas station when my dad still managed it. I think that was probably the last time he had a real chance at being able to manage his own life. Or maybe it was already too late. When we last spoke, Elaine also told me that my dad had always made her uncomfortable, even when they were children. Was he already dangerous back then?

When I look at pictures of him in his gas station uniform, clean-cut and handsome, I have to remind myself that he was still terrible to us. It's easy to forget—just for a second—because I can imagine a different life for the man in the photograph. But no, that's him. There aren't photos of all the harm he did, other than the one of our kitchen sink when he tore the faucet out and broke the kitchen window with it. In that photo, there's plastic where the window glass used to be; the faucet is a mangled mess.

Otherwise, I have hundreds, maybe thousands of pictures from my childhood. We're smiling in most of them because that's what you do—smile for the camera.

I called my mom one night to ask her what happened when Frank shot at her and my father. I know not to call between six and eight, when she and Jack are watching the news or their favorite show. But I try to call at least a couple times a month just to check in, and sometimes to see if she will tell me a story or two.

"I can't remember for sure, but I think Frank had come up to the house for some reason and forgot his shoes. He came back for them and your dad took them out to him. They got into it about something, somehow. Your dad got mad and tried to rip his sideview mirror off the truck. Frank stepped out with a pistol and your dad backed up and told him, 'Shoot me, you son of a bitch.'

"I went outside because they were arguing and I probably told Frank to just leave. I might have told him I was going to call the police. That's when he shot at me. Then he shot around your dad's feet five or six times, like they do in the movies. He wasn't trying to hit him—he was too close to miss."

I felt my eyebrows go up and my eyes widen when she told me this last detail, even though there was nobody in the room to see my reaction. I didn't respond for a few seconds as I tried to make sense of it. I know if Frank wants to shoot someone, he knows how to hit his target. He shot at my father like they were in a Western where the good guy is warning somebody or the bad guy is just showing off. Why would Frank do that? Was he just not ready, or did him and my dad not really want to kill each other? What were they both so angry about all the damn time?

I asked my mom what she thought. "I don't know, honey. It was just one of those crazy things that you can't believe is happening in real life."

So much of my childhood felt like a movie. It was surreal to see my father dragging my mother down the road. Surreal to wake up hearing him say he would kill Grandma and Papaw Caudill if my mom's crying woke us kids up. Surreal to have him flip on my bedroom light and stand over me, and I knew he wanted to see my eyes open but I kept them shut, *played dead*, to protect the people I loved. It was surreal to see him in the upstairs of the addition—the beautiful addition that was destined never to be finished—threatening to kill himself in my future bedroom. None of it made sense. It was easier for me to believe nobody meant these things. It was all pretend, just a bad joke, and eventually the adults were going to reveal their true selves. Some part of me thought, someday, they would laugh and me and George would laugh and I would finally be able to breathe.

I was learning unspoken lessons all that time, though. One of my least favorite memories was when I told my mom we should go back to Dad the day we went to the IGA, after she surprised me and George by asking if we wanted to leave. I didn't know any better and it wasn't my fault that he was able to fool me with his tears and begging. Now I know I was innocent, but I grew up feeling I had played a part—at least that once—in putting us back in danger.

Another memory that still haunts me is when my mom said something a little mouthy toward my dad. I think I was about seven. I asked her in frustration, "Why would you talk back to him? Don't you know what that will start?"

She told me that she was tired of watching everything she said all the time, but I didn't care much about that. I wanted us to survive and I knew that wasn't going to be easy, and I also knew what would make it harder. In that moment, I couldn't understand or care about my mother's voice and what it meant for her to toe the line with him all the time. I *did* know that we were all in it together and that if one of us made him mad, all of us would pay.

I grew up knowing about my mother's motorcycle wreck because her jaw made a popping sound anytime she yawned, and of course, she had to take out her false teeth to clean them. I remember sitting on the couch next to her, asking if my jaw was going to pop like hers did when I grew up. She told me, *no, it shouldn't*, which was a relief. Sometimes she would remove her false teeth to show me that most of them weren't real, and you might think that would be ugly in some way. But sitting there next to her, I wasn't surprised or shocked by how she looked when she showed me the few real teeth she had left—she was beautiful to me.

Back then, I couldn't grasp that she was just eighteen when the wreck happened. Eighteen used to seem like a grown-up age. Now, I wonder why eighteen-year-olds are thrust into adult roles with adult consequences when they're barely grown.

I can see her flying into the fence post face-first. If she hadn't traded helmets with Dave, I wouldn't be here. Her story would have ended. Mine would have never begun. I see her lying in the hospital bed, her face swollen beyond recognition.

That's my mother.

I want to go to her, comfort her, let her know she isn't alone with the beeping machines and a drugged mind and institutional indifference. In some ways, there's no need to. She is here now, alive, recovered long before I was born. At least, her face had recovered.

But in another sense, that version of my mother exists perpetually, through story. *Jenny is in the hospital, sometimes all alone. She's in and out of consciousness. She'll have to move back home.*

I imagine visiting her, thinking I understand her better than anyone else has or could. Maybe I don't, but I have tried to.

I would sit on the bed and sing to her: *You're not alone. I'm with you, I am lonely, too.*

I wouldn't worry her with what all is about to happen, even though everything she is going through will bring me into existence, as well as my suffering. In our life together, I'll see so much that I can't unsee.

There are even things I don't remember that still get to haunt me. The things my mother doesn't remember—they haunt us both. My grandmothers' sorrows trickle and stream through the roots of our family tree. One daughter after the other, born, and for the longest time, reliving days and nights we spent in fear.

Chapter 35

George came to my house last weekend. Now that he's running his own business, building and remodeling people's homes, he has a waiting list a mile long but still drives the hour and a half to help me with projects sometimes. I like hiring him because I know I can trust him.

After doing a couple of other repairs around the house, he figured out why one of our light switches had stopped working and fixed the wiring. We talked for a minute as he was getting his tools together.

"Have you heard anything about Dad?"

"No, you?"

"Not since I blocked his number. I wonder if he's found a place to live."

"Who knows. But I'll see you at Mom's next weekend. Love you."

"Love you, too."

Before he left, I surprised him with a bag of granola that I bought while he was working. He had eaten that kind for the first time at my house about fifteen years ago, when he stayed with me for a week. At that time, he'd needed to get away from trouble that was piling up in Clearfield, where he still lived. I tried to convince him to move away for good, but the only thing he liked at my house was this organic granola. He hadn't found it anywhere else since then. He called me later that night to let me know it was every bit as good as he had remembered.

We talk on the phone every few weeks or so, and for years I've asked George what he remembers from childhood, just like I've asked our mom. He doesn't remember much at all from after he went back to live with our father, or even the time before we left. His most vivid memory is from one time when our dad took him to Carter Caves, which he did fairly often. George loved going to the caves, but one day when he was climbing up a rock to catch up with Dad, he put his hand on a ledge and Dad stepped on it, hard.

"Ow!" George cried out. He looked at our father and waited for his response. But Dad didn't respond. He just looked at George, eyes empty, and turned around to walk away. My brother is still baffled that our father would do that.

"Who doesn't care when they step on their kid's hand? I can't imagine just looking away if I knew I hurt one of my kids." He can't imagine it because that's not in his nature. We spent so much of our lives trying to understand our father's nature, and I think I can *almost* grasp it now. Some things you don't want to understand in the deepest way, though.

George was back recently, finishing some work on my house, and I convinced him to try our local burger place where all the meat comes from a nearby farm. There, we talked over house-made cocktails while we waited for our food.

"Do you remember when Dad used to go to the bootlegger's house?" George asked me. "This was back before Rowan County was wet."

I didn't remember the bootlegger's house, but I did remember how our father used to take us to a variety of houses where he would leave us in the car. "Wait here, I'll be out in just a minute."

He was never out in just a minute. Sometimes, I was lucky enough to have brought a book, but most of the time I just sat there looking out the window, looking for something to stimulate my mind. Thank God for George and the company he gave me.

"Do you still remember the day Mom left him for good?" I asked, hoping it wouldn't ruin our meal. For a long time, I had felt lonely in our family, remembering so much and struggling to break free from the pain those experiences had caused me. George wasn't shutting things out like he used to, though. Just like Mom, he seemed to remember more and was willing to talk about it.

"Yeah," he told me, taking a drink. "I remember them being in the yard and he was hitting her. Mom was screaming, 'Please stop, you're going to kill me!' And he was screaming back at her, 'I want you to feel my pain.'"

"Damn." I couldn't think of much else to say. "We saw a lot, but I hate it that you had to see that."

George nodded. "I've been thinking about that a lot lately, with Mom's back problems. I wonder if some of it was caused by him beating her like that."

Always on the back, where nobody would see.

I've always loved my brother, but I never spent much time thinking about how it felt for him to witness the last time our father beat our mother. I wish I could go to him, too—little George, ten or eleven years old, just a baby. I see him on the couch. He probably woke up because he heard thumping on the porch and against the door—our mother's body. Maybe Dad's voice was loud enough to wake him. The rest would have been another surreal scene, like so many others we grew up with. We were both gentle children, for the most part. We didn't want to fight. Neither of us would have attacked our father in anger. We just wanted him to leave us alone, let us be. We probably would have forgiven him, if he would have just stopped hurting us.

So yes, there's George on the couch, crying and not knowing what to do. There's nowhere to run. He can't fly, can't fight. Nothing to do except endure the horror unfolding in front of him, and then run when Mom tells him to, and pray Dad doesn't catch up to them.

It's easy to forget that he experienced such a thing. He's still so easy to like, so funny and warm. He's laid-back where I am uptight. Everybody loves to talk to him—he makes friends with gas station clerks and coffee shop baristas. I'm guarded and reserved until I'm comfortable, so people have often thought I was stuck-up. The irony.

George and I are both pretty funny, though. We got that sense of humor that comes from tragedy. We've got that going for us.

After the divorce, Dad often told George and me to tell Mom how much he still loved her. He had quit drinking and wanted her to know that. I guess he thought that's what brought out the meanness in him, but it wasn't that simple. Even after he got remarried—to a woman six years older than me—he would talk about how he would always love Mom. Like some George Jones song.

My brother and I were both wild in our teenage years, and we both became parents in our early twenties. We made bad choices and struggled in our own ways. And we're both glad to be alive because we can see so clearly a hundred other paths that we were set on, each of them ending badly. Somehow, against all odds, we were spared from the fate of our father, or even our mother.

My biggest childhood fantasy was that my parents would someday love me like I wanted them to. Maybe they already did—who am I to say what's inside another person? But looking back, there wasn't a single moment of warmth from my father. And yet, he told me endless stories that may have inspired my imagination or simply fed it. My mother was in survival mode—I know that now. Growing up, I only understood that she couldn't focus on me. And yet for all my parents' failings and for all we went without, they somehow managed to give me a lot of books over the years.

About fifteen years ago, I started writing about my life because I had a particular story I wanted to tell. I never set out to get revenge against my father or expose my mother. I thought it was worth telling because nearly all stories have value, don't they? There is something so *human* revealed through them. We are complicated, tragic, beautiful.

The real trick for those of us with messy backgrounds is to learn how to tell the story without making ourselves the hero and victim, all at once. People like to say that writing is therapeutic, but I'm convinced the only way to change—grow, evolve, get better—is to change the story we tell about ourselves.

I grew up certain that my mother didn't love me like she loved George. That's a hard thing to admit, even now. After all we've been through, there shouldn't be part of me that's still five or ten years old, wanting my mom to tell me how great she thinks I am.

And yet, there is. That little Charlie is still there. I noticed her at Christmas last year when my kids and I arrived at Mom's. George was already there—he lives less than two miles away from her. They were sitting at the kitchen table, eating ham and mashed potatoes, laughing about the pictures they had taken with George's phone. He had used a filter to exaggerate everyone's faces.

My mind was already on the drive home and how cold it would be, and what that would mean if we broke down. I needed to stop for gas before I left town. And the gifts I had brought for everyone suddenly seemed inadequate, cheap. There were so many things to care about, I couldn't join in and be carefree with them—not fully. For a moment, I felt invisible but I didn't know how to fix it, just like when I was a kid.

But now I can see the context in which I didn't receive enough love or attention as a child. When I think about my mother, I see a barely grown woman who got married shortly after she nearly died. She had *just* escaped the confines of home and all the terrible, boring safety it offered. She married a crazy person who showed her early on that he was eager to cause harm. And why did she feel trapped so quickly? That I don't know. But that kind of story unfolds all around us, every day.

And then, there she was in a run-down trailer in an isolated holler. In a marriage she couldn't leave unless she acknowledged the possibility of dying there. Every day that she stayed became a gamble.

I never understood before why my mother would have been heart-broken over her miscarriage, knowing how my father went on to treat his children. But now, I see how much she lost. That pregnancy was life-changing and she thought her life was changing for the better. I wonder, when she was pregnant with that first child, if she thought Rob would change once the baby was born. I've been guilty of thinking a man would suddenly become more caring when he became a father.

By then, she might have known her husband wasn't going to be the man she wanted or needed, but that baby could have given her someone to love and be loved by in return. Maybe it would have been a girl and she would have still been excited to name her Charlie and she could have thrown herself into the overwhelming demands and love of a baby.

Instead, she had me, likely while she was still mourning that first child. And what can we give to anyone, even our own children, when we are overcome with grief? Compound that with my father and all he brought to the table. I'm probably lucky to be here.

And watching George with my mom, laughing at those photos, made me so glad Mom seemed to love George so much when we were little. Maybe that's what kept him going, just like books and the woods and Granny kept me going.

Chapter 36

My life now is like a fairy tale compared to my childhood. But the allure of *happily ever after* doesn't embrace the complexity of the human experience.

Some people say that a person remains alive for as long as someone carries their memory. But each person's life and the innumerable choices they make all work like pebbles thrown into a river. The water ripples out from each pebble, creating waves that go on to touch others. Some waves reach the shore and wash over a child's hands as she searches for beauty. Others move through the river body, changing and being changed with each new force exerted upon it.

Every slight, every triumph, each mean look or gentle touch—everything we do creates an effect that ripples outward around us, but also beyond us in time. Some of those choices lead to trauma that is passed along from generation to generation. Others create family mythologies, a source of pride and entertainment for generations to come. And if we can understand the forces that have shaped us, we can overcome any limits they have imposed.

George drove himself and Mom to my house last month for Orion's graduation party. It was a nice little crowd, a mix of Orion's friends from high school and college, friends of mine who have known him since he was a baby, and even some of his college professors. Rose spent most of the evening with Mom and George, while I went in and out of the kitchen to make sure there was plenty of food for everyone. When I took a break to sit down with them, I heard Rose telling them about the wild rabbits.

"Momma found a little nest with these tiny bunnies and it was about to storm. I was scared they would drown and wanted to make them a shelter. We cut up a plastic flowerpot so the mama bunny could get in and out when she wanted, and we put a heavy rock on top of it so it wouldn't blow over. I told Momma we needed to make a home for all the bunnies so they could always be safe. I mean, it's rained other times and we weren't there to protect them—we have to make sure to take care of them now."

"You're so tender-hearted," my mom told her. "Bet you could get Uncle George here to build you a nice bunny house. Ain't that right?"

"Heck yeah!" he said. They were all grinning now. "We'll build a bunny castle. I'll make sure it's all up to code, and you all will have more bunnies than you know what to do with. You'd like that, wouldn't you, Charlie?"

I smiled back at him. "Sure, let's do it up. Just make sure y'all keep an eye on them in case they start getting crowded and we need to build some more rooms." When I stood up to check on Orion, their conversation continued.

"We have to name one of the bunnies Hutch," Rose told them.

"What about George? Or George Jr.? Nobody's been named after me yet."

My mom chimed in, "I think Jenny is a nice name. How many bunnies are out there?"

I walked away, smiling.

A long history of sorrow led to my birth. There isn't exactly a clean resolution to make all that suffering seem okay—no fairy-tale ending after all. But this history reveals how helpless so many people have felt for so long. And in their helplessness, they became parents who could not find their strength or perhaps did not find it quickly enough. I did the same thing—I became a mother when I was still hurting, still broken in many ways.

Maybe the beauty of nature made me reach for a new outcome. Maybe it was God or my granny or the experience of looking at my own children, seeing the incredible depth in their newborn eyes.

Life doesn't have to be a tragedy, mistakes and pain or tedium and defeat. We aren't bound to the past, powerful as it is.

We can be better. We can do for the next generations what we needed done for ourselves. We start by telling a better story.

Epilogue

One of the best things about stories is that they give us access to truths we might otherwise miss. Sometimes, we can see things in other lives, imagined or real, that we can't see in our own. Sometimes those realizations are subtle and so are the impacts within us. Other times, we are saved by them.

The book that helped my mom understand the danger she was in with my father—*Men Who Hate Women and the Women Who Love Them*—is still around, still needed. I found it hidden in plain sight in a laundry basket in our bathroom when I was a kid. All it took to hide it from my father was a T-shirt or two on top of it; he wouldn't have gone through clean laundry. *Women's work.*

I wonder what would have been different if my mother hadn't read that book. Dear Abby wrote a review saying it "could be a lifesaver." And I'm sure she's right. Reading it is what helped break the spell over my mother and let her see that her marriage was a trap. But—and I think this is one of the most important details—it was not unique. There are countless women and men in abusive relationships. So often, they are blind to their own reality.

ACKNOWLEDGMENTS

I am forever grateful to my mother for helping me bring this story into the world. I embarked upon this journey with you because I wanted to understand your story, and I knew it was worth sharing with the world. I also wanted you to have the opportunity to tell *your* story, which you haven't been able to do before. And while this book is not an exact representation of you or your experiences, I hope you feel heard, appreciated, and loved after working through this together.

I am so thankful to and for my children, who are a constant source of joy in life. Aubrey, thank you for reading through this manuscript and making valuable edits. You made an important contribution to this book and I appreciate you giving of yourself to help make this writing the best it could be. Amelie, your presence is one of the best parts of my life. Thank you for all you are and for every minute of our time together. I love you both more than words can tell.

I wouldn't be where I am without the support of Lois Giancola, whose work and guidance helped me find this path and begin the long process of overcoming the pain of my past. Thank you for your wisdom and friendship—I am forever grateful.

Thank you also to Rachel Smith, whose work as a neurofeedback therapist has allowed me to move farther past the impacts of trauma and fully thrive. I am also grateful to Sweetheart Huffine, who has helped me continue to develop and grow spiritually—thank you for what you do and for how you support me and others.

I have so many wonderful friends whose love, support, and understanding enrich my life and writing. To Carla Gover, thank you for always being up for a discussion of language, truth, literature, and all that is beautifully ineffable. To Renee Mikell, thank you for your friendship and wonderful conversations about everything from our precious, sassy dogs to the complexities of loving all the perfectly flawed humans. To Karen Devere, thank you for reading my work and encouraging me as a writer, as well as all the time we get to spend together, enjoying life and each other's company. To Ellen Mitchell, thank you for always being up for a great conversation about wine, cheese, and the human experience—some of my most favorite things. To Jennifer See, thank you for providing me with so much support as I strive for physical and emotional wellness—I am thankful that you are so generous with both your expertise and your friendship. To Maria Wright, thank you for the friendship we share as we navigate motherhood alongside each other, through all the highs and lows. To Angela Anderson, thank you for your depth of understanding and acceptance. I'm so glad you're here. To Kari Major, thank you for our many wonderful conversations and for always being willing to be your authentic self—you are an inspiration.

To my literary agent, Adriann Zurhellen, thank you for believing in my work and for being a wonderful champion of it. I appreciate you so much. Thank you also to Laura Van der Veer, Laura Chasen, and everyone on the Little A team who brought this story to life. I appreciate your thoughtfulness and all the time invested to make this a story with impact.

Finally, thank you to my readers for sharing in a love of stories. I hope this one has a positive impact on your life in some way.

ABOUT THE AUTHOR

Photo © 2023 Erica Chambers

Bobi Conn is the author of *A Woman in Time* and the memoir *In the Shadow of the Valley*. Born in Morehead, Kentucky, and raised in a nearby holler, Bobi developed a deep connection with the land and her Appalachian roots. She obtained her bachelor's degree at Berea College, the first school in the American South to integrate racially and to teach men and women in the same classrooms. She also attended graduate school, where she earned a master's degree in English with an emphasis in creative writing. In addition to writing, Bobi loves playing pool, telling jokes, cooking, being in the woods, attempting to grow a garden, and spending time with her incredible children.